Where We Converge

by A.E. Bross

Where We Converge
Copyright © 2023 by A.E. Bross
Cover Design © 2023 by A.E. Bross

First Edition, 2023
Paperback ISBN: 9798987756119
Ebook ASIN: B0C37R2ZLY

CONTENT NOTE:

This book contains depictions of scenes describing and discussing dissociation (both derealization and depersonalization), PTSD, anxiety, depression, panic attacks, discussion of and reference to child abuse, suicidal ideation, and some violence. Please be kind to yourself.

For RJ.
I like you for more than your face.

CHAPTER ONE

Darius

Darius Adair blinked in the semi-darkness of his apartment, unsure what had woken him. He hadn't been dreaming—he knew this because the only dreams he ever had were nightmares. If it had been one, waking would have been far more abrupt. There was no cold sweat, no nausea, no desperate need to turn on the lights and assure himself that he was safe in his apartment.

Despite all that, he was awake, and the unsettling feeling that something had fundamentally shifted while he'd been asleep sat heavily in his gut. Something was off—reality was *different*—but he couldn't explain how or why. It was subtle, indescribable.

He stilled himself to listen to the world around him. He could hear the muffled sound of traffic on the streets of Chicago beyond his apartment window. The soft sound of heat being pushed from the vents vibrated in the apartment, and the refrigerator kicked on in the kitchen with an insistent hum. There was no noise from the other units around his, though even at their worst, Darius had never heard more than a muted shout and a slammed door through the well-insulated walls.

So, what had woken him?

Groggy and still half-asleep, he rolled out of his tangle of sheets and righted himself, walking the few feet to the bathroom. His apartment, a modest studio, made the journey a quick one. Not bothering to turn on the light, he moved to the toilet to relieve a half-full bladder before haphazardly washing his hands and barely drying them. Biological needs satisfied, he stumbled back towards his bed. The flooring, normally a dark rich oak in the daylight, was cold and stygian beneath his feet. Seconds later, he was back amid the tousled covers of the bed, making himself comfortable.

He slipped beneath the blankets and let his eyes drift shut, feeling the gentle tug of sleep pulling him back. He let it take him, dropping gently towards slumber when he heard a sudden, rhythmic buzzing beside his head. The noise stopped, resumed, then paused again.

Phone. His phone. Someone was calling him.

Biting back a sigh, he turned his head to see the thin line of the screen's illumination on the downturned device. Who would be calling him? Work? He didn't work out in the field, and desk-assigned Monitors didn't regularly get ungodly o'clock phone calls. It could wait until morning. An emergency? He could count on one hand the number of people who would actually call *him* in an emergency. He was close with precisely no one and unimportant enough to be on zero emergency contact lists he knew of. It was more than likely a spam call, someone ringing him to talk about an expired car warranty or some such nonsense.

Still, he supposed he should at least check and see, make sure some apocalyptic event hadn't occurred. Maybe that's what woke him?

He snatched his phone from the nightstand and laid back, blinking to read the bright display.

Nicholas Slavin.

Darius started, then used his free hand to rub the sleep from his eyes. Surely, he had read the name incorrectly. There was no one he knew that was less likely to be calling than Nick.

Nicholas Slavin again flashed on the screen. Confused and distantly annoyed, Darius's finger hovered over the red 'Decline' button on the phone before moving and swiping the 'Accept' icon. "Hello?" he snapped. He was awake enough to be angry, his voice rough from sleep.

"Is this Darius Adair?" The voice on the other end of the phone was surprisingly small. It sounded like a child, though their voice was authoritative for being so young.

"Who is this?"

"Is this Darius Adair?" came the repeated question.

2

"Yes. Who is this?"

"Emily," she said, "Sorry to call so late, but I can't reach your mind, and calling was the only other option."

I can't reach your mind.

Darius unconsciously moved his free hand to the back of his head. The hair there had long since grown over the patch that was once shaved, but the slightly raised skin of the tattoo was still there. He'd had it indelibly marked on his skull, the arrangement of symbols and runes a carefully crafted protection spell to keep his mind safe from any unwanted intrusion. The reassurance of feeling the mark was a welcome one.

"I bet you can't even sense him," The child groaned, oblivious to what might be going on at Darius's end of the call. "Probably not, considering I had to call you, but that's not important right now. You need to find him; he needs your help. I can't do it. Dad's not even here, not that he would be useful, and I heard Trinity talk about you before. *You'll* be able to help."

"Wait, who? Who needs my help? And Emily who?"

"Just hurry." The child's voice was short and annoyed. Then the call went dead.

"Hello?" Darius glanced at his device, saw the call had been ended, and immediately went to his recent calls. He pushed the cheerful green icon next to Nick's number and brought the phone back to his ear.

"You reached Nick Slavin's phone. I don't check this often, so just text," came the decidedly older, masculine voice on the recorded response. Darius hung up, redialed, and again, it went straight to the voicemail message. Emily had probably turned the phone off.

Now much more awake than he had been, Darius's thoughts turned with more clarity. The only child that would have access to Nick's phone would likely be his daughter, Emily Slavin. She would be about eight years old now, considering it had been six years since her mother, Seren, had passed away.

Seren.

Darius had spent the last few years attempting to work through the intricate tapestry of emotions that just the mention of her name brought up. Guilt and shame were always the primary instigators, and he had appropriated hundreds of hours in his therapist's office, trying to grapple with everything that had happened between Seren and himself. He'd spent so much time trying to work through his fractured, riotous feelings to put something resembling his former self back together. In moments like these, it felt like an exercise in futility.

To remember Seren was to bring it all crashing back. His failure. The abuse at the hands of his mentor, Vivian de Winter. What might have happened if Seren hadn't intervened—

Darius viciously cut the thought off, banishing both Seren and Vivian from his mind. He would *not* allow himself to slip into the past, not in the dead of the long, lonely night. Instead, he threw off the covers again and climbed out of the bed with a huff. Now wide awake, he decided to investigate the truth of what Emily had said to him. It would be easy to discern if this was some sort of prank or if someone was in real danger.

He thought back to when he had first woken up, to the sensation that something had shifted. Maybe that was Emily warning him of a very real emergency.

Turning on the lights, he finally glanced at the clock on the wall. 2:47 A.M. He made a disgusted sound but moved to his dresser nonetheless, pulling a shirt on over his bare, scarred chest before he seated himself on the couch. Nerves were already starting to sour his stomach, and he needed to take a few deep breaths, try to concentrate without panicking.

For a mage, Darius didn't practice his craft often. He didn't need to and often found working magic to be triggering, a reminder of what had both sustained him most of his life and almost caused his death.

You'll be able to help.

That was what Emily had said, with perfect sincerity and confidence in her voice. It hadn't sounded like a prank, and as much as Darius wished he could just ignore it and go back to sleep, if someone *was* in danger, he had to help. Not just as a Monitor for the Protectorate but as a halfway decent human being.

4

Damn conscience.

With one last centering breath, he reached to the back of his head, his fingers finding the raised skin of the tattoo beneath his hair. He traced it, visualizing the gesture as the unlocking of a door. His mind, now free of the protective guard, opened to the magic around him.

He was immediately inundated with tides of energy, thrown into the flow of magic with all its currents streaming at different depths and speeds. None threatened to overtake him, as they might be a less experienced mage. Out of practice or not, Darius had been too well-trained to lose himself in the sudden rush of magic. Whatever else his upbringing had brought him, it had created within him an impressive talent.

He could sense almost the entire city, seeing with his mind's eye the consciousness of millions of people. He was careful to keep his distance from them; he had no desire to know their thoughts. The magic he had cast was more of a blunt force tool. Without knowing the mind of the person he sought or having some trace of them, there was no way to narrow down his search to any sort of single object or person. Hearing people's thoughts would do him no good here. No, he was only probing the flow of magic lightly, skimming it for anything that might be an aberration from the usual mental energies found in the mindscape.

He focused on what he remembered of the feeling, the shift that had woken him, scanning the flow of magic and psyche, keeping the sensation of change close to him as he did so. Distantly, he felt a shiver. Not his own, not cold, but in the currents. There was an irregularity, a ripple in the flow.

The irregularity was oddly superimposed, a life and mind laid over the flow but not a part of it. It didn't feel demonic or otherworldly, but it still didn't *belong* on this plane. Darius couldn't find any other way to explain it. He had never experienced anything like it. Curious, he brought his own mind closer to it, and as he did so, he sensed more than he meant to. It was human, or felt human, and fractured in a way that made Darius's head

5

throb with pain. As soon as he could sense the person's thoughts, they became words in his mind.

I don't belong here. Someone, please help me.

CHAPTER TWO

Darius

I don't belong here.

The words rattled around in Darius's head, persistent and grating. He'd had to focus on them if only to better locate their source, but now they wouldn't stop, a relentless repetition of fear and desperation. They pulled at his psyche, and their weight surprised him. They weren't his; they shouldn't have so much hold.

A person's surface ideas were normally just that: quick, fleeting words or images that came and went. But Darius felt saturated by these, his head heavy enough to make his neck hurt. He wasn't sure if he had inadvertently created a stronger mental link than he had meant to between himself and whoever's thoughts were crowding in, but it added to the urgency of finding the origin of the notions.

He tried to bury himself in his wool peacoat, silently cursing at having to leave the warmth of his apartment at such an ungodly hour in order to find the person he had connected himself to. He pulled the thick material closer around him despite knowing it was a fruitless gesture. Very little could protect one from the biting winter night as the wind whipped off Lake Michigan and streaked, serpent-like, through the canyons of buildings that made up Chicago. The brutal gusts cut to the bone, and no fabric could stop it. At least none Darius had found since coming to the city. Nevertheless, muscle memory drove the action, a comforting habit. It helped ease the anxiety of having to open himself to the magic around him. He couldn't hone in on the person who might need his help without doing so, but it left him feeling exposed and vulnerable.

Wandering the city streets alone did not help the sensation. Still, he knew more than enough magic to keep himself from being sensed by the nonmagical. It was the magical he thought he might have issue with. Miraculously, there were no other magical beings about—at least on his route—and he counted himself lucky he would not have to deal with the complications that came with them.

Even the vampires and shades of Chicago knew it was too damn cold out.

He rode the L, sensing each stop, hopping off and hopping on, grateful that the blue and red lines ran throughout the night. The train didn't take him exactly where he needed to go, but it got him a hell of a lot closer than he would have on foot. A ride share had been out of the question; heavens knew how much it would cost to be driven around all night to try and sense a location.

Finally, he found the building he was looking for. It was a rundown apartment building. Not quite a slum lord's holding, but not far above it. He took the two steps at the front in one long stride and tried the front door. Locked. He huffed his annoyance, his breath misting in the air before vanishing into the night. Stepping over to the call panel, he saw there were ten buttons. Ten apartments. What were the odds someone would buzz him in without asking questions? At three something in the morning? He certainly wouldn't hold his breath.

I don't belong here. Someone help me. Help me now!

Darius gritted his teeth against the words. Why could he still hear them? They shouldn't have been with him after he closed the magic. They weren't his, and he had no expectation of being able to continue hearing them—that sort of link wasn't created without the intention of doing so. It also needed to be with someone a mage had some sort of in-person interaction or familiarity with. He had never heard of such a feat outside of ridiculous fairy tale romances. So why now? Why this building?

Why me?

He had thought, given who had called him, that this was about Nick. After all, who else would his own daughter be referring to? But this was an unfamiliar psyche with surprising strength, and the mystery made him uncomfortable.

Frustrated, he pressed the call button for the first apartment. No answer. The second apartment was likewise either empty, its occupants fast asleep, or blatantly ignoring the call button. It wasn't until the fourth call that someone answered.

"Yeah?" came a gruff, exhausted voice.

It was then Darius realized he wasn't sure what he would do if someone actually responded. "Uh...can you buzz me in? I forgot my key," he stammered.

It sounded weak to his own ears, but the frustrated sigh on the other end, followed by, "Damn it, Steve," told him that he had lucked out.

A second later, the front door gave a grudging, guttural buzzing sound. Darius leapt for the door and snatched it open, slipping out of the cold city night and into relative warmth. Relative being the operative word. The lobby was still cold, colder than it should have been for the interior of a building. The tile beneath his feet was smeared with mud and dirt, and the walls bore the same treatment. At least he hoped it was mud and dirt.

I want to go home, and there is no home.

Darius put a hand to his temple. The words or thoughts were coming faster now, harsh and sharp. This close, they were painful, a riotous cacophony in his mind that made his head pound. He needed to find their source.

He moved further into the lobby and found the stairwell nestled at the midway point of the building, off to his right. Without hesitating, he began his climb, taking the steps two at a time. Five floors, two apartments on each floor. He moved past each landing, pausing only to sense whether or not to keep going. He didn't like having to open himself to the magic, each time making the words stronger and more painful, but he had no choice if he wanted to find their source. The words drove him ever upwards until he stood at the roof access door at the very top of the stairs.

Here.

9

On one of the landings below, someone opened their apartment door. "Steve, that you?"

Darius ignored it.

The heavy metal door to the roof proved to be a challenge. Darius knew he wasn't gifted with an overabundance of strength, and the push of the winter winds beyond the door made exiting to the roof even harder than it should have been. The exertion intensified the pounding in his head. Despite the door's hinges groaning and shrieking in resistance, Darius finally managed to open it enough to slip out of the building.

Once again, the icy night assailed him as the sights and sounds of Chicago rushed in around him. In the near distance, the skyscrapers, towers of light, illuminated the murky sky, making it so only the deepest shadows could obscure anything. It was the same brilliant, busy skyline that Darius had fallen in love with when he first arrived in the city, but he couldn't afford to stop and appreciate it then.

Not too far off, he could hear an ambulance siren. Maybe two. Cars driving to and fro, making it only a few blocks before being stopped by a red light. People shouting from a block or two down. Chicago, in all its glory. *And they say New York is the city that never sleeps.*

The building rooftop was one of the higher ones in the area, but only by a story. Slowly, he let his gaze rove across the roof around him, searching for the source of the desperate thoughts until his eyes came to rest on a crouched figure.

The man was sitting hunched over, his back to the half wall that separated the roof from empty space and a five-story drop to the unforgiving concrete sidewalk below. From his vantage point, Darius couldn't tell much about him. The figure's knees were bent, and his chest rested against his thighs, head on his knees. He rocked back and forth, and Darius could hear a whisper of words coming from him.

Darius took a deep breath, mentally steeling himself. He was not good at interacting with people in general, and he had no experience with people in crisis. He felt the innate, awkward anxiety from never being what one might call an emotionally intelligent individual. Still, he had sensed this person from damn near across the city. That meant either the huddled, rocking figure was an extremely powerful creature or something about him called to Darius strongly enough to make the mage feel as if he was meant to be there, whatever the hell that meant.

Darius was going to find out why.

Slowly, Darius approached him, and when he was within ten feet, the man's head suddenly snapped up, gaze finding his in an instant with nearly preternatural accuracy. "Who are you?" he asked, a tremor in his baritone voice.

Darius's steps faltered. "M-my name is Darius, and—"

"Can you spellcraft? Are you a mage?"

The question startled Darius. That was the last thing he had expected to be asked. Maybe that was his mistake. After all, if Darius could sense him so strongly, the man could have been reaching out to Darius.

"The light of the realms," Darius said, testing him with the passphrase. It was something all those who could craft magic were taught, so they could identify others without actually having to use their power.

The man's eyes widened slightly, and he replied, "Is the light of our world." In the semi-darkness, it was hard to exactly make out his features, but when he spoke again, his voice sounded thick with tears and relief. "Can you help me? Please?"

Was this some sort of spell? A trap? Darius turned his head, trying to surreptitiously check his surroundings. He didn't see any indication of some sort of ritual or ambush, but that didn't mean it wasn't there. "I heard you," he managed, finally. "Your words. Your thoughts. I heard you."

If the news meant something to the man, he didn't react.

Darius took a cautious step forward. Then another. When he was close enough, he crouched down, trying to be closer to the other man's level when he spoke again. "Why don't you want to be here anymore? Where are you from?"

The stranger hugged his legs closer to his chest, rocking slightly.

Darius realized belatedly that interrogating the man wasn't a wise course of action. He considered for a moment, then simply asked, "What do you need me to do?"

It was as if his words had electrocuted the man. His head snapped up again, eyes wide in the shadows, but his gaze moved to Darius instantly. He stared, blinked once or twice, and even in the darkness, Darius could see tears falling over his filthy cheeks. After a long pause, the man whimpered an echo of his former request:

"Help me? Please?"

CHAPTER THREE

Darius

It was still dark when Darius and the stranger from the roof made it back to Darius's apartment building. Getting the man down from the rooftop and across town had been much easier than Darius had anticipated. A quick glamour made the man look less disheveled and filthy—a post-grad who'd had a rough night of drinking was far easier to explain than an injured mage in some sort of shock. Not that most nonmagical people would *know* a mage if they saw one, but Darius was nothing if not stringent about keeping that secret.

The stranger hadn't said a word on the ride back to Darius's home. The rideshare driver had been mercifully quiet as well, perhaps sensing that neither of his fares was in a talkative mood or just not the type to start conversations with the strangers who climbed into his car.

Darius preferred the quiet; it gave him time to dedicate to his thoughts. Was this why Emily had called him? To find this stranger? If so, she could have been kind enough to tell him what the hell he was supposed to do now, let alone what this man could have to do with Nick or his offspring. Of course, it might just have been that Emily didn't know who else to call. Darius knew the child was a mage, and maybe, in the dark hours of the early morning, he had been the only one foolish enough to answer his phone.

He wasn't entirely sure what his plan was. Bringing an unknown, possibly dangerous mage into his own home without knowing who he was or what his intentions were wasn't really a logical decision. But the raw vulnerability and need in the man's voice when he had asked for help still echoed in Darius's mind. He couldn't bring himself to take him into

Protectorate custody. They were not the place one brought a frightened and potentially injured person.

That's what hospitals are for, you idiot. Darius groaned quietly to himself.

Of course, bringing him to the apartment didn't solve any of the man's problems either, save for preventing death from hypothermia. Now Darius had to worry about how else to help him. A shower, certainly. Perhaps a change of clothes? The quiet stranger was slightly taller than Darius and not as lean, so the sizing might not be right. Still, Darius was sure he could find something that would be better than the stained, filthy tatters of a blanket the man was in.

In the steady ebb and flow rhythm of streetlamp light that strobed the inside of the car, Darius studied the stranger's features. He looked youngish. Maybe early twenties. His features were sharp and distantly familiar, though Darius couldn't place why or from where. The poor illumination wasn't enough to penetrate the shadows cast by his half-lidded eyes and bent head, short but wild curls hanging over his brow. Darius had to content himself with a half-formed idea of appearance.

A handsome appearance.

Scowling at his wandering mind, Darius paid the driver as soon as he brought the car to a stop. Stepping back out into the early morning, he moved around the car to help the stranger out and up to his apartment. It wasn't until they were both safe inside that Darius allowed his guard to fall if only a little.

With his usual efficient deftness, he moved to his dresser and pulled open the bottom drawer. Rummaging through his clothing, he found a pair of navy-blue lounge pants he'd received as a gift years before. Someone in the office Secret Santa had thought he would get some use out of them. Now, he finally would.

He took the pants and a crisp white tee shirt, pushing the dresser drawers shut. A few quick strides brought him to the bathroom. He opened the door, laid the small pile on the cabinet beside the shower, and turned. "Bathroom is here. Grab a shower and get changed. Then we can work on getting someone to help you."

The man nodded but waited for Darius to move out of the bathroom before he stepped in. He paused, half-glancing over his shoulder. "I'm Morgan." He then closed the bathroom door, disappearing from Darius's sight. After a few moments, Darius heard the shower turn on.

Darius let out a long sigh, running his hands through his disheveled hair. What the hell was he thinking, bringing a homeless person to his home in the dead of night? *Well, dead of morning,* he thought as he checked his watch. Still, it didn't detract from the fact that he had brought an unknown man back to his apartment for no logical reason. Feeling pity for him wasn't a solid enough basis to build an action plan.

And he had touched the man's mind. Darius could *still* feel his thoughts, though not nearly as sharply as before. They had become more and more faded, blurring from clear words to vague pushes of panic and confusion.

Either way, he still *should not* have been able to sense them in any form once he had shut himself off to the magic.

Darius stopped his thoughts before they could become any more confused. Experience as an investigator told him that he needed to focus on the tangible before losing himself in the abstract. He had to put everything that was happening in order and view each fact one at a time.

The first priority was the man's physical health. Spending all that time in the cold, not properly clothed, could not have done much for his constitution. Hypothermia was a very real concern, as was frostbite. Darius didn't think going for treatment at a hospital was going to be an appealing possibility to the man in the bathroom. Mentally and magically, the stranger was on shaky ground. Adding a barrage of unfamiliar emergency room personnel, harsh fluorescent lights, and the sharp antiseptic smell of a hospital might only destabilize him further.

I don't belong here.

Darius turned the memory of those words over and over in his mind. What had he meant? Had those been thoughts of despair and self-harm? Darius couldn't be sure.

Experiencing someone's thoughts wasn't simply hearing someone speaking in one's mind. It could be, if they were trying to directly communicate, but otherwise, it was a difficult and overwhelming magic to work, even for the experienced. At any given moment, a person could have a myriad number of ideas, sensations, and emotions oscillating in various levels of the mindscape. Trying to make sense of that chaos, to truly read someone's mind without their active participation and assistance, was generally avoided.

Darius had a natural gift for crafting mindscape magic. It was why he had initially joined the ranks of the Protectorate, and the training he had received honed that innate talent into a keen skill. He had been one of their best Indagators, with the help of his mentor.

He had taken no small amount of pride from that work, and that pride had been his greatest weakness.

After Seren's death, he had done what he could to distance himself from that work. He had come in from the field and taken a desk job as a Protectorate Monitor. It was safer. His only responsibilities were to document anything Indagators did in the field. He became an office worker, and he was fine with that. No more regular mindscape work. No more unnecessary risks. He had also painstakingly designed a ward and had it tattooed on his skull to keep others out of his mind. For fuck's sake, he wasn't supposed to *hear* any thoughts that weren't his own unless he was deliberately pushing past the seal.

He growled and let himself drop onto the couch, head in his hands. Distantly, he could still hear the sound of the shower, and he was thankful he had at least some time before he'd have to pull himself—and a plan— together for the sake of the stranger.

I don't belong here.

The words were so clear, so sharp, painful even. Every word was cut out of profound bewilderment, desolation, and panic. They were visceral, and Darius wondered how much longer the man would have stayed on the roof before ending his own life.

It was a dark idea, and he pushed it away. He didn't want to contemplate such things.

16

Instead, he returned to the idea of taking care of any medical needs the man might have. Darius would need help there. He had little experience with healing, magical or mundane. If there was no cut to put disinfectant on and cover with an adhesive bandage, then it was beyond his understanding. Even then, he wasn't the ideal person for the job.

But he knew someone who was.

Pulling out his phone, he brought up the screen and navigated to his contacts, swiping through until he found the number he was looking for. He pressed the 'Call' button and brought the phone to his hear.

After the first ring, the line clicked. "Hello?" The warm, feminine voice on the other end of the phone sounded sleepy. "Who is this?"

Darius faltered slightly, not immediately recognizing the voice that answered. "I'm looking for Ines. Ines Moore."

"You found her."

"This is Darius Adair."

There was a pause, and then, "Darius? You're still alive? Where have you been, and why the hell are you calling me at five in the freaking morning?"

Darius rolled his eyes. "Of course, I'm still alive." He shook his head disapprovingly as if she could somehow see him, then remembered that she could not. "I'm calling because I have a bit of a problem, and I was hoping you could help."

There was amusement in her voice when she replied, "What type of problem could you possibly need my help with?"

Darius wasn't sure how to word what he wanted to say. *I picked up a homeless guy who needs a physical* was wrong in so many ways. "I, er, have someone here—"

"You're an adult. I don't care what you do with your free time," she interrupted, yawning.

"I have someone here that needs medical attention."

"So, bring them to the hospital. Call 911 if it's an emergency."

Darius let out a long, frustrated sigh. "I would have if I thought that was a wise idea," he said through gritted teeth. "I have a mage here who

17

needs medical attention without making a scene or drawing unwanted scrutiny."

Her tone was instantly suspicious. "This isn't official Protectorate bullshit, is it?"

"No, it is not."

She let out a long breath. "Darius, I just got off an hour ago from my overnight shift. Can it wait?" There was no teasing in her voice anymore, only exhaustion.

"I don't think so. He might be hypothermic or injured. Might have frostbite."

Another pause, then a sigh. "You *should* take him to an ER, but I'm feeling generous. Text me your address, and I'll be over as soon as I can. If he's bad, I'm calling an ambulance—no arguments. There had better be coffee, tea, or legal stimulants of some nature there when I arrive, too, or so help me." She disconnected the call without saying goodbye.

Darius stared at the screen of the phone as it went blank, then tucked it back into his pocket. Coffee was an excellent idea. He pushed himself up off the couch and moved toward the kitchen, his thoughts on brewing a strong cup of dark, caffeinated goodness, when a sharp cry from the bathroom stopped him in his tracks.

What now?

CHAPTER FOUR

Morgan

The world was made of pain.

Was existence only this agony? Had there ever been anything outside of it? Somewhere in the recesses of his mind, he thought he remembered there had been, but he couldn't recall anything beyond this torment.

The cold hurt, warmth hurt, light hurt. Everything was injured and cut, bleeding his mind and his body. The only thing that didn't stoke some form of suffering within him was *his* voice. The man who had found him on the roof. *His* presence in Morgan's mind was the one thing that was neutral.

Had he said his name? Morgan couldn't remember. He longed to be a version of himself that could recollect a name. Or maybe he didn't have that ability yet? Shouldn't he, by now? Time and space weren't right around or in him. Was it because he had come back? Would it ever be right again, or was he wrong and broken now?

Traveling through time had been the shittiest thing Morgan had ever done. He should have known it would be. Unmaking himself to travel through the time-space continuum, to remake himself at a different point, wasn't an act that would go without reality hefting serious consequences on him.

Now, if indeed Morgan was in 'now,' he found himself standing in a bathroom. It was sleek and minimalist with no frills or accessories. How had he gotten there? Hadn't he been outside in the cold?

Him. He brought me here. The thought reassured Morgan, but he reached behind himself and locked the bathroom door anyway. He felt safer that way.

He couldn't remember why he was in the bathroom. He looked around, trying to recall. A heaviness in his bladder gave him one suggestion, and he moved to the toilet to relieve himself. That's what bathrooms were for; he recognized that much. Once he was done, he shifted a step or two back to catch his reflection in the mirror. He didn't know himself. Covered in grime, hair a mess of greasy and matted curls, he couldn't see the light brown skin he was used to seeing, the smattering of dark freckles across his nose. He could see his eyes, though, the same sharp, light brown as his mother's. Their familiarity gave him comfort, and he clung to it, even if he couldn't remember his mother beyond the color of her eyes.

A shower. The shower could be the reason why he was in the bathroom. There was a clean set of clothing on the cabinet beside the sink. Those could be for him. He moved to the faucet in the shower and turned it on. He dropped the ragged blanket that had covered him and put a hand into the water to test the temperature before he stepped in completely.

The water pressure stung, and the heat set his nerves tingling. He thought he could picture a memory of a hot shower feeling good. Would it ever happen again, or had he imagined the memory?

For the time being, he hurried through trying to wash the grime and filth off his skin. He used the soap he found in the shower to wash his hair and body. He saw what looked to be expensive shampoo and conditioner but didn't bother with it. The fewer things he touched, the less he experienced, the less he hurt. He rinsed the suds from his aching body, wincing as each little popping bubble felt like a wasp sting, and made sure the painful water had sluiced him clean before turning it off. The faucet felt cold and sharp, and he hurried to snatch his hand back.

Now that the water had stopped, Morgan felt at least some of the pain lift. He stood in the bathtub, watching the last few droplets fall from the showerhead.

Get out. Towel. Dry.

He did these things mechanically. If it wasn't for the tingles of pain all over his body, he wouldn't know that he had stepped out. The bottoms of his feet hurt with every step he took. It was like walking on knives despite the smooth, cool tile. He grabbed the towel and began to chase the droplets of water from his skin. The towel felt like sandpaper, and his skin screamed as he dried himself. The air in the bathroom was growing cool, and once his legs and backside were dry, he stepped into the pants that the man had given him to avoid the chill.

What was the man's name? The man who was helping him? Had he forgotten it already, or had the man not offered it? Morgan's memory was jumbled, and he couldn't recall either way. Christ, he just wanted his mind to settle. Would it ever settle again? Had it ever been settled?

That was when he brushed the towel over his right collarbone and froze, agony making it hard to breathe. The skin near the spot was swollen and misshapen. Something was nestled under his skin that didn't belong there. He moved to run his hand along the lumpy skin, and the slight touch felt like he'd set fire to himself. He whimpered and leaned hard on the sink. In the mirror above it, he caught his reflection. His clean skin looked ashen, his freckles dark against it. He looked drawn. Sickly.

Get it out. It isn't supposed to be inside you. Not anymore.

He reached up and pulled open the medicine cabinet behind the mirror and rifled through, looking for something, anything, to cut whatever it was out of him. There was nothing. A set of nail clippers, a fancy electric razor, but nothing that could cut the alien thing out of him.

Frustration and panic rose like bile at the back of his throat, and without warning, he gave a harsh shout, slamming the medicine cabinet door shut.

An instant later, there was a change in the atmosphere, a flare of magic. Morgan could sense it even if he couldn't see it. Suddenly the door behind him, the one he had locked, opened, and the man—*what is his name?*—was standing in the doorframe, concern on his pale face. "Are you all right?"

"I have to get it out," Morgan explained, pushing past him and out into the small apartment.

There was nothing of use to his left. A couch, television, and two large windows meant to give a generous view of the city streets beyond and below—nothing that could soothe the pain. Instead, it made it worse, the icy gray morning beyond the windows sending a painful chill through Morgan. He could swear it had been summer only a day or two before, and the oppressive heat of the memory beckoned to him as a welcome alternative to the cold darkness of the world outside. Was it even real?

Was this?

To his right was a kitchen, modern with a large center counter. It was the kitchen that might provide his salvation. He moved to it, his bare feet making almost no sound, and he began pulling out drawers, searching. "Where do you keep them?"

The man—*Darius, that's his name!*—hurried to catch up with Morgan's erratic movements. "Where do I keep what?"

"Knives. Scissors. Something sharp. I need something sharp," Morgan blurted, wetting his lips as his search became more frantic. He pulled each drawer out with more force, slamming the contents around recklessly and creating a cacophony of sound that he felt slice into his mind. Everything was sharp, but nothing was the right kind of sharp. "I need to get it out!"

Then Morgan saw the block of wood with handles sticking out of it. Knife handles.

Darius saw him notice it, too, and suddenly he was moving. "Whoa. Whoa!" He quickly, put himself between Morgan and the knife set. He put his hands up in a cautious gesture meant to keep Morgan at a distance.

Morgan was already moving forward, though, ignoring him and reaching for the knives.

Darius's hand came in contact with the lumpen flesh on Morgan's collarbone, and Morgan's shoulder caught fire from the electrifying pain. He pushed Darius away even as white-hot agony coursed down his arm. Morgan fell, landing hard on his good side—if any side of him could be considered good. It jarred him, and torment shot down his arm, paralyzing him. He made a strangled noise as he tried to breathe through it, to fill his lungs in spite of the constricting pain that made everything so tight, so immovable. He finally managed it, letting out a low sob once he had the air to do so.

Darius knelt in front of him. Dark brown eyes sought out Morgan's own and, once they found that gaze, he held it. "Let me help you," Darius said, his words so thick with sincerity that Morgan could feel them against his skin. They weren't pain, like everything else. They weren't sharp. They felt solid and warm, and it was comfort when everything around him felt jagged and broken.

"It all hurts," Morgan admitted in a choked voice. Everything was razor-edged, and it was exhausting. "Thoughts, light, cold. Everything." He could feel tears streaming down his face, hot and burning against his skin. "This…" He pointed to his collarbone. "This needs to come out. I have to get it out."

Darius studied the raised, angry-looking skin without touching. Then he let out a long breath. "I called someone from a hospital to help—"

Panic surged in Morgan. Everything was so ruined, and hospitals had questions. Doctors had questions. Morgan couldn't answer them. He had no answers. "No, no hospital, no doctors, no..." He trailed off when Darius held a hand up.

"No actual hospital. She's a friend, a healer, and a nurse, so she will be able to look at this and see what needs to be done."

"It needs to come out," Morgan insisted, his own voice like needles in his ears. "Out."

Darius continued, "She'll be here soon, and she can help." His gaze never faltered, and after a moment, he added, "I trust her completely."

Morgan was frightened. He needed something to hold onto in this storm. Staring at the man who had saved him, the man whose words didn't hurt as much as the rest of the world, he nodded. If Darius said he trusted her, then Morgan would trust Darius. It was all he could do amid the tempest.

"Why don't you lie down?"

Morgan nodded and moved to stretch out on the floor, but Darius stopped him. "I meant in the bed." He sounded both impatient and embarrassed.

"Oh," was the only thing Morgan said. He slowly pushed himself to standing and wavered, pausing for the wave of nausea and pain that accompanied the movement. Darius put a gentle hand on his elbow, supportive. When Morgan could, he trudged the few steps from the kitchen, around the false wall made with a bookshelf, and gingerly sat on the bed. With another deep breath, he laid down, letting a small sigh escape him as the soft mattress cradled his body.

"Better?" asked Darius, leaning against the bookcase.

Morgan nodded, but even as he did, thoughts crowded in, almost as sharp as the pain and just as disjointed. Memories, maybe, but they were jagged and cut ceaselessly at each other and him. He gulped for air as the combination threatened to overwhelm him. "I can't...I can't quiet my mind."

Darius froze, and Morgan noticed. Beyond the mess of his own mind and body, Morgan still noticed the shadow of panic that passed over Darius, locking him up. Why? What did Darius fear?

Did Darius fear him?

Morgan reached a hand out, though he was unsure if it would be accepted. Everything happening, that had happened or would happen, was trying to surround him, to drown him. He needed an anchor. "I need help. Something. Make it quiet. Can you make it quiet? You're a mage, right? Everything is so loud."

A long, silent moment stretched between them. Finally, Darius asked, "Are you sure?"

Morgan nodded, tears slipping from his eyes, the trails they made rivulets of pain. "Please?"

Darius moved to sit next to Morgan on the bed, their hips brushing. He put a hand to Morgan's forehead, and Morgan felt his cool touch as a relief, a balm to the burning heat of his racing thoughts. After a second, Darius moved his thumb over Morgan's forehead, tracing a letter or sigil. He was casting, and even as Morgan realized this, his thoughts suddenly quieted. They didn't vanish, but it was as if a layer of calm had been dropped over top of the chaos. The world seemed quieter, softer, and less ragged.

Morgan's eyes drifted shut, and a profound exhaustion washed over him in warm waves. He hadn't realized how tired he was. The sensation was bone deep.

"Thank you," he said or tried to. He wasn't sure if he managed to speak the words before he sank into dark, welcoming sleep.

CHAPTER FIVE

Darius

Anxiety roiled nauseatingly in the pit of Darius's stomach as he gently eased his hand off of Morgan's forehead, dismissing the magic that he'd used to effectively blank the man's thoughts. The look of pain, vulnerability, and raw panic that had shone in Morgan's wide eyes haunted Darius. Never had someone been so unguarded, so *honest* in his presence, and the responsibility it placed on Darius's shoulders was frightening. It felt intimate in a way that stripped him of his defenses, sending a confusing blend of excitement and anxiety through him.

Darius had the opportunity to get a better look at the man. With the soft lamp light cast across his clean face, now that he was washed and at least partly dressed, Morgan appeared both less threatening and less broken. He was attractive. Dark freckles were sprinkled across the bronzed, light brown skin of his face, and his exposed shoulders and chest had the same. The muscle there was toned but not overly so. This was someone who was used to activity, not long hours at the gym.

As he continued his cursory examination, Darius's gaze fell on the deformed skin against Morgan's collarbone. It looked inflamed and painful. Darius resisted the urge to probe the injury more closely. He was curious, but with basic first aid and nothing else, he knew he would make situations like this worse, and Ines would kill him if he did.

Sure that Morgan was asleep, Darius pushed himself to his feet and moved into the kitchen, keeping his footfalls light. He checked his watch. If Ines's estimate was accurate, she would be at his door in just under twenty minutes.

All of a sudden, the reality of what was going on rushed in on him, threatening to overwhelm him. He had brought home someone in pain and need, neither of which Darius was used to dealing with. He had *taken responsibility* for the welfare of this person. And if that wasn't enough, he felt a connection to this Morgan, and historically, people he felt connected to never fared well.

He leaned over the dark marble counter of the kitchen island and took a deep breath, steadying himself as his stomach churned in time with his thoughts. He shut his eyes tightly against the nausea, willing it away.

Coffee. Make the damn coffee.

Forcing himself to concentrate on that single task, he retrieved a pitcher of filtered water from his refrigerator and used it to fill the reservoir for the twelve-cup coffee maker on the counter. He counted as the water filled and was careful not to overfill or spill any. Next was the coffee. He counted again—four heaping tablespoons in the filter. He wasn't even sure he would have any, but the routine was where he found solace. The repetition, the quiet counting, helped him feel less overwhelmed. By the time the coffee machine was gurgling and the apartment was filling with the warm aroma of dark roast, he was feeling much better.

The small intercom by the door buzzed. Ines. Without even checking, he pressed the 'open door' button. Belatedly, he admonished himself for not confirming it was her. He remembered his own escapades earlier that morning, tricking whoever that poor man had been in the apartment building, the one who'd buzzed him in, thinking he was someone named Steve. He forced himself to push the thought away. There was already enough to be anxious about; he didn't need to add more to the list.

His logical brain told him that he was being ridiculous, but he couldn't keep his anxiety from dwelling on the possibility of having allowed an unknown into the building. Then a knock came at his door, interrupting the mental feedback loop. On the small video screen next to the intercom, he could see a familiar face, and he sighed in relief, pulling the door open.

Ines was a shorter woman, five foot two inches of pure audacity with forty-five years of sarcasm thrown in. Brown and black ringlets streaked with silver tumbled to her shoulders, and a healthy flush filled her cheeks.

She shrugged off her coat as she walked past him, dressed in an oversized purple hoodie and pair of faded blue scrub pants that sported errant spots of dark brown at the bottom of one pant leg. Darius hoped it wasn't blood, but the alternative wasn't great either.

"Long time no see," she said, her gaze moving around the apartment before coming to rest on him. "Small place, but nice. I figured you for more of a penthouse sort of guy."

"Not on my salary." Darius shrugged. "Coffee?"

"Where's the patient?"

"Asleep on the bed."

Ines nodded. "All right, coffee first."

"How do you take it?"

"Black, like my soul," she deadpanned.

Darius chuckled as he found her a large mug and poured the dark liquid into it. He handed it to her, then poured his own. The silence in the room was starting to feel oppressive, though judging from how Ines sipped the hot brew, she didn't notice. Still, Darius felt the need to fill it. "Rough shift?" he asked, the words moving awkwardly through his mouth.

Ines didn't notice. "Every overnight is a rough night. Last night wasn't too bad. Heart that needed emergency surgery, few flu cases, but nothing critical. A little girl who cut her hand helping make dinner. They all left the ER, one way or another, feeling much better than they had prior," she said with a self-satisfied grin.

"Helps to have a mage for a nurse."

Ines's casual shrug fooled no one, especially when her eyes were shining with pride. Ines Moore could heal the sick and mend the wounded with the best of them. This was because she had dedicated her life to the magic of the cycle. Life and death. Regeneration and decay. She embodied both sides of the coin. Her first calling was to heal, but that made her no less formidable than any other mage. Darius knew never to get on her bad side. She had a temper and could hold a grudge with the best of them, magical or not.

She was also one hell of a nurse.

"That makes sense," Darius replied. He brought his coffee to his lips but stopped when his stomach rolled at the smell. Grimacing, he put the mug aside and grabbed a glass from the cabinet. He poured himself some water, added a few ice cubes, and sipped, hoping it would settle his gut and his nerves.

Finishing the sizeable mug of coffee in far less time than Darius thought it should have taken, Ines set her mug on the counter and clapped her hands together. "All right. Let's see what we've got."

She hopped off of the stool and moved further into the apartment, striding past the bookcase and into the bedroom area. Darius followed and was close enough to hear her sharp intake of breath when she first saw the sleeping Morgan. She glanced back to Darius, eyebrow raised. "Well, now I see why you brought him home instead of to the hospital."

"Oh?" asked Darius, confused by her smug expression.

"He's *pretty*," Ines teased, elongating the word and waggling her eyebrows.

Darius spluttered. "Ines, this is serious."

"All right, all right, cállate, por favor," she said, waving a dismissive hand at him. She moved to the bed and sat down beside Morgan, who stirred but didn't wake. She gently took his wrist, pinching it between her thumb and her index and middle fingers, finding a pulse and counting it out while she watched her watch. Darius observed her quietly, arms crossed, waiting to see what she might discover. Once her initial examination was over, she took a deep breath and closed her eyes. Opening them again, her normally brown eyes glowed with a faint, copper light. Mage light. She was using her spellcraft to sense and examine Morgan.

One of the first lessons taught to anyone who could craft magic was how to sense it in others. Most channeled this through their eyes, granting them a sort of magical sight that could be used to see another mage, their aura, or magic crafting. It had the noticeable side effect of making one's eyes glow, and it was the reason the passphrase had been created centuries

29

before. This way, spellcrafters didn't have to worry about alarming mundane people.

"Darius, what's going on here?"

"What do you mean?"

"I mean, his aura is cracking at the seams. I've never seen one so damaged. Did you not see this?"

"What?" Darius took an involuntary step back. He'd never heard of such a thing. He didn't work in auras. "That can happen?"

"Apparently," Ines breathed. She shot Darius a quick glance, then rolled her eyes. "I said damaged, not dangerous. At least I don't think it is. Not to us anyway. Auras aren't really my thing. Whatever this young man went through, it must have been hellish." She shook her head, turning back to him. "Physically, he looks just... Wait..." She squinted, moving closer to him and further examining his collarbone. "What the fuck is that?"

"It's what I was hoping you could help with."

"You buried the lede a bit here." Ines pursed her lips. "You didn't say anything about him having something *under his skin*. I'm a nurse, not a surgeon."

"Well, today, you might have to be both. He was ready to cut it out himself," snapped Darius, his patience wearing thinner by the moment. "I doubt he'll be any less motivated when he wakes up, and he could seriously hurt himself. I'm sure as hell not qualified to take care of him either, yet here we are."

Ines, not one to be snapped at, whirled on him, pushing herself to her full, though diminutive, height. "I don't even know what it is, Darius. It could be any number of things: a cyst, a burn, some sort of cancer, or other growth."

"No, he said it wasn't supposed to be there."

"Well, neither is cancer, is it?"

Darius clenched his jaw, taking a long and audible breath through his nose. He could feel the last remnants of his patience evaporating around him. Despite her size, Ines was a force to be reckoned with, and he wasn't sure he had the wherewithal to withstand her. "He said it had to come out. Said it didn't belong there, and it needed to be cut out."

"Then why didn't you take him to a hospital?"

"I don't know!" Darius barely kept from shouting as he threw his hands up in frustration. Suddenly, the words were pouring out of him, sharp and angry. "He asked me not to? Something felt off about him? I couldn't know if he might hurt people? Maybe I thought getting to argue with you would be the highlight of my ungodly early morning? Take your fucking pick." Before she could interrupt him, he gestured to the man. "You said yourself that his aura was badly damaged. Would *you* risk him around people who can't protect themselves from something like that? He's a mage. I have no idea what he can do, intentionally or not. Hell, what would you do if you woke up confused and hooked up to all sorts of machines? I don't know how stable his mental state is, and I couldn't take the chance!"

Ines blinked and tried to hide, of all things, a smile. "Okay, cálmate," she said. With one last look at Morgan and a long, drawn-out sigh, she crossed her arms over her chest and nodded. "Get me a sharp knife, the sharpest you have. Then I'm going to need you to hold him down. This isn't going to be pleasant but, hopefully, I can make it quick."

CHAPTER SIX

Morgan

Morgan was ripped from sleep by hot, biting agony slicing into his collarbone. He tried to cry out but choked on the scream as he attempted to sit up. He couldn't. He was being held down, subjected to the torture by steady, powerful hands. He tried to struggle, to fight for escape, but pain and exhaustion made his attempts useless.

He forced his eyes open, sleep forgotten as the pain shifted. It was a serpent of agony, coiling and digging into the bone. He gasped, working his throat to let out a strangled moan. His hands dug into the arms of the person holding him down, desperate for escape from the excruciating torment. Who would do this? Why would they hurt him? He wasn't sure where he was, but when he looked up to see who was holding him, it was someone he knew. *Maybe.* Someone he thought he knew, then?

Distantly, he could hear the muffled sound of voices. One was feminine, attempting to soothe, repeating something he couldn't make out. Her tone was comforting but brought him no relief. The other voice, male, was louder and more authoritative. *Don't fight*, it said. *You're safe. We're almost there.*

The voice was familiar to Morgan, somehow. He tried to listen, tried to calm down despite the burning pain snaking around his clavicle. He squeezed his eyes shut, gritting his teeth against it.

There was one more stab of agonizing pain and then nothing, a sudden emptiness where the pain had been. Morgan thought he heard the distant sound of metal against ceramic. The hands that had held him down were gone. He breathed deeply, eyes wet with tears, trying recover from whatever hell he had woken to. He didn't want to move lest the pain return.

Before he could wonder what had happened, a gentle warmth washed over his injured collarbone. He knew the sensation. Or did he? It was milder than pins and needles, a soft vibration that soothed away the hurt. It felt like spellcraft, like healing. He relaxed into the glow. It was withdrawn a moment later, but he *felt* much better.

With the pain gone, he grew drowsy. Sinking back into the soft sheets and comfortable pillow, he dozed off and on. He could hear the two voices talking but only caught bits and pieces of the conversation.

"It was wrapped *around* the collarbone? How is that even possible?" came the more familiar voice. Morgan liked that voice. It was authoritative but soft. He knew its owner had a name, but his exhausted mind refused to give it to him.

"We work magic," came the woman's voice. "Anything is possible."

The only response Morgan heard to the statement was a heavy sigh. Then he felt himself drifting again. He wondered what they had meant. What had been wrapped around whose bone? Were they talking about him? His body felt too heavy to move. The idea of even sitting up to ask the voices was exhausting, and he was *so* comfortable.

He dropped into a deeper doze than before. Time passed. Or maybe it didn't. Morgan couldn't be sure. It felt like time was different everywhere. Around him, within him. It was all so disjointed. Was it just his perception of it that was so scattered, or had he damned himself to a very real space-time continuum hell?

~

When he opened his eyes again, it was to an apartment lit with the dull gray light of a clouded day coming in through the windows. He felt less pain, though a strong ache thrummed through every fiber of his being. It was an improvement.

Absently, he moved a hand to his collarbone, fingers brushing tentatively at the skin where he had had... What? What was it that had been there? He traced the outer curve of the bone but stopped, hissing in pain as his hand touched a thin line of what felt like scabbing. It still stung, but it wasn't the same desperate pain from earlier. This was duller, less urgent—the slow, burning itch of healing.

He listened to me.

Morgan remembered his frantic words to…Darius. Yes, that was the man's name. Darius had listened to Morgan's need to remove the thing from beneath his skin.

Morgan sat up with great care, feeling hundreds of aches and pains as he did so. Still, he felt *better*, and he would take that victory. It made him restless, though. Swinging his legs over the edge of the bed, he pushed himself to his feet despite the discomfort.

The apartment around him was quiet, and for a moment, he wondered if he was alone. He kept still, trying to listen beyond the white noise of the refrigerator and the soft hiss of heat coming from the vents. Just beyond those, he could hear a rhythmic breathing. Quietly, he crept toward the couch, where it was coming from, and saw a man lying there, asleep.

Morgan recognized him immediately. This was Darius, the man who had found him and brought him in from the cold. *My hero.* Morgan smiled at the thought and felt heat in his cheeks. There were few who would take a stranger off the streets, get him treatment, and give him the bed. Whoever this Darius was, he was an amazing and kind person.

Not wanting to wake him, Morgan quietly padded toward the kitchen area. It wasn't far. He saw a necklace laid out on the smooth countertop and stopped to examine it. He knew instantly that this was what had been under his flesh, around the bone. The chain, gold, was washed clean of the blood that had to have covered it when it had been pulled from his flesh. A small, red stone set in a simple pendant hung from it.

He didn't recognize the necklace so much as he *knew* it on some intangible level. The stone in the pendant was a garnet, his mother's birthstone. Had she given it to him? He didn't think so, but he couldn't recall exactly. If he was being honest with himself, he was having difficulty calling up memories of any events with any sort of clarity or order. His recollections felt as adrift as his sense of time. The more he tried to grasp at them, the quicker they would float away. Did they even belong to him? Did he have any memories?

What if he didn't? What would that mean?

Everyone has memories, don't they?

Panic rose in his gut. They *did* belong to him; they were *his* memories. He tried to force a recollection, a realization on himself, but the quiet, insistent voice would not be silenced. *What if they aren't? What then? If you don't have memories, are you real? Can you be real without them?*

If he wasn't real, then what about the world around him? It was strange. There was nothing that felt familiar to him, nothing that felt *real*, except the necklace. He stared at it, wanting to pick it up, to wear it, but worried that somehow, something would stop him. There would be some invisible barrier between him and it, and he would discover he couldn't touch it if he reached for it, or worse, that he or it wouldn't be real, and trying to get it would shatter the fragile illusion around him. The thought held him frozen in terror.

"I see you're up," came a crisp, sharp voice that cut through his panic.

He turned so quickly that it took a second for the world to catch up in his vision. Darius stood beside the couch, looking disheveled from sleep but also relieved.

This was the first time Morgan was able to get a good look at the man. He was a bit shorter than Morgan's own six-foot stature but lean and reedy. His hair looked like it had once been in a shorter style but hadn't been cut in months. His skin was a pale sort of olive, and his fatigue made it look pallid and sallow. His dark brown eyes rested easily on Morgan, and Morgan couldn't help but find him handsome. The thought was a welcome one and briefly calmed his anxiety until he suddenly wondered whether Darius was real or Morgan had somehow created him.

Panic spiked astronomically, and Morgan felt his throat tighten. The reaction must have shown on his face because Darius's sharp features softened. "What's wrong?" he asked. "Are you all right?"

"I—" Morgan's mouth was dry, and he couldn't swallow. Couldn't breathe. He looked around, trying to inhale past his contracted throat and get a grasp on his rapidly worsening panic. "A-am I really h-here?"

Confusion flashed in Darius's eyes but was quickly replaced with calm. When he spoke, his voice was even and reassuring. "Yes, you are."

"I don't feel like I am. Nothing is connecting me. Why aren't I connecting?" With each word, Morgan felt the truth more and more. He was coming apart. The sensation of pins and needles pricked at his fingertips, but the discomfort didn't help ground him in his skin. It was alien to him. He shook out his hands, trying to chase the feeling away.

Darius didn't flinch. "All right. How about you look around and tell me five things you can see?"

Morgan blinked at the question. It made no sense. Nothing made sense. "Five things I can see?" he repeated, looking around. If nothing made sense, then everything made sense, including Darius's request, and Morgan had nothing to lose by answering him. "The uh...the kitchen counter. A mug." The mug sitting beside the sink had a grumpy face on it. Morgan would have chuckled at it if he could. That was two things. He needed three more. "Kitchen sink." He moved his gaze towards Darius again. "Large windows," he added, nodding towards the two behind Darius. "And you."

"Good," Darius said, his voice still calm, though the corner of his mouth twitched with the hint of a smile. "How about four things you can touch?"

Morgan clenched his jaw, fear leaping in him. What if he couldn't touch anything? Things had to be real to touch. He had to be real to touch them. What if he wasn't?

He stood still for a moment longer, then tentatively reached a hand out and touched the wall. It was cool, ever so slightly rough, and he trailed his fingers over it lightly. "The wall," he said, the words coming out in the rush of a relieved sigh. He looked down, and for the first time, he realized that he could feel the floor beneath him. It was hard wood and felt slightly striated under his feet. "The floor."

Now he was actively searching for more to reach out and touch. It anchored him. He took two steps toward the sink and turned it on, letting the steadily warming water run over an outstretched hand. "Water," he said and felt a grin lifting at his mouth. It turned into a gasp when the water got too hot, and he had to snatch his hand back. He turned it off, feeling sheepish but also relieved. The pain, the sensation of hot and cold, reassured him further. "And a burn. I feel a burn."

"It isn't too bad, is it?" Darius asked, taking a cautious step forward.

Morgan shook his head. He felt himself coming down from his panic or being distracted from it. Either way, it was lessening.

"What about three things you can hear?"

Morgan took a deep breath and closed his eyes, listening. Distantly, he heard the sounds of traffic beyond the building as well as movement in the building. Nothing distinct, but the hum of activity was there. It made him feel a part of something. Connected. If he listened very carefully, he could even hear Darius breathing. The same sort of breathing that he was doing. Calmer, even. "Traffic outside. People upstairs. You." He felt his face heat at the last word and didn't open his eyes.

Darius encouraged him further. "How about two things you can smell?"

Morgan tilted his head back quietly, eyes still closed, and took a deep breath. "Coffee," he murmured, and suddenly, he remembered—he *remembered*—how long it had been since he'd had a good cup of coffee. Suddenly, his mind seized on that, and it was all he wanted. "And coffee," he repeated, opening his eyes to meet Darius's gaze with a grin.

Darius finally gave a small smile. "Then let's get you some."

Morgan stood aside so Darius could move past. He circled around to the non-kitchen side of the counter and watched as Darius reached up to pull a plain gray mug out of the kitchen cabinet, filling it from the coffee maker. "Do you take anything in it?" Darius asked.

"Do you have anything?" asked Morgan. Given the coffee to focus on, he found himself able to concentrate.

Darius nodded and opened the fridge, examining the contents. "A bunch of creamers," he hesitated, then on a sigh that felt like it was saying *oh well*, he began to list them. "French vanilla, hazelnut, sweet cream, Irish cream, amaretto, cinnamon roll—"

Morgan was quickly becoming overwhelmed by the choices. He interrupted Darius there. "Cinnamon roll sounds fine."

Darius put the steaming mug and the creamer in front of Morgan, then retrieved a spoon for him. He stood there awkwardly a moment longer before busying himself with pouring his own coffee.

Morgan mixed the creamer into his drink, watching the swirling white of it vanish, turning the dark liquid a lighter shade of brown. Tentatively, he sipped at it and let out a small sigh. His panic had mostly abated for the moment, and he was intent on maintaining this calm, which meant focusing on one small thing. As he took another sip of the warm brew, he let the feeling of it sliding down his throat and warming his center consume his thoughts. It was comforting and quiet. He needed that.

"How are you feeling?"

Darius had his dark eyes trained on his coffee when Morgan looked up at the question.

Morgan took another drink. "Better. How did you do that?"

Darius shrugged, though his expression was tight and awkward. "Something I learned in dealing with my own issues. Grounding can help some people get through them."

"Did it help you?"

Darius shrugged again. "Not really, no."

The two men drank their coffees in silence for a few moments. Morgan was grateful for some time to recover. The anxiety still sat at the edges of his mind, ever-present and trying to creep its way back into his thoughts, but he kept his focus on the mug in his hands, on the physical act of swallowing his drink, on how the heat from it felt as it warmed him. Concentrating on small things kept him from being overwhelmed by everything else.

"All right," Darius said, breaking the quiet of the kitchen. "If you're feeling up to it, I would like to talk."

Morgan felt the anxiety slide back in. Only a little, but enough to make his heart pound uncomfortably hard against his chest. "What about?"

"You."

Morgan sighed. "I was afraid you would say that."

CHAPTER SEVEN

Darius

Darius watched Morgan's reaction carefully, gauging to see if the younger man was in the right place to talk. He had no desire to traumatize him any further, and if he saw even a hint of panic, Darius would wait. After a pause, Morgan nodded but turned his eyes downward to study the mug in his hands, and he said nothing further.

Darius made a mental note to proceed with caution. Darius was no stranger to panic attacks—having or recognizing them—and had some tools to employ to help diffuse them. Seeing Morgan so stricken had reminded Darius of his own struggles, and he'd tried to help with the first mental activity that came to mind. Grounding was the first thing Darius had ever tried on his own journey. It met with little success, but he was happy it worked so well for Morgan.

Darius knew how difficult that terror could be. He hated how his own mind could make the world around him sharper and more injurious than it was. If he could help someone else find their way out of that, he would.

Darius nodded towards the living room area of the apartment. "Come on. Sit wherever you will be comfortable. Don't worry. This isn't an interrogation." He pushed off the counter and led the way to the couch and coffee table. Grabbing two coasters, he put his on one and offered another to Morgan, who moved to sit on the couch. Morgan nodded but held onto his mug, his fingers tight. Darius dropped the coaster on the coffee table for him, then moved to stand by the window.

"What would you like to know?" Morgan asked. He looked nervous, but his voice was strong.

Darius exhaled, his back to Morgan, watching the grayness of Chicago beyond the glass. "What's your name? Full name."

"Morgan Campbell Slavin."

Darius could see his own eyes widen in the window's pale reflection. Each name hit Darius with a strange sort of force he hadn't been prepared for. It was as if someone had reached into his own troubled past to pluck them with deliberate care, assembling them with a design to injure him.

Morgan had been Seren's last name. That alone wouldn't have been much more than a coincidence, but Campbell was the last name of Seren's best friend, Trinity. Slavin was Nick's last name. *Morgan Campbell Slavin.* What were the odds of the three of them ending up together in one man's name? Darius's logical brain told him there was at least some chance, but everything else screamed that there was no way it was a fluke. None.

Anger sparked up inside him, but he controlled it, instead turning to study Morgan. He couldn't keep the doubtful expression from his face, though. "Is this some sort of joke?"

Morgan's grip tightened on the mug, though he kept his gaze firmly downward. "No. My mother named me after her best friend, who died before I was born. She gave me her family name as my middle name, and finally…" He trailed off, and Darius could see he was struggling to finish his thoughts. "I have my father's surname."

"Who are your parents?"

"Trinity Campbell and Nicholas Slavin."

"Excuse me, what?" Darius blurted out, unable to keep his calm and collected exterior.

There was no feasible way that Trinity Campbell could be this man's mother. She was not thirty yet. Nick Slavin himself was in his early thirties, Darius's age. It was impossible for them to have created Morgan, who had to be at least in his early twenties.

His mind worked to try and find possible solutions to the problem it had been presented with. He had to remind himself that Morgan had been through something traumatic. Perhaps it was affecting his memory or perceptions. It was possible that he *knew* Trinity and Nick and was drawing connections where there could not be any.

41

A.E. Bross

"I, um," began Morgan, interrupting Darius's thoughts, "I know this is going to sound ridiculous, but it's the truth." He looked up, locking eyes with Darius. "The absolute truth."

Darius met his stare, unwavering. There was a raw, vulnerable honesty in Morgan's face, and Darius had no doubt that the man was being candid. He looked very much to Darius like he would be a terrible liar. Whether what Morgan was saying was the reality of the situation or not, it was what he believed true.

Still holding that gaze, Darius noted the color of Morgan's eyes. Their tone hovered somewhere between light brown and hazel with amber flecks that caught the dull Chicago light coming in through the windows. *Beautiful.*

Darius immediately banished the thought. Carefully replacing his neutral expression, he waited for Morgan to continue. When he didn't, Darius offered some encouragement. "Well?"

"Geez, there's no way to say this without sounding completely nonsensical," Morgan said, embarrassment coloring his cheeks. He took a breath, glanced away, then said softly, "I'm from the future."

Darius blinked, the words not registering. Slowly, gradually, they sank in, and he blinked again. "That isn't possible," he said, each word drawn out to give him some space between them to think. It didn't help. No amount of consideration could force the words 'I'm from the future' to make any additional sense.

Despite part of his brain reassuring him that time travel was ridiculous, the investigator in him turned the possibility over in his mind. It wasn't that time travel was impossible, theoretically speaking. However, attempting it was considered a severe violation. Time travel was taboo, forbidden by the Protectorate. They had outlawed it centuries before—by a majority consensus of mages—and made a point to revisit the concept every decade or so to reevaluate the possibilities and dangers. The conclusion was always the same. The possible repercussions to the overall timeline, the innocent, nonmagical people, and magic in general were projected to be too catastrophic. There had been those who tried it in the past but usually to no greater end than causing themselves inordinate suffering or death. If they survived, it was normal to suffer from spectacular side effects.

Tunguska had been the closest any spellcrafter had ever come to the full weight of those attempts. Before that, the dancing plague, and so on, all the way back to the Lupus supernova in 1006 B.C.E. What had become of individuals was worse. Some had severely damaged their auras and minds. He knew of at least one instance where a mage was driven mad and went on a killing spree until the Protectorate had quietly stepped in and removed him from the equation in 1888. Other mages had been torn limb from limb, unable to contain the sheer power and forces needed to complete such a task. Their very physical forms had been sundered because of the attempts, to say nothing of what may have happened to their souls. Stories ran the spectrum from mundane failure to bizarre and apocalyptic scenes of chaos and destruction, but many remained entirely unsubstantiated.

Whatever the truth, the reality was that it was forbidden.

Darius studied Morgan, who was staring into his mug, and recalled what he had felt the night that Emily had called, when she had sent him on his errand to find Morgan. He remembered that sensation of something having profoundly shifted. There was also what Ines had said when she had first seen him.

I mean that his aura is cracking at the seams. I've never seen one so damaged.

It was a tenuous thread at best, and Darius wasn't one to pin his theories on tenuous.

There was also the necklace that had been placed beneath the man's skin and muscles. Darius had never heard of that outside of certain old necromancy rituals. Morgan was clearly alive, with no indication that he had been otherwise. Besides, there hadn't been true necromancers for ages. Not since Oliver Barlow and his group in New York more than a century ago, and that had been an entirely different can of worms.

A knock sounded at the door.

Both Darius and Morgan turned to look, and Darius was immediately on his guard. He had so few visitors that any knock was a suspicious one. He had never put any sort of magical protection on his home. He eschewed the cloaking spells and misdirection glamours that some of his co-workers often used to keep the mundane humans from seeking them out. They often had the side effect of making those who experienced them feel unwell, and he had no desire to cause illness to the unsuspecting people around him. Darius tended to keep to himself and keep others at arm's length, no extra magic needed. It kept people away well enough. So, when the knock came again, Darius found himself wary of whoever the hell that was at his door.

He hadn't called anyone. No one should be able to get into the building without being buzzed in. That didn't preclude people from slipping in before the door was closed behind a resident on their way out, but why *his* door?

He took a step towards the point of egress. Morgan was clutching his mug in a white-knuckle grip, the cooling coffee all but forgotten. He stared at the entrance, then looked to Darius, eyes as wide as saucers.

A muffled voice came from the apartment hallway. "I know someone is in there," it said. It was oddly small and young. Confused, Darius strode to the door and pressed a button on the display beside it.

A fish-eye angle image popped up from the camera the complex put on each resident's entry, and Darius saw a young girl standing just outside. Most of her was obscured by a thick winter coat, and half her face was blocked by a thick scarf wrapped around her small shoulders. Dirty blonde hair stuck out from under her winter hat and fell awkwardly over the scarf, and sharp, blue eyes looked out from under a young but discerning brow.

Cautiously, Darius opened the door a crack and peered through the opening. "Can I help you?" he asked.

"It's about time!" the child said, sighing heavily. She pushed the scarf away from her mouth so she could be better heard. "Are you going to make me stand out here forever?"

"I think you have the wrong apartment. Where are your parents?" Darius tried, sounding a bit more dismissive than necessary. Something about the girl's voice was familiar, but he couldn't place it, but he didn't want to get distracted from his current situation. He needed to get back to the business of finding out more about Morgan.

The girl—Christ, she couldn't have been more than eight years old—checked the number on the outside of the door, then turned her sharp gaze back to him. "No, I'm right where I'm supposed to be. Don't know where Dad is. Mom's dead."

She said the words so matter-of-factly that Darius was at a loss for how to respond. He took a step back, and the young girl took the opportunity to slide in between Darius and the door, making her way into the apartment.

"Hey!" Darius snapped, but his exclamation was drowned out.

Morgan, who had been kneeling on the couch, leaning on the arm of it to see what was happening, suddenly gasped and leapt up, arms wide. The little girl needed no second invitation. She ran and threw herself into Morgan's arms, holding him tightly. Morgan dropped to his knees and began to sob. The little girl just held him, smoothing his hair and kissing his face.

Darius closed the door to his apartment slowly. The scene, though touching, did little to clear his confusion, and he wasn't sure how to ask just what the hell was going on.

After a moment, the girl looked up at him. She didn't stop comforting Morgan, but those sharp, familiar eyes were on Darius, unwavering. "I know you haven't seen me since I was small. I'm Emily," she explained, "and this is my little brother."

45

CHAPTER EIGHT

Morgan

The violent mix of relief and sadness that washed over Morgan when he saw the young girl took him completely by surprise. At first, he wasn't sure if it was her past all the winter garb she wore. When he was, he hadn't even been aware of moving. One second he was on the couch, and the next, he was on his knees on the hard floor, embracing her and sobbing like a child. Seeing Emily, a young, innocent Emily, who didn't have the world on her shoulders and who hadn't spent most of her life helping Morgan's mother raise Morgan, to keep him safe, was an emotional shock he hadn't been prepared for. His image of his older sister had always been the eternally worried defender, making sure they were safe, doing what was necessary to keep them going just one more day, and sacrificing her own well-being for others. She would give someone the shirt off her back, then scoff and insist it wasn't cold.

The last time he had seen the Emily from his time, she had been—

What? What had she been? His brain shied away from dwelling on it, and he didn't know why. What was it that he was afraid of remembering?

Regardless, he wanted to think about the vibrant, intelligent eight-year-old currently holding him in her tightest hug and telling him that everything would be all right. He didn't know how she had recognized him. He wouldn't be born in this timeline for another year or so. Then again, his sister had always been preternaturally intuitive, even for a mage. Apparently, she had been so as a child as well.

"How did you get here?" Morgan asked when he was finally able to speak. He huffed a laugh and helped her untangle herself from her scarf and hat.

"That is an excellent question," Darius snapped, moving around them to sit on the couch. He all but snatched up his coffee. He took a long drink, but when he spoke again, his voice was softer. "Does your father know you're here?"

Emily moved back from their embrace and threw Darius a stormy look, pulling her coat off of her shoulders and leaving it where it fell. Morgan could all but feel the indignant anger rolling off his sister. Darius either didn't feel it or didn't care. The mood in the apartment was thickening with tension, and it sparked Morgan's anxiety. He felt more grounded, sure, but with the man who had saved him and the girl that was his sister's past self squaring off against each other, he felt his heart rate increase. He didn't want there to be friction. Not now.

He cleared his throat, and both Emily and Darius looked at him sharply while he moved back to sit on the couch next to Darius. He wiped his eyes again and gave a weak smile to them both before picking up his coffee. It was lukewarm now, but he sipped it nonetheless. "Darius, this is my sister," he said, trying to sound cheerful, despite how cracked his voice was from crying.

"Emily Slavin," Darius clarified, his jaw tight, face pale. "Emily Seren Slavin." He said each name with a harsh curtness as if wanting to drive the entirety of it home.

"That's my name, don't wear it out," was her retort, in a classically annoying sing-song voice.

"Wait, y-you know her?" Morgan asked weakly. Confusion blossomed, fueling his anxiety. How was Darius connected to all of this? Vaguely, he also heard the tightness in Darius's voice and wondered what was there to cause it. It felt like the more Morgan tried to clear up, the murkier everything became.

"*Older* sister," Emily specified with a small smirk. Then her gaze dropped, and her shoulder fell a bit when she turned back to Morgan. "Yeah, he knew Mom. My Mom. And he knows Dad and Trin."

"You knew my dad's first wife?"

"They weren't married," Darius said, jaw somehow tightening even further. His words were low and gravelly, scraped through his teeth. "And yes, I knew—"

"Anyway," Emily interrupted, moving to stand in front of Morgan and smiling. "You look good. Better than I would have thought after a trip like yours."

It took everything for Morgan to look into her young face. He didn't see any of the signs of age he was used to seeing in his sister. The worry lines that had been permanently etched into her expression from years of concern. The child before him wasn't *his* Emily. No, this Emily was still a seed of a person. A haughty, precocious eight-year-old seed, but a seed nonetheless. It both amazed him and deeply saddened him. She was all hope and discovery, and he would never see the sister he had grown up looking up to again. He pushed away his grief and asked her, "How do you know all about this?"

"I dreamt about you when you remade yourself here. I saw how it hurt, what it took." She put a small hand on his forehead and looked into his face, bright blue eyes, her mother's eyes, searching his. "You're not all right, are you?"

Morgan was at a loss for how to respond. Could he tell a child how badly broken he was? How could he explain that his mind was scattered, and his body felt like shards of crushed glass loosely glued together? Would her young mind grasp what he was trying to say? His barely did. Was that fair? She saved him from having to decide, though, by continuing her own explanation.

"I called him to go find you. On an *actual* phone," she said, nodding in Darius's direction. "Something was blocking me from just dream-speaking it to him."

Darius scoffed into his coffee but said nothing. At least nothing understandable.

Emily shrugged, though she was obviously annoyed at Darius's manner. "And, well, here we are." She opened her hands and looked around. "In this tiny apartment, with a rude Protectorate Monitor," She sobered a bit. "You look pale. How are you?"

Before he could reply, everything around him froze.

Morgan blinked, unsure of what was happening. Then Emily started to move, but *backward.* Her movements were awkward, alien, a jolted juxtaposition of what she had been doing. She was speaking, but her words were garbled and unintelligible. She was progressing in reverse. He glanced at Darius, saw him picking up his coffee and sipping it, but the gesture was off because he, too, was moving in reverse order. Time was rewinding around Morgan. He was seeing everything backtrack, sliding in time and space.

He squeezed his eyes shut, trying to ground himself in that moment, to keep himself in the here and now. It felt like he was being torn in two. One steadily dwindling part of him was in the present, but another part was being dragged backward. He was back in the bed, excoriating pain wracking his body. Then he was in the shower, then back in the car with Darius. Time moved back and back, and with each second, Morgan felt more alien to it all.

He broke out into a cold sweat, and his head swam. The nauseating sensation that the world around him was shifting and that he wasn't connected to it in any meaningful way was physically painful. The ache from the night before returned, thousands of needles against his skin, burning him. He was unnatural, not from this time, this world, and reality wanted to make him pay for it.

Why won't it stop? How do I stop it?

He put his hands over his ears, trying to shut out the sounds that ran backward around him. He clenched his closed eyes so hard that it hurt, and he doubled over. He had become unmoored. Despairing slithered in. How would he ever—

"Morgan!"

The sound of his name in a sharp, authoritative tone snapped him back, bringing everything into a jarringly vivid focus. He opened his eyes. Nothing was shifting. He was still in the apartment. Emily was kneeling on the floor next to him, a hand on his knee, tears in her eyes. Darius was in front of him, sitting on the coffee table, holding him at the shoulders to keep him from falling.

"I—" Morgan started, voice hoarse. He felt hot tears stinging the backs of his eyes.

"Just breathe," Darius instructed, holding Morgan's gaze. "Breathe."

Morgan nodded, sucking in air and exhaling it in jagged breaths. He focused on the feeling of Darius's hands on his shoulders, of Emily at his knee, the couch under him, the floor beneath his feet. Anything that was solid and connected him to the here and now. After a few minutes of this, he felt his body relax if only a fraction.

"Better?" asked Darius.

Morgan nodded. Darius sat back on the coffee table, finally releasing his shoulders, and Morgan felt a distinct loss at the broken contact. He let out a soft sigh and leaned back into the couch, letting the soft cushions cradle him. He was suddenly exhausted.

Darius shook his head and lifted his phone. "I'm calling someone."

"Who?" asked Emily, moving to sit next to Morgan. She took his hand in both of hers and squeezed it, blinking away tears. "Who is going to be able to help with all of this?"

"Trinity," Darius replied as he unlocked his phone.

The name hit Morgan hard, knocking the wind from his lungs. His mother, Trinity. Except not truly his mother, not yet. Not in this timeline. Morgan's chest tightened with anxiety. What would he say to her? How would he react?

Emily shrank into the couch as if trying to hide in it or behind Morgan. Under her breath, barely loud enough to hear, she said, "I'm going to be in so much trouble."

Darius didn't seem to care. With a few flicks of his thumb, he dialed the number and held the phone to his ear.

"What happened?"

Emily's whispered question drew Morgan's focus away from Darius and back to her. "What?" he asked.

"You went somewhere before, in your head. We thought you were going to pass out. You weren't breathing, not right anyway. What happened?"

"I just... It felt like time was warping and moving backward. Everything was rewinding."

Emily gave him a sympathetic look and squeezed his hand again. "It's okay," she whispered. "I'm here."

To have the young version of his older sister consoling him was a bizarre mix of comfort and amusement. Still, he would accept it. He was in no place to pick and choose where he found his aid, especially with the consequences of his actions being so extremely detrimental. He remembered his Emily squeezing his hand in much the same way, the small gesture meant to bring the quiet reassurance of her presence. He patted young Emily's clasped hands and offered a weak smile. "Thank you."

Darius finished his phone conversation and breathed out a long sigh before turning to look at the two siblings on the couch. "Trinity is on her way." He eyed Emily suspiciously before holding his phone out to her. "Call your father. Tell him where you are."

"He won't answer. Not from your number," she said, shrugging. She made no move to take the proffered phone. "I even deleted the call I made, just in case."

"Try," Darius insisted through gritted teeth.

Huffing a sigh, she leaned forward and snatched the phone from him.

"Will you be all right if I just take a shower?" asked Darius, his attention now on Morgan. "Do you need me out here?"

Morgan wanted to ask Darius to forgo the shower. He wanted the man to stay with him, to help him stay grounded if he began to feel that horrendous disconnection, but he had already disrupted Darius's life so much as it was. "I'm fine," Morgan said, hoping he sounded convincing. "Go ahead."

Darius studied him a moment longer.

"I'm with him," added Emily, insulted at Darius's hesitation. It suggested she might not be enough to keep him company. Morgan suppressed a smile. She had shown up at Darius's door only a few minutes before but was acting every inch the older, protective sister.

Finally, Darius nodded. "All right. I'll leave the door unlocked. Come and get me if you need me." He moved to the closet and pulled out some clothing. Once satisfied, he crossed the room in four or five strides and vanished into the bathroom.

As the door closed behind him, Emily turned to Morgan. "Why don't you lie down? I'll be right here next to you. I'll keep you safe."

I'll keep you safe.

The words echoed in Morgan's mind, in his heart, as the memory his mind had hidden from him suddenly blossomed before him. His Emily, lying on the ground, bloodied and whispering that it was up to him, that she couldn't keep him safe anymore.

"*I know you can do this,*" she had said.

Those had been her last words before she'd died.

CHAPTER NINE

Darius

When the bathroom door clicked shut behind him, Darius had to resist the urge to slam his fist into it. By nature, he wasn't a violent person, but then fate had seen fit to not only drop Morgan fucking *Slavin* into his lap but Emily as well? Emily, who had her mother's name.

Emily Seren Slavin.

Darius hadn't the foggiest idea of how he was supposed to approach any of this. He couldn't leave Morgan to his own devices. Darius still wasn't sure about this whole time-traveling business, but it was as clear as day that Morgan believed it. Emily Slavin, damn her, seemed to think that Darius was perfect for the job of caring for Morgan. After all, it had been her phone call that had started this mess.

Well, she thought he was the next best person after herself, of course.

Absently he rubbed at the back of his head, turning the shower on with his free hand. He needed to think, to work through his thoughts on what was happening around him.

Darius's relationship with the Slavin family was complicated at best and abysmal at worst, and even those descriptors would be gross oversimplifications of the situation. After all, he had been intimate with Seren Morgan, who, unbeknownst to him, had been *engaged* at the time. To Nicholas Slavin. Darius had been completely in the dark. Seren hadn't mentioned anything.

None of that mattered to Nick.

Darius groaned quietly to himself, the sound vanishing into the steady hiss of the shower. Now, Morgan Slavin, alleged son of Nick and Trinity, who asserted he was from the future, was most definitely in his apartment and needing his help. It wasn't even as simple as giving him help. Darius would need to investigate his claims, the possibilities of time travel, and how it had been accomplished if he even believed it was possible.

Darius had never made a study of the magic that governed space and time. His mentor had eschewed the practice of dedicating oneself to more than one or two magical studies. After all, as Darius had been told time and time again, he had the advantage of being under the tutelage of a great mage that specialized in spellcraft of the mind and should behave with the requisite amount of respect and deference to her wishes.

He sneered at the description.

He had been under the supervision of a twisted, self-interested woman who had used her magic to manipulate all those around her. Him becoming almost as skilled at mindscape spellcraft as her had been a side effect. Viviane de Winter had only wanted to use him for her own ends, and she would have succeeded had it not been for Seren.

And Seren had died because of it.

He clenched his jaw, his teeth grinding painfully against each other. He didn't want to think about Seren. He *never* wanted to think about Viviane.

Angrily he stripped out of his t-shirt and pajama pants, stepping into the shower. He hadn't tested the water, and it was hotter than he had expected. He hissed in response and increased the cold water until the shower was comfortable enough to wash and shave in.

Darius couldn't stop thinking about how Morgan had looked only moments before. He'd gone deathly still, his eyes glazing over and his face going the color of pale ash. Then he'd pitched forward, limp and unresponsive. It was amazing that Darius had been able to catch him before he cracked his skull on the coffee table. He couldn't get the image of Morgan looking so much like death out of his mind, and Darius had to admit that it had frightened him deeply.

He shut off the water and stepped out, toweling off quickly so he didn't drip all over the bathroom. He took his time, though, with getting ready. The morning ritual of showering, dressing, teeth brushing, and the rest gave him some measure of normalcy, of calm. He would take what he could get. He watched himself in the mirror as he did it, mechanically putting toothpaste on toothbrush or putting product in his dark hair. His thoughts kept going to Morgan, then Emily, and inevitably to Seren.

It had been six, almost seven years, and it still wasn't behind him.

Had he even tried to move on? Or had he gotten stuck in his grief?

His chest constricted with the thought of that anguish, and he wrestled to push it away. He couldn't afford to think too deeply on the subject. He might start to fall apart. He had in the past, and he wouldn't do that when there was another man falling apart in his own damn apartment. Not to mention the daughter of his dead friend and her angsty almost-husband shooting him death glares while he tried to figure out just what the hell was going on.

Hadn't he had enough excitement in his life already?

The sound of raised voices managed to float in through the closed door, though Darius couldn't make out quite what was being said. He let out a long, harsh sigh, then took a deep breath, straightening his back and squaring his shoulders. No one was going to do this for him.

Emerging from the bathroom, he was greeted with the sight of Morgan sitting forward on the couch. Emily stood opposite him, the coffee table separating the two of them. Her arms were crossed over her chest, Darius's cell phone clutched in her small hand. "—I already tried," she was yelling. "He won't pick up the phone."

"Maybe if he sees the number twice, he'll know it's urgent," offered Morgan, tone thin with exasperation.

"He won't. He doesn't even *like* Darius."

"So much that he would ignore multiple phone calls?"

Emily laughed so hard that Darius was amazed it didn't cause pain. "Yes! I wouldn't answer it, either! Dad doesn't like him!" She was practically singing the words at this point.

"Why not?"

"Why would he?" Emily snapped. "What's to like?"

"You know I can hear you," Darius said, trying to keep his temper in check.

"So?" asked Emily, completely confident in her insult.

"All right, all right!" Darius said, raising his voice to be heard above them. "Enough." He stalked to Emily, hand out. "Phone."

She glared at him, then slapped it into his open palm with more force than the action really required. Darius was starting to gain a grudging respect for her dedication to being a little brat. Ignoring the sting in his hand, he took the cell phone and redialed the number. It rang, rang, and then went to voicemail. Once Nick's disinterested greeting finished, and the beep indicated it was recording, Darius spoke. "Emily, *your* Emily, showed up at my door. I would think—"

That you'd care more about your only child.

The words almost came out, but he stopped himself, breathed, and said, "I'll ask Trinity to give you a call about this, too, just in case you're not answering voicemails." *Or you don't bother to listen to mine.* Again, Darius kept the words to himself. Emily was, after all, less than three feet from him, and he couldn't imagine what she might feel if he was overly disparaging towards her father or hinted that Nick needed to show he actually cared about the girl.

A notification pinged on Darius's phone not a second after he finished his call. The ID flashed *Work*. With a quick flick of his thumb, he typed in his pin and opened the text message.

ALL MONITORS AND INDAGATORS REPORT IN AS SOON AS POSSIBLE.

It was an automated message, something that went out when administration wanted everyone's attention. It didn't happen often, and Darius couldn't fathom what might have come up. He tried to ignore the sinking sensation that it was connected to Morgan. He thumbed the screen and selected an automatic response, acknowledging that he had received the message. He had wanted to wait until Trinity arrived to even contact work, but with a broad order like that going out, he thought it would be unwise to delay.

"Something wrong?" asked Morgan, concern in his voice.

"Don't know," admitted Darius, studying his phone. "That was work, but they were non-specific as to why they were contacting us. They just want everyone in."

The phone chimed again in his hands. This time, the ID read *Sibyl Diluna*. His partner. He barely managed to bite back a groan as he opened the text message. She only ever texted him with an invitation to events—which he never accepted—or she knew that something interesting was going on. Darius wasn't the type to attend many social events and never knew why she continued to invite him, but given the timing of the text, he had to assume it was in regard to the alert that had just gone out.

He liked it that way.

SIBYL: Dare, are you on your way in? Did you get the text message?

He hated that nickname. She insisted on calling him that, despite numerous attempts he had made to get her to stop. Now he glared at the word, annoyance building.

"More work?" asked Emily, curiosity in her tone.

Darius nodded before responding to the text message.

DARIUS: Yes. I'll be in shortly.

He slid his cell phone into his pocket, biting back an annoyed groan. He could have delayed a bit longer after the alert, but leaving Sybil on read would not have worked out in his best interest. Now that she would be on the lookout for him, he knew he didn't have much time to waste. Sybil was the type of person to make comments if someone stepped out of line, including something as inconsequential as being later than she felt they should be. She very much enjoyed commentary on others' behavior in general and was never shy about her opinion. There were times when he wondered if she was aware of the passive-aggressive habit or if it was an unconscious one she had picked up somewhere along the way in her life. He could imagine her sighing dramatically and making comments under her breath about how late he was and how misplaced his priorities seemed to be.

Being partnered with the office gossip was a less-than-ideal experience for Darius.

Still, she did good, thorough work. He certainly didn't *like* the woman, but he didn't have to. He just had to work with her.

"My partner. I have to go into work."

"Oh," Morgan said softly, and Darius could hear the disappointment in his voice.

"Don't worry," he said as he moved to his wardrobe and plucked a dark vest from a hanger. Sliding into it, he buttoned it quickly before donning a black blazer that matched. "Trinity should be here soon, and she's going to have a look at you. I'll be back as soon as I can manage." He checked himself in the wall mirror and nodded. Despite the chaos of the night and earlier morning, his reflection betrayed nothing of the last few stressful, fruitless hours. All Darius saw was himself, work-ready. Maybe a bit tired. When he turned, he caught Morgan looking at him. Morgan quickly looked away, a blush creeping across his face. Darius wondered what he could have seen to bother him.

He was about to ask when the buzzer sounded, and he moved to the intercom. "Trinity?"

"Yep."

He pressed the entry button, listening to the sound of the buzzer over the intercom before it went silent.

He grabbed for his heavy wool coat and scarf, being sure to bundle against the cold outside. A pair of leather gloves completed his winter armor. Slipping his phone, wallet, and keys into his pockets, he quickly answered the door when Trinity's knock came.

Trinity had been Seren's best friend. They had known each other since childhood, and for a while, they had been connected at the hip. Trinity was the order to Seren's chaos. After Seren's death, Trinity helped Darius deal with the aftermath. She had tried to help him cope with the loss, and when that failed, she found him a list of mental health specialists to try and stubbornly checked up on him until he was seeing someone. He was grateful for her perseverance. In large part, it gave him back his life.

She was taller than Darius remembered, only an inch or two below his own five-foot-eleven. She had a round, open face that was as quick to smile as frown. Despite her being shorter than Darius, she probably outweighed him. She was built broadly and was curved in ways that said both plus-sized goddess and that she would mess up anyone's day when pushed. She had deep brown skin, and her hair, braided into small, tight braids, was pulled back in a loose ponytail at the nape of her neck. As she stepped into the apartment, a smile bloomed on her face. "Darius, it's been too long. Would it be all right if I gave you a hug?"

He nodded, though the affirmative was less than truthful. He wasn't overly fond of physical contact, more from past trauma than anything else, but as she wrapped him in her embrace, he felt a fraction of his stress melt away. Perhaps his lack of fondness came from a deficit in positive examples. He wrapped his free arm around Trinity's shoulder and squeezed, the warmth a welcome one. Maybe he would have to try seeking out these experiences more often. Especially with Trinity. The woman gave exceptional hugs.

He felt a pang as he thought of how he had drifted away from her. Hell, from all of the people who had helped him.

Her warm greeting assured him there were no hard feelings. She stepped back from the hug and examined him, her dark eyes taking in his dress and expression. She offered him another smile. "How have you been?"

He shrugged a response. Her warmth made him feel small and humble. He felt like he wasn't worthy of her good graces. "As good as can be expected, I suppose."

She clasped a comforting hand on his shoulder. "We can't do much more, right?" Her eyes then drifted over his shoulder, and she raised a brow. "And you, young lady," she said, addressing Emily, "shouldn't be here without your Dad or I knowing about it."

Emily leaned against the wall a few feet behind Darius, intently studying the floor. "It's not like he cares," she said, in a voice that was half defiance, half sadness.

For the first time since Darius had met her, Emily actually seemed like a small child to him. Beyond her precociousness was a vulnerable little girl. His annoyance towards her softened if only just a bit. She was still a bit of a brat.

Emily's response apparently had the same effect on Trinity, who let out a resigned sigh, but said nothing.

"All right," said Darius, remembering he actually had to be at work, and as soon as he could before his partner started asking questions. He strode forward, beckoning Trinity to follow. "This is Morgan. Morgan, this is Trinity and…" He trailed off when he saw how ashen Morgan still looked. "Are you all right?"

"Y-yes," Morgan stammered. "I'm fine."

Darius hesitated. He hadn't considered the effect meeting Trinity might have on the man. After all, Morgan believed her to be his mother. This meeting might be traumatic. He cursed his own emotional ignorance but wasn't sure how to correct the error now. He hadn't meant to exacerbate things for Morgan.

Trinity glanced between Darius and Morgan. Her expression changed to a reassuring one, and she put a hand on Darius's arm. "Don't worry, I can handle this. He'll be safe."

Darius glanced between them for a moment longer, then nodded. "Fine." He turned to Morgan. "You're welcome to stay as long as you need." As he walked to the door, Trinity followed. He spoke in a low voice to her. "Just lock up if you and Emily leave before I'm back. Make sure he's safe and good before you do. He's been experiencing panic attacks, and once, it looked as if he was going to faint. Don't hesitate to call or text me or Ines if something happens. The spare key is in the kitchen cabinet, on the inside of the door. Take it in case you need it." He stopped, his hand frozen on the doorknob. He gave her a meaningful look. "And Trinity? Thank you."

She gave him a nod and a smile, then closed the door behind him once he left.

Darius quickly headed to the stairs, trying to shift his brain from worrying about Morgan to preparing himself for whatever was so important that the Protectorate had ordered all of its investigators in.

CHAPTER TEN

Morgan

Morgan sat on the couch, mouth agape, staring at Trinity.

He barely heard Darius leave. In fact, the man had virtually ceased to exist to Morgan; his world had become the woman who closed and locked the apartment door. Morgan felt as if reality around him had slowed, but not in any tangible or disconcerting way. This wasn't the panic-inducing, warping of his sense of time and space. No, this was the grinding pace his emotions were bringing his existence to. A heightening of sensations. The kind of time movement that happened when earth-shattering revelations had made themselves known.

This was Morgan staring at the woman who, in his timeline, had been his mother.

She looked younger—so much younger—than he could ever remember having seen her. It wasn't long after this time that she would have him, but to see her face free of hypervigilance and worry was to see an almost entirely different person. Her hair was in tight braids. In his lifetime, he had only ever seen her hair in its natural coils, free and in a halo framing her face. Her skin, so much darker than his, was the same warm, earthy tone he remembered.

Her smile, which had initially been serene though tentative, vanished, and her lips became a worried line. "Oh no. What's wrong?" she asked.

It was then that Morgan realized he was crying. The moment he realized it, he completely lost control. He began to weep in earnest. If seeing Emily as a young child had hit him hard, seeing the woman who both had been his mother his entire life and hadn't yet become his mother left him completely undone. He tried to offer an apology, but the force of his own emotions, his grief and frustration and loneliness, wracked him, and he couldn't stop the sobs that tumbled out. He covered his face with his hands, unsure if he was hiding it or just trying to keep himself from falling apart. Either way, it wasn't working.

Then he felt arms embrace him and realized that Trinity, his *mother*, had wrapped him in a hug.

If he'd been drowning in the depths of his own emotions before, he was now dragged into their deepest chasms. Relief, despair, and grief warred within him. Unconsciously, he wrapped his arms around her and clung to her, his sobs loud and unrestrained. He couldn't have held back if he tried.

They stayed like that for a stretch of time. Morgan wasn't sure how long. Trinity rubbed his back and whispered soft shushing sounds, as if he was a child. He didn't mind.

After a little longer, his sobs thinned, and his eyes dried. He sat back, wiping his face of tears. Emily stood next to him, a wad of toilet paper in her hands. "I couldn't find tissues."

Morgan chuckled and accepted the proffered toilet paper. He folded it as best he could and blew his nose, trying to fix his complete mess of a face. He pushed himself off of the couch and moved into the bathroom, tossing the toilet paper into the waste basket before coming back out, a heavy sigh escaping him. As he returned to the couch, he saw that both Emily and Trinity were seated and looking at him, both of them wearing identical looks of concern.

Trinity spoke first. "Can you talk about it?"

The words sent nervous waves through Morgan, but he nodded. He thought about sitting for it but then decided to stand. Maybe pace. Anything to expend some of the anxious, emotionally charged energy that was building inside.

"My name..." he trailed off and shook out his hands, trying to get himself steeled against the grief and anxiety roiling within him. "My name is Morgan Slavin. I'm from a point in the future, and I came back to stop...*something*." He threw his hands up with the last words. He wished he knew what it was. If Emily, his Emily, had known, she hadn't been able to share the information with him before it had become impossible.

"The future?" Trinity repeated, an eyebrow raised. She glanced from Morgan to Emily, who nodded with all the gravity an eight-year-old could muster.

"I know, it is a lot," Morgan hurried to add.

Trinity turned back to him. Her eyes narrowed slightly. "All right, say I accept that. What is the something?" she asked.

"I don't know," he said, exasperated. "Something big. There was some event that threw off the divide between this reality and one of the ones beyond. At least that's what I was told. It led to them bleeding into each other. It was apocalyptic."

Trinity kept her tone even when she continued questioning him despite the growing presence of incredulity on her face. "And you don't know what caused something so catastrophic?"

"No, I don't, Mom. I'm trying here."

The title had tumbled out of his mouth without him realizing it, but it struck him hard. From the look of shock that blossomed on Trinity's face, it had a similar effect on her as well.

"I'm sorry, what?" she spluttered, suddenly far less composed. She pushed to her feet, eyes wide. "What did you just call me?" She didn't sound angry, but shock and curiosity were at war in her voice.

Oh no. Morgan frowned, moving his gaze to study the faux wood flooring beneath him. He hadn't meant to drop the information on her like that. "You're my mother," he blurted out, only making things worse.

Trinity blinked owlishly but said nothing. She was too stunned to speak.

"He's my brother," announced Emily, bounding to her feet. She puffed her chest out with pride, a broad smile on her face. "My *younger* brother. Well, technically, half-brother."

Morgan could see Trinity turning the idea over in her mind. Realization dawned slowly, but when it did, her hazel-brown eyes went wide and she stared at Morgan.

It seemed realization also dawned on Emily. She turned towards Trinity and blurted out, "That means you and Dad had the sex to make a baby! I thought he only did that once, with Mommy!" There was a note of horror and disgust in her voice. "Gross!"

Trinity ignored Emily's accusatory shout, never taking her surprised eyes from Morgan. They held wonder and doubt as she stepped closer to him, putting her hands over his. She didn't break her stare, and her eyes flashed with an earthy, reddish light as she cast. He wasn't sure what magic she was working, but within a moment, the light faded, and tears welled up to replace it. "How is this possible?" she asked, her voice a harsh whisper. "Your aura is a mess. I can see parts of us both, but it's so torn—"

"I don't know all the ins and outs," Morgan interrupted, matching her volume with his own rasp. "I just know I had to do it. I had to do something. Had to come."

She dropped his hands and opened her arms wide, inviting him into another hug. "Oh, my poor boy," she said softly. "How are you still standing with an aura like that? You've been through so much."

Morgan nodded silently and stepped into the warm embrace. He had to fight against the tears that threatened to fall once again. He wanted to speak. He wanted to get this story out. He needed to.

Trinity sensed the need because she ended the hug. "All right, how about you tell Emily and me all about it, hmm?" She looked around, then checked the watch on her wrist. "I'll get us something delivered. How about something with hot chocolate?" She waggled her eyebrows at Emily, who nodded enthusiastically. "But don't think I forgot about you sneaking out on your father, young lady. I thought he had a few more years before that became a problem."

Emily immediately sobered, disappointment darkening her young face. "Yes, ma'am," she said, her voice quiet.

"But first, hot cocoa," Trinity said. She thought a moment, then clarified. "And a talk, young lady."

Morgan sat on the couch and waited, trying not to listen in while Trinity scolded Emily. To be honest, it wasn't much of a scolding. Morgan had a feeling that it wasn't the first time something like this had happened, and Morgan had no issues figuring out why it might not be Emily's first adventure. Nick, Emily's father—and in reality, Morgan's own father as well—sounded as if he was too busy to notice that his daughter was gone. Morgan very much doubted that the man didn't care. The problem was more than likely that he cared too much and didn't know how to manage it.

It was why, in Morgan's own timeline, Nick was dead and had been since Morgan was a baby.

He had died by suicide the year Morgan had turned two, early enough that Morgan had no memories of him. His timeline's Emily had always spoken of their father in wistful tones, hurt but not angry, and had always called him a man whose sadness was too much. On nights when Morgan's sadness at his passing frustrated him, when the strange emptiness it left despite Morgan not having known him got to him, Emily would tell him about his father. About how he played the guitar, how he'd loved Seren Morgan so fiercely that her death ate him from the inside out, and how he'd quietly left the world one night because of it. This tender description had always soothed Morgan, but seeing now what younger Emily was going through, he wondered how she had managed to grow into such an understanding adult.

The scolding—which turned out to be a soft talking to—ended with Trinity offering a hug to the young girl. Emily took it without hesitation, holding fast, and Morgan couldn't help but smile. In his timeline, Emily had treated Trinity as her own mother. She had inherited the role when Seren had died, and Trinity wasn't one to shrink from responsibility. Morgan could see that their relationship had started when Emily was young and only strengthened from there.

The buzzer sounded, indicating that their delivery had arrived, and within minutes, Trinity, Morgan, and Emily all had steaming to-go mugs filled with artisanal hot cocoa, the few food containers forgotten in a bag on the counter in favor of the chocolatey brew. It was only then that

Morgan remembered his coffee, now cold and alone on the coffee table. He brought the mug to the sink and dumped its contents down the drain before returning to the living space.

"Now, tell us everything." Trinity's words were soothing as he sat down beside her on the couch, her tone kind and questioning rather than demanding.

Morgan nodded, took a steadying breath, and began to speak.

CHAPTER ELEVEN

Darius

The cold morning air did little to soothe Darius's mood. He took the time to stop and get himself a dark chocolate mocha. The past few hours had been a roller coaster, and he needed caffeine and something resembling comfort. If he had to put up with being called into the office on top of everything else that had happened, he was going to enjoy *something* about it. He also ordered a plain coffee, no sweetener or creamer, for his partner. The last thing he could tolerate was having Sibyl on his case, especially because she would more than likely be in before he was. Coffee would be his best chance at a distraction.

Drinks in hand, he quickly walked the rest of the way towards the Loop. Turning the corner, he ducked into his office building and breathed a sigh of relief as warmth once again surrounded him. The building he worked in was generic enough, a product of new innovation with glass walls for the outer offices, making it glitter in the dull January light. It was deliberately designed to resemble and blend with the other businesses found in that part of Chicago. Darius strode through the lobby, past the bank of elevators, and into the stairwell. Six stories of stair climbing was what Darius considered his morning workout. He had never been one for hitting the gym—wasn't his thing—so stairs and some light weight work at home kept him in good enough shape. Plus, the climb would give him time to think.

As soon as he had that, his thoughts immediately returned to Morgan Slavin and the chaos that had been his life for the past eight hours. It wasn't even noon yet. As he climbed, he turned everything over from beginning to end. He wasn't in the habit of leaving people to die when he could directly act to stop it, but those direct acts were usually along the lines of bringing a person to the right authorities. A hospital or a homeless shelter, perhaps. A hotel or diner, at the very least. That was usually the end of it, on the exceptionally rare times it even came up.

So what was different about Morgan?

He felt connected.

As he hit the third-floor landing in the stairwell, he gave out a rueful chuckle. Charity and compassion had never been his strong suits, and feeling any connection of any kind was rare at best. Being standoffish, prideful, and thinking of himself above others—those were his strengths. When he had shared that thought with his therapist, the psychologist had suggested that he was also quite talented at self-deprecation. Darius couldn't argue.

Still, this felt so out of character for him. He could have—*should* have—reported the incident to the Protectorate. There were procedures which one followed when recording incidents that involved mages. Darius should have followed them, but something held him back. He wanted to protect Morgan, not just from what was plaguing him, but from the admittedly cold and detached investigation of the Protectorate. A gut feeling told Darius that secrecy was best, and he hated gut feelings. Listening to them was a horrible way to lead one's life. He was a Protectorate Monitor, for fuck's sake; he was supposed to gather the facts, put them in logical order, and make rational decisions after weighing the evidence on all sides. Most of all, he was supposed to report them. He usually did.

The sixth-floor landing came before he knew it. He shouldered through the door and into the hallway. The navy blue industrial carpet was familiar and comfortable. The receptionist at the front desk spared a single glance up, then returned his eyes to the computer screen in front of him. "Mr. Adair," he offered by way of a noncommittal greeting.

"William," Darius replied, with the same amount of interest. He didn't slow down.

The Protectorate employed mages in many different areas of study and expertise, and this was his. The Indagator and Monitor section of the

Protectorate was probably best compared to nonmagical law enforcement. Indagators were field agents who followed up on reports of magic being utilized in ways that were illegal. This could be anything from openly displaying magic to mundane people to dabbling in forbidden spellcrafting arts. Monitors were then given the information that Indagators gathered and did the fact-checking, background research, and information gathering that could be done from the office in order to present a full and complete account of any magical events that crossed their desks. Unlike nonmagical law enforcement, the Protectorate had fewer issues where excessive force and brutality towards minorities and marginalized people were concerned. Magic transcended the mundane societal bigotry baked into nonmagical institutions through no small effort of the founders as well as every current member. The Protectorate accepted and respected all cultures, backgrounds, races, and creeds. No one was employed by them that could not accept that.

The Protectorate only ever involved itself in magical matters, and if someone called everyone in, then Chicago more than likely had a serious magical issue on its hands.

This floor of the building housed the Protectorate Monitors. Here, they researched and observed activity that had proven harmful, depending on Indagators for information from out in the field. It was set up with a series of offices along the outside and a few open-air conference areas in the center. Most of the office areas housed two monitors who had been partnered together, for a total of eight agents in the separate spaces. One of the unused rooms had been converted into a staff lounge area with a kitchenette and a couple of tables. The last and largest of the work areas was occupied by the Lead Monitor, who oversaw the entire floor. The walls of every room were made of glass, and each office had similar contemporary furniture to give it a uniform appearance. Natural light gave the space an abundance of illumination but also sent a very clear message: everything could be seen. There was no hiding anything.

"About time!" Sibyl said, turning her chair to face him when he stepped into their office. Her hair, dyed a vibrant auburn, was pulled back in a ponytail that was only successful in keeping half of it tamed. Her skin was a shade that she herself likened to porcelain. She was one of those people who took great pride in their appearance and made sure others knew it. He dreaded the sunnier months, if only because he had to tolerate daily complaints as to how difficult it was to keep her skin out of the sun.

Sibyl Diluna had been his partner for nearly half a decade. When Darius's life had blown up six years earlier, Sibyl had been one of the people who were there to witness at least part of it. Back then, she had only just started with the Protectorate, a novice Monitor assigned to keep an eye on Darius's comings and goings. The Protectorate had been suspicious of Viviane de Winter, his mentor, but without proof of wrongdoing, their hands were tied. She had pull in the higher echelons of the Protectorate, and any suspicion on her part would mean an end to investigative efforts. The Protectorate had decided that Darius would be the easier subject to keep track of. He had resented the Protectorate for their meddling at the time, not knowing how it would help save his life.

While Sybil had helped Darius in the end, she was also the Monitor who contributed most to the case against de Winter. In fact, it had played a large role in her making a name for herself as a Monitor in the Protectorate ranks. After the situation had come to a head, Darius was taken into custody until his innocence could be proven. He had heard that, in his absence and with Seren no longer living, Sibyl's recounting of the case painted her in a very advantageous light. He didn't know if those rumors were true. He hadn't been in the frame of mind to judge them. Once Darius had been cleared of wrongdoing and reinstated within the Protectorate, the Lead Monitor at the time had partnered them together, thinking that Sybil could 'keep an eye' on him. Darius hadn't felt it his place to object. He had, after all, been the one in the wrong. Besides, he found Sybil to be a capable Monitor, if not occasionally irritating.

He offered her a shrug and put the large coffee in front of her, watching her pale blue eyes light up. She practically snatched the cup up and took a long, deep breath, smiling dreamily. "All right, distraction achieved. Anything in it?"

"No. Just black coffee."

Her dreamy smile widened. "You know me so well. Need to get some creamer!" She hopped up and pushed past him, hurrying to the break room.

Alone in the office, Darius took his time removing his coat and hanging it on the peg on the wall. He dropped into his office chair with a sigh and took a long drink from his coffee. He wasn't looking forward to finding out what Administration had called them in for. He was unsure if he was hoping for it to be nothing of real interest or something he might be able to sink his teeth into. It might help distract him from his current situation.

He knew he shouldn't want a distraction. Morgan was in trouble, and Darius hated to admit it, but he wasn't sure how to help him out of it. Not until he had a better handle on the truth of Morgan's claim. He hoped Trinity might be able to shed some light on it. She was one of the most talented gnosis and cycle mages he knew. If there was anything to be gleaned from Morgan's aura or spirit or whatever else that Darius was rubbish at reading, he was sure Trin would find it.

Hell, he thought she would make an excellent Indagator if it wasn't for her immense dislike towards and distrust of the Protectorate itself.

He couldn't blame her. His own mentor had been one of the highest-ranking members of the elders within the Protectorate, and she had committed atrocities with that power. The only reason Darius still held any trust in the Protectorate was that he knew how well de Winter had hidden her intentions from everyone, even himself. The Protectorate had also picked up the pieces and helped him do the same. He was grateful.

Besides, dwelling on the past wouldn't do him any good with his current problems.

Despite not knowing what his next move should be, Darius still felt himself drawn to Morgan. He doubted the pull was magical in nature. Besides his own skill with identifying magical means of mental influence, if Morgan was attempting to manipulate him, the symbols tattooed on his scalp would prevent it. Even a talented, well-trained mage wouldn't be able to get past the protection without considerable difficulties, not least of all Darius being alerted to the attempt.

No, this was something different. It was emotional. He wanted to help. He wanted to do more than he would normally be able to, the disconnected way that a Monitor could help in a magical situation, with fact finding and data collating. Maybe Darius saw a bit of himself, the scared and misled person he had been. Or maybe he just liked Morgan? Either way, he wanted to assuage Morgan's fears and try to help him find peace in a world that seemed too foreign and hurtful to him.

It was then that Sibyl came back in, sipping at her coffee. She raised a wry eyebrow at what she saw on his face. "What's up? You look, I don't know," she waved a hand in the air before continuing. "Distracted? You never look distracted."

He shrugged and opened his laptop, letting his silence answer the question. He frequently did that and always seemed more than happy to draw her own conclusions. Darius had no desire to tell her anything about what had transpired in the last eight hours, either in his thoughts or in his apartment. He worried that her next attempt at ingratiating herself with superiors would be with any information he might share. He didn't want the information to find its way to their higher-ups before Darius was able to weigh the pros and cons further. Certainly not before Morgan was feeling better.

Sibyl sat down at her own computer, adjacent to him, and studied him, drinking her coffee and squinting. Her scrutiny was relentless until she suddenly gasped, shooting back up to her feet. "Wait a minute! Did you do what I think you did?"

Darius sighed. He'd heard this tone of voice before. Not with him but with others around the office. She thought she was onto something, and there would be no stopping her now.

"Depends," he replied, trying to sound casual. "What do you think I did?"

"Did you get laid?" There was a pause, then she dropped her tone to a more conspiratorial volume and hissed. "You *did*, didn't you? Come on, share the details. Who is he?"

He hated the way her tone changed when she asked these questions. She had gone from slightly suspicious to the television stereotype of a workplace gossip monger, and the way she suggested him having found a masculine individual made him want to cringe. It was the unabashed excitement of someone who thought gay people were somehow still a novelty.

Strictly speaking, he *had* found himself a man. He knew that wasn't what she meant, though. Still, he cursed himself as he felt his cheeks warm. He hoped it wasn't noticeable. "No."

"You're blushing, Adair!" she said, grinning widely. "You got yourself some."

His hopes dashed, Darius forced himself not to groan. "This entire conversation is completely inappropriate," he managed, wishing she would drop the subject.

"Excuse me," she snapped. She strode to the door and swung it shut, though softly enough to prevent it from slamming. "We've been partners for years; this is an entirely appropriate conversation to have. You need to give me details!"

Darius clenched his jaw. He *would not* be giving her anything remotely resembling the slightest of information. Years ago, when they had first been partnered, she had insisted on going to a local bar—some dive named Elysium—to talk. Eager to have everything out in the open, Darius had informed her that he was bisexual. It was as if she had heard 'gay,' and she ran with it. While it had stopped her from making any more flirty remarks to him, thank goodness, the biphobia and erasure were sharp pinpricks when they arose. Her actual response to his sharing had been to insist that she knew he had to be gay, that his relationship with Seren had been a fluke, and that she knew because Darius hadn't been attracted to Sybil herself, so he *must* be gay. That behavior had been all he needed to inform him that she was not a person worth confiding in, regardless of how much 'ally' paraphernalia she insisted on showing him when Pride month rolled around. While it resulted in a more professional and distant relationship, it also meant that he was forced to endure her conclusions when she did leap to them.

He had considered reporting her for harassment on more than one occasion, but he vacillated on whether or not it was worth the trouble.

"There are no details. Nothing happened," he replied, tone even and uninterested.

Before she could speak again, there was a knock at the door. Sighing in frustration, Sybil snatched at the handle and opened the door.

One of the office assistants stood on the other side. Darius immediately remembered their first name was Baylee, though he couldn't place their surname. Of course, nothing said they had one. The assistant offered a small smile. "Lead Monitor Powell wants everyone at conference table one as soon as possible."

"Thanks, Baylee. We will be right there."

Sybil glared at Darius, but he ignored it, instead pulling a notebook and pen from his desk and moving past his partner before she could offer any sort of argument.

Darius hurried to grab a seat at the large conference table at the far end of the room's center. There were three conference areas, all situated in the center of the office, all surrounded by glass walls. The Protectorate had become big on transparency within the last century or so. Perceived transparency, at least. Darius was sure that there were still more than a fair share of backroom dealings and quiet investigations. Not everyone was a safe person to entrust information to.

His co-workers filed in quietly, everyone taking a seat. A few others had notebooks, as he did. One or two had brought their laptops. Sybil eventually dropped into the seat beside him, coffee noticeably absent from her hand. She wore a faint scowl but said nothing to him. In fact, there was very little conversation among any of his colleagues, aside from a few hushed and curious whispers.

Everyone settled as soon as the meeting was called to order. Ty Powell, Lead Monitor for the Protectorate's Chicago branch, was a commanding presence despite being slightly shorter than Darius. He was lean, with a slender face and short blonde hair kept in a professional cut. His eyes were a sharp blue as he looked over the people at the table, taking them all in. Only the head of their department for a little over a year, he still managed to draw respect and admiration from the people he led. He wasn't feared but fiercely respected and had a reputation for being an advocate for his workers as well as himself. Darius had heard that once, before his post here, a Monitor had dared to dead name him, acting as if Ty being a trans man was a fact that could be used against him. The man was gone the next morning, transferred to a lesser post and ordered to attend six months of diversity training or risk losing their standing in the Protectorate for flagrant discrimination and harassment. The Lead Monitor wasted none of his patience on those who didn't deserve it, and Darius felt both safe and proud to be working in his unit.

"All right, everyone," the Lead Monitor said, stepping to the head of the table. "Apologies to call some of you in on days off, but all hands on deck are required."

There were a few 'yes sir's, but for the most part, everyone remained quiet, waiting for him to continue.

"In the early morning hours, the Protectorate's Cosmology people registered a substantial surge or surges of magical energy. They're not sure yet if it was one powerful one or multiple, and they're sifting through the data and residual space-time magic while they can. As of right now, there's no direct explanation or culprit, and the energy is apparently unlike anything cosmology has seen or can explain." Ty grinned. "We all know how much those folks love something they can't explain."

"Is it dangerous?" asked Baylee, from their place at the end of the table. They looked and sounded worried.

Ty's smile became reassuring. "So far as they can tell, no, but I wouldn't let my guard down."

A feeling of dread was settling in the pit of Darius's stomach, but he remained quiet, his expression a cool mask of mild interest and neutrality.

Ty continued. "For three to four hours afterward, there was a strong amount of..." He trailed off, holding the paper he was reading from closer. "Disruptive energy being emitted from a number of different locations, each ranging from one to five city blocks." As he spoke, he gestured, and the table's surface lit up like a map, highlighting a number of areas in the metropolitan area. One of the areas was a rough match to where Darius had found Morgan, but he wasn't sure what the others were for or what could have occurred to set them off. Had Morgan tried to break through the timeline at multiple points?

"Sir?" came a question. "What kind of disruptive energy?"

"They didn't specify in this report."

That drew a few quiet comments and some mumbling around the table.

"I'm sure they'll get us the information as soon as they have it," Ty said, clearing his throat to quiet the group. "After that time," he continued, "the energy ceased and hasn't reoccurred since." He sighed, resting a hand on his hip. "I'm going to be moving Monitors specifically onto this case, as our Lead Indagator has increased the number of Indagators investigating as well. She's out in the field right now, but any questions can be funneled through me. Some of you will be putting current assignments on hold to shift over, while others will be called on to take on a bit more work to help keep us from falling behind." There were a few unmuffled groans, and Ty nodded. "I know, but the Protectorate has agreed to extra pay for the trouble, so there will be overtime available for all those who are looking for it."

He began to list off Monitors who would rendezvous with Indagators to begin working on this assignment. Darius was relieved that neither he nor his partner's names were called. "The rest of you will be receiving work from the reassigned individuals by the end of the workday. Also, after today, everyone should consider themselves on-call. Hopefully, this is nothing, but it could be a whole hell of a lot of something, and I don't want to be caught unaware. If you have any questions, you know where to find me. Dismissed."

Darius stood, mechanically moving back towards his office. Sybil followed, and as soon as they were in the office, she turned to him, excitement in her pale eyes. "What do you think it was?"

"Just what the lead monitor said," Darius murmured with a shrug. He would *not* be saying anything more to her.

She pursed her lips and pondered for a moment before speaking again. "I wonder if it's the Ascendant?" The Ascendant were a group of mages who thought they were gifts to the Earth, sometimes literally. In the past, they had been one of the strongest associations within the mage world, and they acted as if humanity was there to cater to their whims. Millennia before they had ruled over others and had no qualms about destroying those who couldn't perceive magic. That was the lore, at least. Currently, they were considered a terrorist organization by the Protectorate and most mages.

"They've been quiet lately," Sybil was saying. "Ever since, well, your thing with de Winter."

Her words were casual, but Darius felt like he had been doused with ice water. The reminder of his former mentor's connections, of just the woman himself, was enough to knock him sideways. The blood drained from his face. To hear the name spoken aloud was jarring. He had thought it plenty of times. How could he not? Hearing the words, the palpability of the sound was immense and crushing. He shuddered inwardly as a wave of memories crashed in around him.

"This doesn't feel right," he remembered saying.

"Darius, this is part of your training. You must endure. Just relax." Had been her response.

He'd been twelve at the time. Twelve.

He tried to shut out the memory of her voice, low and smooth. Even just the recall of it conjured heart-rending shame. He should have known better. He should have done something.

No, he tried to tell himself. *You were a child; you couldn't have known.* He clung to the words, repeating them silently, over and over, even as his world seemed to contract.

Sybil gasped, her hand moving over her mouth. Maybe she had seen his reaction, or maybe she was just remembering the trauma he had endured, but either way, her expression had transformed into one of remorse. "Oh shit, I'm sorry, Dar. I didn't even think."

"It's fine," he said. It wasn't. He clenched his jaw hard, trying to fight the wave of nausea that threatened to overtake him. "It's fine. It's in the past." This wasn't how he had intended to have to get through the workday, but he wouldn't let some thoughtless comment from his partner completely dismantle him.

He excused himself with a mumbled, "I'll be right back," and hurried to the restroom, splashing cold water on his face. The frigid shock helped cut through the panic clouding his mind, and he repeated the gesture twice before he wiped the excess droplets away and raised his head to meet his reflection's dark gaze.

He looked pale. He wasn't a man who had a lot of color in general, but the anxiety and panic made him look an almost sickly shade of white. The dark circles under his eyes did little to alleviate that look. If he couldn't figure out how to look a bit less like death, he would be fielding questions all day about whether he was feeling well or if he should perhaps consider going home early. He couldn't stand the thought of that. First and foremost, he didn't want this to define him, to keep him from being able to do work that he enjoyed doing.

He was dependable, reliable, and he did not let something that happened more than half a decade ago continue to drag him down. Secondly, and more distantly but still an important aspect of his reasoning, he didn't want to raise the slightest specter of suspicion. He still had a mage claiming to have traveled back in time holed up in his apartment. If this power surge had been Morgan breaking through to a time and space other than his own, Darius had no desire for that information to get out. Not yet, anyway. He still needed to get a solid grasp on what exactly was going on with Morgan. If possible, he'd want to help protect the man. He was vulnerable and alone, and Darius knew what that felt like. He'd had Seren, once all those years ago. Now, he would be that support for Morgan.

He nodded to his reflection, determination quieting his anxiety. It wasn't gone, but it was manageable, and that was all Darius needed.

CHAPTER TWELVE

Morgan

"I'm not even sure where to begin," Morgan said, turning the styrofoam cup of piping hot chocolate around in his hands. The soft *shhh, shhh, shhh* sound that the bottom of the cup made against the countertop soothed him. He wasn't sure he had the strength to go through all of this again, even if it was just retelling what had happened.

Across from him, Trinity and Emily both sat on stools. The studio apartment didn't boast a dining table, but the counter was designed to seat at least four. Trinity quietly helped Emily get situated on her stool, which was a bit bigger than she was used to. Once the young girl was comfortable, Trinity took a sip of her coca and followed it with a quiet nod. "Why don't you try from the beginning. The very beginning."

Morgan took a long, measured breath. He felt as if he was on stage, expected to perform, and he wasn't sure how he could fulfill the role. "Well, I guess my beginning is you getting together with Dad."

Trinity coughed, choking on her cocoa.

Emily giggled. "Trinity and Daddy sitting in a tree, K-I-S-S-I-N-G," she sing-songed, bobbing her head back and forth before hiding her smile behind her cup.

Trinity, eyebrow arched, gave the child some expert side-eye before she spoke. "You do know what comes after K-I-S-S-I-N-G, right?"

Emily thought for a moment. Realization quickly dawned, and she made a face. "Eww, are you going to talk about sex?"

Morgan started at the frankness of Emily's question. That was literally the *last* thing he wanted to discuss with his sister or his mother, regardless of what timeline he was in. Trinity didn't bat an eyelash. She just nodded her head slowly to Emily, an expression of the utmost seriousness on her face.

"Eww," Emily said again. She looked at Morgan, then back to Trinity. "Can I borrow your phone? Do you have any games on it?"

"Yes, you can, and only the two you installed last time," came Trinity's wry reply. Still, she pulled the device from her back pocket and handed it over to the girl.

Emily snatched it and grinned. "Thank you! If you need me, I'll be on the couch with the phone volume up all the way." She expertly hopped off of the stool and gingerly grabbed her mug. With slow, careful steps, she made her way toward the living room area, disappearing from view on the couch after placing the mug on the coffee table.

"All right," Trinity said, her voice lower and her eyes trying to see if Emily was settled in. When she was satisfied that the child wasn't eavesdropping, she turned back to Morgan. "Hopefully, that's a bit more comfortable. Just keep your voice down if you can." She smiled.

Morgan nodded, relieved that she'd had a plan. It was a small relief to not have younger ears listening in. It wasn't a story for children, and Morgan wasn't sure he could sugarcoat it enough to get it to one.

Trinity reached across the counter with both arms, hands turned upwards. She could see he was struggling and offered him comfort he could take hold of. He put his hands on hers, marveling at how small they seemed in his. He remembered them being bigger. Or had he just been so much younger the last time he had held them? Seeing their hands together made him feel secure. She wouldn't lose him. Wouldn't let go.

"Something happened this year, in 2022," Morgan began, voice low. He was trying to think, to put his thoughts in a sort of order to help tell this, and it took all of his concentration. "Or maybe something was supposed to happen and didn't. Whatever it was, it had a ripple effect in the pattern of magic. We just didn't know it." He took a few long, steadying breaths and continued, never letting go of her hands. "It began to affect people's minds, everyone's minds. Mages and the unmagical alike. It was worse for mages, though, because we're all connected to the magic. The more magic that was worked, the worse it got. It just seeped into everything."

"How?" asked Trinity.

"We all know that the nonmagical mind protects itself, right? If someone witnesses some small spell craft, their mind brushes it off or chalks it up to the closest logical explanation. Except magic was everywhere. It seeped into *everything*. Spells were ostentatious and unpredictably overpowered, and even when someone wasn't working magic, it was overloading them, like radiation or something. Eventually, it was out of control. Mages were fighting in the streets. Unmagical people started manifesting and accessing magic, but they weren't *mages*. They became something *different*. They could use magic, but it tore their minds apart. It rotted everything.

"It got so bad, and it was everywhere. The Protectorate was infected. Their agents fell with everything else. It wasn't just Chicago, either. The world was ruined. It had spread." His voice cracked. He could feel himself shaking but couldn't stop. "Then, everything went silent. No communication, no nothing. So, Emily and a few others, we all—we all came up with a plan to try and do what no one else had ever been able to do. It was the only thing we could think of."

"Send you back in time to stop whatever it was that started it all," Trinity supplied.

"No," Morgan said. "Not at first. The original plan was for Emily to come back or go back or whatever. But she... she..." he trailed off. He couldn't bring himself to say, out loud, that she was dead. It would be too final. It would hurt too much. He took a shaky breath.

Trinity gave his hands a squeeze even as she glanced past him to check on young Emily. Then her gaze moved back to his, and her expression was one of kind comfort. There was no skepticism to be seen. She believed him. Actually believed him. She squeezed his hands and nodded. "All right, and what about you? Or maybe I mean us? What was your story growing up?"

Morgan pressed Trinity's hands with his before drawing back, wrapping both hands around the to-go cup of hot cocoa. The beverage within was still hot, and the warmth radiated into him. He sighed heavily and took a long drink. "I was born maybe a year and a half from now, I think. Dad died by suicide when I was really young." Despite Emily being out of earshot, Morgan lowered his voice further. He couldn't imagine having her hear this. "After that, it was just you, Emily, and me." He smiled at the cup in his hands. "It was good. Fun. Aside from what was slowly going on in the world on a wider scale, our little family was pretty damn good. When I was sixteen, y-you—" He stopped, his body physically refusing to say the word *died*.

The interruption threw off his thoughts entirely. He lost track of where he had been in his story, and the confusion unstuck him from his place in the world around him. Panic crawled up his spine, sticky and prickling.

Then Trinity was there, her hand over his on the cup. Without him realizing it, she'd left her own seat and now stood next to him, her free hand on his shoulder to steady him. He tried to focus on the feeling of her. She had done the same thing to him when he was younger, when he felt sick or afraid. One hand over his, one on his shoulder. There to catch him if he fell but giving him the strength not to. He felt the anxiety subside. It didn't vanish entirely, but it had diminished to a manageable degree.

"You good?" asked Trinity quietly.

"I think so," Morgan replied, drinking his cocoa and using the smell and taste to ground himself. "I'm twenty-six. It took about twenty years or so for everything to get bad enough that it was noticeable, and by then, it was too late. Five- or six years' worth of trying to fight these strange, twisted people who were using magic but shouldn't be able to. It would devour them. Corrode holes in their brains. It's not even an exaggeration. They were husks of magic and rage. The magic just ate through them." He shook his head, his shoulders sagging. He could remember how hollow those husks had been. Skin peeling, eyes empty but for a single, small pinpoint of light. "We had to do something, and that's when we hatched the plan. It's when we decided to punch a hole through space and time and chuck someone through." He laughed mirthlessly at the way he described it. Just open the way and throw. His voice was barely a whisper when he said, "It came at a price."

Blood everywhere. There was blood all over him, and none of it was his. Shrieks in the distance. Then someone—Cady maybe— shouted that they had to do it. There was no time. He threw himself into the casting circle. The chanting, the screaming, the whipping wind and the wailing. Then there was burning, so much burning. Every atom of his being was being seared to near nothing. Incinerated into nonexistence. How could it hurt so—

His world had been unmade. Nothing around him was real. Or was it him? Was he not real?

Morgan stumbled back, distantly hearing a clatter and bang. He didn't know what it was. He didn't know where he was. All he felt was the agony. He thought there was a muffled shout, maybe. Then he was falling. He heard his name, and then he wasn't falling.

Then he was lying on the floor, his body splayed, his head resting on something soft. A pillow? Had he dreamt it all? He blinked, and as his vision cleared, he saw that Emily and Trinity hovered over him, twin expressions of concern on their faces. Emily's eyes shone with tears.

"You with us?" asked Trinity.

"Yes," he said, his voice a rasping whisper. He cleared his throat and nodded, trying again. "Yes. What happened?"

"You fainted," Emily said, her voice shaky.

"What were you feeling right before it happened?" asked Trinity.

"I was remembering the casting," he said, doing his best not to call up the memories again. He closed his eyes and brought his hands up, palms resting on his forehead. "How it *felt*." It had been horrible. Even now, he could sense the ripples the magic sent through his entirety. When would this subside? Would it ever? Tears stung his eyes. "What did I do to myself? Am I always going to be like this?"

Trinity shrugged. "I don't know, kiddo. I don't know."

Her unsure answer didn't comfort him, but hearing the nickname she used gave him a small glimmer of warmth. His mother had always called him kiddo.

"Do you think you can sit up?" she asked cautiously.

Morgan nodded but didn't immediately move to do so. Instead, he took a few long breaths, steadying himself. Slowly he sat up, needing assistance when he did so. "Give me a second," he murmured, the room spinning lazily around him. Once it stopped, he nodded to Trinity. Her grip was right under and around his upper arm as she half-lifted him to his feet. He was feeling more light-headed than he thought, and he nodded toward the couch. "Can you help me over?"

Trinity nodded but worry furrowed her brow. She walked beside him to the couch and lowered him down as he moved to sit. Emily moved to sit beside him, wrapping his arm up in an embrace. "Are you all right?" she asked, eyes wide.

"I don't know," he answered truthfully.

Trinity crossed her arms over her chest, thinking. "All right, you should get some rest. I'll shoot Darius a text and maybe call Ines and see if she can come check on you in a bit." She turned to Emily and flashed her a smile. "Come on, kiddo, get your things."

"I don't have any things," she said.

"Your coat? Scarf? Did you wear a hat and gloves?" Trinity huffed, shooting the girl an exasperated glare. "Get them together and go wait by the door. I just need to say a few quick things to Morgan."

Emily nodded, but before she climbed off the couch, she rose to her knees and planted a gentle kiss on Morgan's temple. "Feel better. I'll see you soon." The whisper was so serious, so solemn, that Morgan could feel those tears threatening again.

"Bye," he said, his response feeling small in comparison with his sister's.

As she wandered to the door, Trinity turned to him. "I want you lying on this couch, doing nothing, until Darius is back or Ines calls up from the door. She was here before, right?" Morgan struggled to remember. Distantly, he had a recollection of another person, a woman. He thought she was Ines. At his hesitant nod, Trinity fished her phone out of her pocket and unlocked the screen. "Good. She can come by again. Your aura is…" She trailed off, looking for the words to explain what she had seen. "It's bad, I won't lie. Don't use any magic for a bit. It needs time to heal," she said, finally.

"But it will heal?"

"I think so, yes." She nodded, emphasizing her answer. "Ines might be able to help you with the physical stuff for right now. I'll tell her to call Darius, and you can all work out a time for her to drop by."

Morgan nodded and laid down across the couch, tugging one of the throw pillows from its spot and under his head. He let out a long sigh. Trinity's voice was beginning to sound distant as she made her phone calls. It was a soft, pleasant constant as he lay quietly, trying to keep himself calm. He heard Trinity and Emily call another goodbye from the door, then the door close, the lock clicking home.

He let out a soft, choked sigh and closed his eyes against the nauseating tangle he had, with the best of intentions, made out of his life.

CHAPTER THIRTEEN

Darius

When the sunlight—gray as it was—vanished for the day, Chicago turned bitter. The walk home, despite being short, was an unpleasant one. Puddles of slush were hardening to ice and the air was sharp with a winter breeze that sent people fleeing indoors. Darius made it a point to stop at the coffee shop on his journey home if only to snatch a few minutes of relief from the cold night. He still played the phone conversation he'd had with Trinity over in his mind, trying to make sense of it.

Morgan's aura and the magic that flowed around and through him was a mess. According to Trinity, it had been torn to shreds and stitched back together, and she surmised this was a result of the magic craft that had sent Morgan back in time. He had needed to literally break himself down in order to pass through time the way he had, and the reconstitution afterward left him whole, but precariously so. She thought it might be why Morgan was in such bad condition, his physical form still recovering from the havoc that magic played on him.

"It looks like it will improve. It was slowly stitching itself back together when I saw it, but it is going to be a slow process," Trinity had said.

"Have you ever seen something like this before?"

There was silence on the other end of the line, then, "No, I haven't. It's scary. I did see it trying to mend itself, though. He has to give it time to do that. Have him avoid crafting spells for now, along with anything else that might affect his aura."

"Got it," he agreed. "Anything else?"

"I left him sleeping. I called Ines. She said she'll be there when she can. She also mentioned sending you a personalized bill?"

Darius chuckled. "I'm sure she did."

"Keep me posted about him," Trinity had concluded. "You know Emily will come knock down your door if you don't."

Less than fifteen minutes later, Darius was in his building and at his apartment door, still trying to shake the January chill. He fumbled with his keys, finally managing to unlock the door. Once he was in the apartment, he shut the door behind him, making a point to lock it as well.

The apartment was dark. Not a single light was on. He blinked, trying to give his eyes time to adjust from the harsh fluorescent hallway light. Once they did, he saw that some illumination filtered in from the city beyond the windows. The drapes had been opened wide, and a warm orange glow from the streetlights filtered in, along with the faint strobing of the cars driving down the street far below.

He unshouldered his messenger bag and laid it quietly on the floor next to the counter. He didn't want to wake Morgan if the man had managed to get some more sleep. He removed his shoes and moved quietly through the kitchen. Once past it, he rounded the bookshelf to check the bed but saw it was empty. Confused, he turned to the couch.

Morgan was more dark shape than person. He was curled up on his side, legs pulled tight against his chest and head tucked in. He was facing the back of the couch, his back to the world. Darius had no expression by which to judge what had happened. Was he asleep? Was something wrong?

"Don't worry, I'm not asleep." Morgan's hoarse whisper was dry and rough, stifled with tears that either had been shed or were waiting until the dam broke.

"What's wrong?" Darius asked, reflexively concerned at the gravelly tone of his voice. "Did something more happen?"

For a long time, Morgan didn't answer. The quiet stretched between them. Just as Darius was about to give up on a response, Morgan spoke.

"I made myself wrong."

The words were so quiet and muffled by the couch cushion, Darius wasn't sure he had heard them correctly. "What do you mean?"

Morgan shifted. When he spoke again, his words were less garbled. "I made myself wrong." His voice hitched. "I did this *thing*. I came back to help. I thought I could help, but it changed me. It changed my magic. I'm different. Scattered. Bits and pieces where a whole used to be." He hugged himself tighter, and Darius could just make out his shoulders moving, shuddering with quiet tears.

Darius let out a long sigh and sat down on the couch, giving Morgan some space but still offering the comfort of proximity. He was at a loss of what to do or how to soothe him. He had no idea what undertaking the feat that Morgan had would do to a mage's psyche, their aura, even their very connection to magic. In his schooling, Darius had heard many a philosophical discussion of the possibility of time travel. It had been a lot of abstract talk by tutors and scholars that he hadn't understood and didn't mean a damn thing in the practical sense. Darius was out of his depth, and it made him supremely uncomfortable.

Morgan sat up, though most of his features were still lost in shadow. "I don't think I can fix it. I don't think anyone can. Who would want to try? No one wants a broken person. I don't know how to pick up the pieces. I don't know if I even have the energy. Who would want to if I don't?" he was crying now, his words wet with tears and tumbling out in a rush. "It's too much work."

Darius felt the words in his chest, a physical blow that sucked the oxygen from his lungs. Years before, he had thought something similar. He was broken. There was nothing there worth saving, and even if there was, who would think him worth the trouble. He had been used and betrayed by his mentor, had lost the person he loved, and had been left to pick up the pieces on his own. He knew how lonely it felt. He racked his brain for something to say or do. Almost without realizing it, he shifted closer to Morgan and held out his arms. The other man, distraught, took him up on the unspoken offer.

Darius pulled him into a tight hug, wrapping his arms around Morgan and holding him tightly. It felt silly, but Darius held on as if letting go meant abandoning him. He licked his lips and forced himself to speak,

89

regardless of how awkward it might feel. After all, he had only known Morgan for a handful of hours, but here he was, the only port in the storm. "I know this is hard. I've had to do it, too." His voice, already a rasp, cracked. He couldn't go down that road. Not yet. "I'm here to help, all right? I will help you pick up those pieces."

Morgan stiffened in his embrace, but after a moment, he relaxed, and a second later, his body resumed its shaking as he quietly sobbed. Darius held onto him until the tears subsided, determined to show him that he was not alone. Morgan finally leaned back, sniffling. His face was flushed, his eyes rimmed red and swollen from tears. Darius was surprised at how strong the urge to wipe them away was. Instead, he gave Morgan a small smile. "Better?"

Morgan nodded, meeting Darius's gaze.

The air between them was suddenly charged, sparking with a tension that took Darius by surprise. His breath caught in his throat, and he couldn't look away. For the first time in a long while, he felt a warmth growing in his chest. A connection. It had been all of a day and a half of knowing Morgan, but still, there was somethi—

Morgan leaned forward and captured Darius's mouth with a kiss.

Darius froze, fighting not to jerk away from him out of sheer surprise.

Morgan must have felt the reaction. He pulled back a fraction of a second later, stammering apologies. "I'm sorry. I thought... I mean, I should have asked, and we were so close, and you were being so..." He didn't seem to be able to complete a single thought, much less speak it.

Darius recovered first, putting his hands up. "It's all right," he said, forcing the words out. He could see Morgan building up again, and he wanted to avoid it.

"Oh no. Oh hell, are you even queer?" Morgan blurted out, his eyes once again filling with tears. "I am so sorry, Darius."

"Stop, stop, stop," Darius ordered, trying to keep his voice calm though raising it slightly to be heard. "Relax, okay? Yes, yes, I am queer, all right? Breathe."

Morgan nodded frantically but didn't look any calmer.

Darius took a deep breath and stood up. The surprise had sent adrenaline surging through him, and he now had nowhere to go with it. He needed to move, to try and free himself from the excess energy. He looked around nervously, his mind grasping for something, anything, to fill the silence between them. "Do you want something to drink?" he asked, striding to the kitchen. "I have water. I can brew some decaf. I also have tea?" As he went through the motions of collecting what he would need for tea, he repeated each step to himself quietly, drawing calm from the routine.

"Water is fine," Morgan murmured, voice weak.

"Ice or no?" Darius turned on the electric kettle for his tea before he retrieved a glass for Morgan.

"Yes." It sounded more like a question than an answer to one.

He used the time he had until the water boiled to calm the rest of the way down. Choosing a relaxing herbal blend of tea, he sweetened it, then brought it and Morgan's water back into the living room. He handed the glass to Morgan but didn't sit back down. Instead, he moved to the window, looking out at the lights of Chicago beyond the glass and taking a taste of his tea. "I'm bi, so you don't have to worry." He breathed and took another sip from his mug, enjoying the lingering warmth as he braced himself for what came next. "I'm also demi."

Morgan blinked, took in what Darius said, and took a large gulp of his water. He seemed to understand it in stages, and his eyes widened a bit more with each stage completed. When it all set in, he looked away, studying the cup in his hands and avoiding Darius's gaze. "Oh. All right. I'm sorry. I should have asked. Or not actually assumed something like that at all. I mean, I've known you a few hours, that's it." He sounded disappointed but not upset.

Darius thought the disappointment was almost worse.

The nervous energy in Darius's body had dissipated almost entirely. He took another long drink of his tea. "I'm not great with emotions and relationships, but...but I feel as if I like you. Or I'm starting to, but definitely not ready to get, uhm, physical. I'm not there yet." Every word

91

felt like he was prying it from the depth of his psyche. Still, he wanted to speak them, even if it was uncomfortable. "It's hard to explain."

Very few of his partners, regardless of gender, seemed to understand the concept of being demi, and explaining it was always this strange mixture of apprehension and annoyance. It wasn't *that* difficult of a concept. To need a connection before it went further, before he could feel that physical attraction—that was it. Simple, right? Yet here he was, cheeks burning with embarrassment and perhaps fear of being rejected just for the way he was.

It wouldn't be the first time.

Morgan's expression changed, and his gaze moved to meet Darius's, a wide smile spreading across his lips. "Wait... You like me?" he asked, his face practically glowing.

Darius let out a small laugh. "Well, I think there's a connection forming between us," he admitted, slightly flustered. *I want there to be a connection.* He could feel heat rising in his face, but he kept going. "I want to help. I know that much."

"Thank you." Morgan smiled. "For telling me and for offering the help."

"Thank me once I've actually helped."

Morgan shrugged, but his expression didn't change. "You already have."

CHAPTER FOURTEEN

Morgan

Morgan didn't think he'd ever been so embarrassed in his entire life.

He'd *kissed* Darius.

The *one* person who was helping him.

Well, that was a bit of an exaggeration. There were others helping, too. Trinity and Emily were on his side as well, and even Ines, who had shown up to the apartment about an hour after Darius had gotten back, was firmly in his corner. The first thing she had announced upon walking into the apartment was that she had been given strict instructions from Trinity to take a full set of vitals and see if there was anything else she might be able to do, be it magical or mundane.

"Who am I to argue?" she asked, eyebrow arched and with a wry smile. "It's not like any of you think I have a life. Besides, Trinity can be frightening when she needs to be."

"She's barely half your age," Darius retorted.

"Don't you know? The older you get, the stronger your sense of self-preservation."

Darius rolled his eyes but gave no other reaction.

It was strange, seeing people in the past. Or, Morgan supposed, should he start calling it the present? Still, having memories of Trinity and Emily being so much older, and seeing them in his now-present, younger, and so different, was jarring. They didn't have the weight of tragedy and despair rounding their shoulders and pulling them down. Morgan was thankful for it, but it also made him worry. What if he couldn't stop whatever event that had ruined so many lives? What if he couldn't even figure out what *it* was? He assumed that it had to be something substantial and that—hopefully—it hadn't happened yet. Still, so much was weighing on his shoulders, and failure was not an option.

There was also another worry. In the other timeline, where he had met and known Trinity, and Emily, and Ines, there had been no Darius. At least not that he could remember. He assumed Darius could have distanced himself enough from Trinity and the rest so as not to be in their circles. He also could have died. The thought made him nauseous.

Whatever had happened, Morgan had never known him. He considered telling Darius as much, but would it matter now? By coming back, Morgan had changed the timeline. It was entirely possible that nothing that had happened in his own timeline would happen again. After all, Morgan traveling through it fundamentally changed events. What he had known as his own timeline probably didn't exist anymore. He groaned to himself. He hated trying to wrap his head around time travel.

Ines pressed her stethoscope against the inside of Morgan's elbow, just below the cuff she took his blood pressure with. "Sit up, both feet on the floor."

Morgan did as he was told. "Sorry to keep making you come back here," he murmured.

Ines shook her head dismissively. "Don't even worry about it." She leaned in, a cynical expression on her face. "I don't have much of a life these days. Between the nursing shortage and my innate talents, I'm basically just going from work to home and back again a few hours later." She shrugged. "One more servant to the great god of capitalism."

Morgan nodded, still feeling bad to have to drag her back. That, mingling with his chagrin at having thrown himself at Darius, kept him quiet for the rest of exam, which only consisted of a check of the lymph nodes, a listen to his heart and lungs, and a quick aura glance. "It's probably still too early for things to be getting easier for you, huh?" The look on her face told him that she hadn't liked what she had seen in his aura. She glanced at Darius. "Did Trin say anything about it?"

"Just that she hadn't seen anything like it," Darius answered, voice flat. "She said it looked like it was trying to reknit itself and that he shouldn't try spellcraft for a bit." He sounded irritated, and he shrugged. "That's all I know."

"Oh, you mind magicians and your insistence on one-track studies. Your mentor ought to be slapped upside their head."

Darius's face darkened instantly, and Morgan felt a pang of worry for him when he spoke again. His tone was tight, anger and fear pulling it taut. "There are a number of things that ought to have happened to my mentor."

To her credit, realization quickly dawned for Ines, and she shook her head. "Shit, Darius, I'm sorry. Don't mind me. I have an issue with not having a filter between my brain and my mouth." Despite her attempt at a joke, the apology was sincere.

"Regardless, whatever Trinity saw, it certainly seems to lend validity to Morgan's story."

"Which is?"

Darius turned his gaze on Morgan, who wanted to disappear into the cushions of the couch. He had felt drained enough as it was explaining it all to Trinity, then to Darius. After all, who would believe someone raving about time travel? Especially when accepted magic at the time forbade such an act from even being possible.

Ines also turned to look at him, and Morgan heaved a sigh. There was no putting it off, it would seem. "I came back from the future. To stop some event that happens and sort of plunges Chicago, the U.S., and much of the world into darkness."

The silence that followed his admission was heavier than he could have imagined it being.

Ines broke it with a small laugh. "Well, that's one I hadn't heard." She shrugged and finished packing her things up.

Morgan blinked and looked up at her. "You believe me? Just like that? No long explanation?"

Ines shrugged again. "I've seen stranger. Hell, I've been inside stranger. Call me if you're ever neck-deep inside a demonic womb that is ready to rend the barrier between worlds by birthing its abomination into the realm of humanity."

Morgan looked at Darius, trying to figure out if she was joking, but Darius's expression told him that she was not. Before he could say anything, she raised a hand and shook her head. "Don't ask for particulars, kid. I have no desire to get into the details. I just mean that I'm open-minded." She stood and shouldered her bag. "I'm at the hospital tomorrow, but then I'm taking a few vacation days. I have a feeling that things are going to get complicated soon, and I want to be available for them."

"Are you sure?" Darius asked. "I don't want you to have to give up money from a shift."

"With the vacation time I've earned? I could be gone six months, and they'd still have PTO they owe me." She grinned. Offering Morgan a quick wink, she moved to the door. "Call me if you need me, all right? Morgan, be careful when you're getting up from sitting or lying down. You might get light-headed or pass out if you're not." Turning to Darius. "I think, once his aura settles down, he'll probably feel much better. I can't find anything physically wrong with him. Blood pressure's fine. Pulse is fine. Without lab tests or scans, that's all I've got. I'm only a nurse."

"And a mage," Darius argued.

Without skipping a beat, Ines continued. "And a mage. You do know that we're all still human, yes?" she asked, eyebrow raised. "Anyway, I can't sense anything wrong with him, outside of his aura, but if it persists, bring him into the hospital, and we can get some actual tests run."

"You can't just—"

Ines took her turn to interrupt. "Darius, do you have any idea how complicated a circulatory system is? How about the limbic system, hmm? Magic and spellcraft are great, but I am one person, and there are so many amazing technologies now that make that work much, *much* easier. Trust me, there are times you want a blood test or CT scan and not a mage." This was obviously an argument she had had before. She didn't sound annoyed, but her tone spoke volumes as to how any contradiction would mean a fight.

Darius raised his hands in surrender, which Morgan was thankful for. He had no doubts that the woman could easily take Darius in any sort of conflict, magic or no.

"Fair enough," Darius was saying. "Do you need cash for gas?"

"No, but thanks. Might take you up on it if this becomes a habit." She moved to the door, waving haphazardly over her shoulder to the two of them. "Take care. I'll call and check in on my break tomorrow."

"Good night," Darius said, following after her to make sure the door was securely shut.

"Thanks again," Morgan called, hoping his words carried before the door to the apartment closed.

And just like that, Morgan was once again alone with the man who he had kissed without consent. Damn it, why weren't the couch cushions swallowing him up?

Darius let out a long sigh and moved into the kitchen, placing his mug in the sink. He retrieved a glass from the cupboard and filled it with water from the refrigerator dispenser. "Do you want a refill?" he asked, glancing Morgan's way.

Morgan shook his head, his face heating when he felt Darius's gaze. Morgan's glass of water sat, practically forgotten, on a coaster on the coffee table. The ice had melted completely.

Morgan wished he could put this guilt out of his head. He took Darius at his word; he had a feeling that if Darius was admitting that he might like Morgan, then it must mean that it was the beginning of something. This wasn't a rejection so much as a delay, to wait and see what formed. Morgan could respect that. Still, he was mortified that he hadn't thought to ask. The Trinity from his own timeline would have some strong words for him if she knew. She'd taught him about consent, and half of it had flown out the window when Darius had been close enough to touch.

His lips had been so warm.

Morgan pushed the thought away as Darius came over to the couch, putting his drink on a coaster on the coffee table and taking a seat next to Morgan.

His nerves getting the better of him, Morgan stood up, stammering, "I should probably lay down on the..." But before he could finish his thought, the world around him swam and lurched, threatening reverse. *No*, he thought, trying to somehow hold on tighter to the present moment, to his place in the timeline. The feeling of being unmoored faded, but the dizziness forced him back down to the couch, his head resting on his hand. Ines's warning to him echoed in his ears, and he kicked himself for trying to move so quickly.

"Are you all right?" Darius asked, half rising.

"Yes, just light-headed," he murmured on a sigh. *And annoyed at being a burden. And still embarrassed at my behavior.* The list went on and on. "Maybe I should stay on the couch for a bit longer."

Darius nodded, thinking. "Do you want to watch something?"

"Huh?"

Darius pointed to the television on the far wall.

Morgan thought about it. A distraction might be a very good thing. "That would be okay. Just, nothing too, uhm...too..." He trailed off, unsure of how to describe what he was thinking. "Harsh? Loud?"

"I think I know what you mean." Darius nodded and turned on the television, revealing a number of apps and options. He was quick with the remote, and in an instant, the beginning of some sort of nature documentary began, all about underwater sea life.

Morgan had never really been able to watch television in his time. It was a relic of his younger years, before the world had turned upside down. The nostalgia of it was odd. He shifted a bit to find a comfortable position, blinking away the residual dizziness that clung to him. He wanted to be able to focus on the show, to let the calming monotone of the narrator carry him away from his worry. He continued to fidget, trying to get cozy but still struggling.

"Here," Darius said. He adjusted and opened an arm, inviting Morgan to draw in close.

"Are you sure it's all right?"

Darius nodded, though his voice had a nervous edge to it. "If it's all right with you. Just watching the show, though."

Morgan could live with that. In fact, closeness was just the thing he thought he needed. He moved in until he was against Darius, resting his head on the man's shoulder. Darius's cologne smelled of bergamot and sandalwood and made Morgan think warm, safe thoughts. He liked it. He also found it easier to relax with Darius's arm draped around his shoulders. Sighing into the sensation, he finally turned his attention to the aquatic exploration on the television screen and the soft, soothing voice of the narrator. He fell asleep to the calming sight of a bloom of sea nettle jellyfish swimming quietly through the deep, blue Atlantic.

CHAPTER FIFTEEN

Darius

It's not me.

The whisper scraped at the back of his mind, pulling at the jagged scars of poorly healed wounds. It was garbled, distorted, as if he was hearing it at a great distance through water. It scratched and clawed, determined to be heard.

Then he was back there. The ruins of what had been an ornate office. The mahogany was charred, black with soot spattered with blood and viscera. The air was so thick. How could anyone breathe? His mentor was gone, destroyed by the power she had tried to call from parts beyond. Half of the building was gone with her.

Half of Seren was gone, too.

What remained of what had been Seren dragged itself towards him, unnaturally long arms clawing at the floor beneath her, sinew stretching and popping while slivers of opalescent steam rose from her raw flesh. Where she still had skin, it was an unnatural grayish blue hue. Her head lolled impossibly to the side, neck broken. Her eyes were dark pits, and at the center of them, a cold, silver light glinted like dying starlight.

Darius, that's not me.

Fear clawed at Darius, thousands of shards piercing him, rooting him to the spot as the husk of Seren came closer, the wet sound of blood and dragging entrails sloughing against his nerves. She was getting closer, and closer. And the gun, the gun his mentor had given him to *deal with* Seren before the ritual had been disrupted—it was in his hand. He couldn't bring himself to squeeze the trigger. He couldn't kill her.

Darius opened his eyes to be greeted by the plain white of the ceiling above. He was on the couch. He'd fallen asleep sitting up. Lifting his head, he stretched his neck from side to side to loosen the stiff, angry muscles. He could only move so far, though. Morgan's head rested on his shoulder, and he was softly snoring. The sound brought the ghost of a smile to Darius's lips.

As Darius looked at the sleeping man, he took a minute to study his features. He could see bits of Trinity and Nick in the sleeping man's face. He had a scattering of freckles across the bridge of his nose, cheeks, and forehead. They made him look younger, as did his peaceful expression. Darius realized he hadn't asked his age. He probably should. He made a mental note to come back to it later.

Morgan's brown curls were a tangled mess, more a halo around his head than laying the way it should. Darius found himself wondering if he ever tried pinning or tying the hair back or did he let the dense curls fall where they may.

Darius was wondering a good number of personal things about Morgan and was puzzled as to why he was wondering them.

Well, not entirely. He *knew* why. He could try and claim that he wanted to help, that he was curious about the mystery event that Morgan had come back to stop, or that he needed something to distract him from his own somewhat bleak existence. He could do all that, but he knew he would be lying to himself, even if only by omission, and he generally didn't care to.

He liked Morgan. The kiss the night before had been abrupt, startling, but being so close, so intimate, had sparked something in his chest—not to mention below his belt. He wasn't sure if he could develop feelings on so short an acquaintance, but he couldn't deny that he felt a pull. The tug at his mind and at his heart that brought him back to Morgan. He had felt it the night he had found the man, when he had opened his mind to hear his pleas. He had felt it when Morgan had so earnestly asked him to ease his mind the first time so that he could sleep. Darius felt it now, while Morgan lay resting and vulnerable against his shoulder.

He was beginning to feel *other* things from his proximity to Morgan as well. He shifted slightly, adjusting to help relieve the pressure, then snatched at one of the throw pillows and put it on his lap to hide his stirring arousal. The last thing he needed was Morgan waking up to that, especially after the night he'd had.

Letting out a deep sigh, he turned his head to look at the windows of the apartment, hoping to distract himself. The shades had been left open the night before, and they looked out onto a gray Chicago day, damp, heavy snow falling lazily over the city. The scene did little to motivate him to begin his morning. He tried to turn to see the time but couldn't quite make out the clock on the microwave in the kitchen. He thought it said somewhere in the six o'clock realm, which meant he had time before he needed to leave for work.

"Oh no," came Morgan's hoarse voice. Darius glanced down to see him looking up, cheeks decidedly crimson despite his darker complexion.

He sat up so quickly that Darius had to push himself back to avoid colliding with him.

"Oh no!" Before Darius could say anything, Morgan was up and moving to the bed, putting his head in his hands and groaning as he sat. "I am so, so sorry. I can't even explain how sorry I am. I did not mean to get this intimate. After I did that yesterday, and you said what you did, and I just—"

Darius wasn't sure what was happening, but he could see that as Morgan spoke, he became more and more frantic, his breath coming faster on each word. He was working himself into a panic.

"I fell asleep on you, and I didn't mean to be so forward, and—"

"It's all right," Darius tried to interrupt. He strode around the couch and to the bed, sitting beside Morgan. "You're all right."

Morgan looked up over his hands, eyes red and wet. "Y-you're sure? It's all right?"

"Yes," Darius said, surprised at how much he wanted to reassure him. "It's fine. All you did was fall asleep."

"On your shoulder. After you asked for space."

Darius smiled. "I promise you that I didn't take it as any sort of advance. Just exhaustion. Besides, I offered the comfort."

"Right. Yeah. Yeah, you did. Thank you." Morgan wiped his eyes and laid back on the bed, groaning. "I am such a disaster. Also, I think I got up too fast."

"Why? What's wrong?" Darius asked, amusement vanishing to be replaced by concern.

"Dizzy," he said, but his voice didn't waver. "A bit nauseous."

"Not faint?"

"I don't think so. If I am, I'm in the right place, huh?"

The quiet joke made Darius smile.

Without looking, Morgan asked, "How does it look?"

"What?"

"My aura?"

Darius took a long breath, consciously making the effort to shift his eyesight, opening it to the patterns and flows of the magic around him. It could be jarring, but the transition for Darius was smooth, a strange sort of stepping outside of his normal senses in order to perceive more.

Seeing auras wasn't a difficult thing to do, though 'seeing' might be a misnomer. There was a sight aspect to it, but also a sensation of it, a fleeting tactile echo. Sensing an aura was what most mages learned first. It was one of the few things one could use magic for and not risk blatantly affecting the world around them. It helped mages identify each other, though not as subtly as the phrases he had spoken to Morgan upon first meeting him. Using magic to see another mage's aura, even to just identify them, was still using magic and tended to alert any other mages in the area, not to mention other creatures of the paranormal world. Safer not to use it when out and about in public.

Of course, seeing something and understanding something enough to change it were two entirely different things. Perceiving an aura was to appreciate it, to understand the colors and echoes around a person. Darius knew there were those who worked with auras, to change or heal them, but the only skill he had was to know what was considered 'normal.' Even then, he could only detect bigger changes or shifts, not more minor discrepancies.

Auras were always a difficult thing to describe. If one were to describe it by sight, it might be a myriad of colors. Just as the mind and soul can consider more than one idea or feel more than one emotion, the aura frequently embodied a multitude of shades in different chromas, each flowing and ebbing into the next. Darius knew a few. Boredom, contentment, fear, even dishonesty could be read on an aura. That was what he had most experience in. They were the more important indicators to Monitors and Indagators alike.

Of course, sight was only one instance. There was also sensation, the tactile feeling of the air pressure changing or the wind direction shifting. Sound was another. Even taste, at least he'd been led to believe that. He didn't experience it quite on that level. He wasn't sure he ever wanted to.

Morgan's aura was a great deal more confused than any Darius had discerned before. Not that there was confusion in it, but the aura itself was discordant and chaotic. The colors and feelings shifted, swelling and ebbing the way Darius had seen others, but there were strange counter currents in the surface, areas where two flows met and swirled in miniature whirlpools that were nauseating to look at. They were difficult to tolerate, and he blinked, letting his mage sight slip away in favor of the nonmagical.

"That bad?" asked Morgan, voice sad.

Darius shook his head. "No. I mean, I'm not an authority. I know more of the mind than of spiritual or emotional energies."

"Emotional energies don't occur in the mind?" Morgan asked, hiding a shy smile.

Darius was surprised by the ridiculousness of his own statement and the question Morgan had posed. He thought for a moment. "They do, and they don't. They exist in that uncertain area where the mind meets the spirit meets the heart." In truth, it was something that mages had squabbled over for eons. He certainly didn't have the answer, either. "What I studied was more the logical, unemotional works of mind spellcraft, which is why I am out of my depth." He put a reassuring hand on Morgan's shoulder. "If Ines and Trinity say it'll get better, then I suggest we believe them. My aura work is limited to gleaning whether or not someone is lying."

Morgan's brow furrowed. "Why?"

Darius realized that the two of them hadn't had much time to really talk at all since he had helped Morgan home. He felt his cheeks heat, remembering how he had blurted out his emotions from the night before, especially because he had known Morgan for such a short time. Was it wise to open himself up to feelings like that on such a short acquaintance? Darius wasn't sure. Of course, wise or not, it was already done. He wanted to continue to be open. He was tired of keeping himself locked up. Here was Morgan, someone new, who didn't know the person he once was, when he had been young and misled. Judgment couldn't hang on Morgan the way it clung to those who knew what had happened and how he had been so manipulated all those years ago.

He felt like it might be his only chance.

"I work for the Protectorate. I used to be an Indagator, but I've shifted to a position as a Monitor. Office work, fact-checking, and surveillance to keep nonmagical humanity safe from magic they have no defense against."

Morgan was looking at him as if he wasn't sure if Darius was upset or relieved about the shift from field to desk work. "I'm...sorry?"

Darius chuckled dryly. "I think it was a good move. Not as dangerous, and I enjoy the research aspect of it." He shrugged.

"Oh, then that's all right, yes?" Morgan offered a smile.

"Yes." Pushing himself up, Darius moved to his dresser and pulled open the drawers, withdrawing a crisp button-up shirt, pressed pants, an undershirt, boxer briefs, and socks. He piled each atop the other in a neat, orderly pile. With his hands busy, his mind worked.

"Did you report me to the Protectorate?" asked Morgan.

Darius stilled for a moment, then shook his head. "No. I think it's wise for you to recover first. Then we can discuss what to do about the Protectorate and whether they can help."

Morgan nodded, relieved, and Darius resumed getting ready for his day.

He would have to check in at the office, see if anything had been discovered. The more he thought about it, the more he wondered if the power surges that the Lead Monitor had briefed them on could be related to Morgan's appearance in the current timeline. Darius didn't remember sensing them when he had searched for Morgan through the mindscape. Granted, he hadn't been specifically searching for them, but he couldn't shake the certainty that he still would have felt something so strong. He wasn't sure where that left him. He was trying to figure out if he could, or should, share the information. He had only told the people he *knew* he could trust completely. Well, them and Emily. He knew Sybil wasn't in that circle of trust, but he wondered if the Lead Monitor might be a candidate for it. He was the kind of man who put loyalty and the safety of others high among his priorities and might be exactly who Darius needed to speak to about all of this.

The trick would be getting to him without Sybil getting suspicious that something was up. She was naturally inquisitive and rarely respectful of personal boundaries. Still, he was confident he would be able to find some window of opportunity to speak to his superior without Sybil finding out the subject matter.

After that, he could cut the day short and perhaps take Morgan out somewhere to purchase some clothes. Maybe an inexpensive phone so that he had some window to the world to help him adjust.

It would certainly be a more pleasant way of spending the day than working.

"It sounds like you're giving me more opportunities to embarrass myself," Morgan murmured his response when Darius explained the idea. "Are you sure? I can't pay for anything."

Darius held up a hand. "Don't worry about it."

"But—"

"Pay me back once we get things figured out and you on your feet," he insisted. "Rest for the morning. I need to head out to work, check-in, and get a few things done. I can be back by one."

Morgan considered it a moment before nodding his assent. "All right, but please don't let me embarrass myself again."

Darius smiled. "You haven't embarrassed yourself yet," he reassured.

Morgan blushed again and nodded, lying back on the couch quietly. Darius couldn't help thinking how good he looked on it.

CHAPTER SIXTEEN
Morgan

Morgan spent the morning trying his best to tidy up, taking small breaks in between tasks to lie down when nausea or dizziness made it too difficult to stand. He wanted to keep his hands occupied, even if it didn't keep his mind from wandering. Doing tasks and being active helped keep him progressing through time in the correct direction, or so he thought. Of course, Darius was a fairly neat individual, and Morgan found himself with very little to do, taking care of small bits of cleaning that might have been overlooked. It didn't keep him occupied for long.

He took care of the drinkware from the night before, washing them and leaving them to dry while disregarding the dishwasher itself. It was empty and felt wasteful to run for a couple of mugs and glasses. He also made himself a sparse but satisfying breakfast. An egg, over hard, and a piece of dry toast. He was feeling better than he had been on the previous day, but he didn't want to push it. He was excited about the prospect of going beyond the apartment. The space was small and beginning to feel claustrophobic, which only added to his uneasiness.

Or maybe it was that he still had no idea how he was going to stop whatever the hell it was he had come back to stop. He didn't even know what it *was*. Emily, his timeline Emily, was supposed to have been the one to go back, not him. She'd known all the ins and outs. He was a poor substitute. He wished she'd had time to tell him more before she had died.

He froze as the memory and grief unfolded in his mind. The night they were going to try and send someone back, send Emily back. They'd been attacked mid-spellcraft, husks of people drawn to the power they were calling up. *Blood, there was so much blood. "Em, you all right?"*

"You have to do this, Morgan. I can't. Not anymore." She'd been coughing. *Coughing up blood. Coughing up blood meant her lungs—*

"I know you can do this."

He put aside the half piece of bread and pushed the plate away, appetite vanishing with this new recollection. With his mind starting to settle, his memories were bubbling back to the surface with increasing frequency and strength. His own trauma washed over him in a wave of grief he hadn't been prepared for. Elbows resting on the countertop, he put his head in his hands and took a deep, shaky breath. He heard the nearly silent sound of tears hitting the counter surface, and he blinked at the haze of mourning that clouded his vision.

Wiping at his eyes, he tried to convince himself that his head wasn't swimming, but the strength of the heartache wouldn't be wiped away. His whole being seemed to contract with the force of his guilt and grief. The feeling was harsh and unforgiving.

I don't belong here.

Here doesn't belong around me.

Anxiety and panic shot up his spine, and he felt instantly disconnected from the world around him. No longer a part of anything, he was unmoored. His fingertips were numb. He couldn't feel the counter beneath him. Was he breathing? Did he need to breathe?

He remembered what Darius had said when this happened before, when he had felt unreal. He needed five things he could see. His eyes flitted over the apartment, and he quietly counted the first five things that popped out to him. The onyx-colored cabinet pulls in the kitchen were the first sight he clung to. The next was a handwritten note on the refrigerator to see a Dr. Lee on Thursday. The handwriting was neat but long, half-artistic. It had to be Darius's, and Morgan thought it fit him somehow. He pushed the thought away, trying to focus on the rest of the exercise. He laid eyes on the half-finished remnants of his own breakfast, the gray day beyond the windows, and the untouched bed across the apartment.

What came after that five things he saw? He struggled to remember as his vision swam.

Four. Four. Four what?

"Four things you can touch," he murmured. He splayed a hand open and slapped the counter, the sting of connection with cool marble beneath his fingertips cutting through the numbness. He pushed himself to his feet, feeling the vibration of the stool against the floor and the solidity of the floor beneath his bare feet. He moved towards the bed, dragging the back of his hand along the wall, the drywall subtly textured against his knuckles.

He climbed into the bed. His panic was beginning to ebb, and with it, the sensation of being disconnected began to fade. He told himself it would, but he still continued the exercise that Darius had given him.

Three things he could hear. That was next. There was the distant din of traffic. Then the soft whisper of sound that the blankets and sheets made as he pulled them back and slipped beneath them. He imagined Darius sliding into the bed each night, the day dragging him toward sleep. That thought was far more calming than him finding the third sound, his own ragged breathing as it slowly evened out. A long sigh escaped him as the soft bed cradled him.

Drawing the blankets up over his shoulders, he nestled into the bed, and relief began to seep into him. The dissociation was passing, and he found himself beginning to relax. Eyes closed, he dozed off before he could consider two things he could smell.

CHAPTER SEVENTEEN
Darius

Darius was in a decidedly foul mood by the time he strode into the Protectorate building that morning. Sleeping upright on a couch, no matter how comfortable, did not make for a good night's rest. He was on edge and worried about Morgan. The walk to work had also given him the time to stress, more and more, about his work partner, his boss, and how well he would be able to get his message across. He had even skipped his usual coffee on the walk in, his anxiety already simmering. He didn't want to add caffeine to that mix, no matter how tired he felt.

As he strode through the lobby and towards the stairs, he turned over in his mind how he might explain his speaking independently with Lead Monitor Powell to Sybil. He could claim some medical issue came up, but that might incite more curiosity than anything. He could perhaps angle for an issue with his pay. Protectorate HR and payroll weren't the smoothest of machines, and there was no shortage of issues that came up every now and again. That would be something to discuss with a superior, wouldn't it? Darius was having trouble checking his frustration. Every scenario he ran through made Sybil more interested in his business, not less. She was a Monitor, for fuck's sake; she was trained to sniff out inaccuracies in people's stories.

He had no worry about what he would say *to* Powell once he had gained a meeting. He would be straightforward with him. Darius knew Powell was someone to be reasoned with, and that was exactly what he would do. The Lead Monitor didn't appreciate beating around the bush.

Darius tried reminding himself that he didn't have to share anything about this meeting with Sybil. The regular laws of employment applied here. He knew any meeting between his manager and himself would be

111

confidential. He also knew it wasn't always as simple as that, and frankly, if he tried to invoke such reasoning against her, she might become even more suspicious. If she thought he had some lead or intended to try and get ahead with their boss, it would cause problems.

He was still trying to figure out just how to handle the situation when he reached his floor and exited the stairwell into the office. He nodded to William, who ignored him, and strode by, arriving at his office to realize that Sybil wasn't there.

Surprised, he checked behind him, then looked towards the center conference areas and the other offices. He didn't see her anywhere on their floor. Sybil was one of those individuals who was always the first one into the office. Usually, the first one to leave the office as well, but one couldn't fault her for that when she practically opened the place. He did see LM Powell in his office, speaking with an Indagator, and Darius thought he should send the man a message, maybe set up a time to meet.

Slipping his phone from his pocket, he checked to see if he had missed a call or text from Sybil, something to tell him why she wasn't in. There was nothing. Confused, he stepped into his office and shrugged off his coat, putting it on the hook on the wall before taking the seat at his desk, opening his laptop, and booting it up. Once he was signed in, he opened a chat window on the intraoffice portal and used the small dropdown to address it to the lead monitor. He quickly went about typing his message.

D. Adair: Sir, I need to speak with you on a topic of the utmost importance—

As he typed, he heard the distant *ding* of the elevator door. He had a poor view of the lobby from his desk, but he thought he saw the red hair and pale complexion of his partner coming from the elevator banks. He suddenly had very little time to finish his message before risking discovery.

—however, this meeting needs to be as discrete as possible. At your nearest convenience, please—

Sybil pushed the office door open, and Darius quickly pressed 'SEND' on the message, cursing silently at being unable to finish his sentence completely.

He closed the chat window as Sybil bustled in, her voice sharp and cold as she snapped, "Fine. I understand. I will speak with you later." Darius leaned back, taken aback before he realized she was on a call. She put a hand to the small Bluetooth speaker in her ear and pushed against it so hard he was amazed she didn't hurt herself. She let out a frustrated groan and shot a glance his way for the first time that morning. "What?"

"Nothing." He raised his hands in a gesture of surrender. "I'm sorry, is something the matter?"

The look in her ice-blue eyes sent a chill down his spine. Besides the annoyance in them, there was a sharp edge of condescending anger, as if she was deciding whether or not he was even worthy of her notice. It was an intimidating glare.

It vanished in an instant, and she let out a long sigh, offering him a shrug. "Just some personal shit," she explained vaguely. She hung her coat on the hook next to his and fell into her own office chair. Darius offered her one last sideways glance before returning to his own computer. Within seconds, the office was filled with her typing. She was banging each key as if it had personally wronged her. Rather than inquire again, Darius thought it wiser to simply ignore her.

Twenty minutes later, a knock came at the door. It was Baylee. They offered a quick good morning before announcing that Lead Monitor Powell wanted to speak with Darius. Their usually energetic expression was pulled down by worry when they added, "He did not sound pleased."

Sybil perked up, curious at the added information. As Baylee nodded and retreated from the office, Sybil's expression of curiosity transformed itself into a look of smug self-satisfaction. "What did you do?"

Apparently, the possibility of him getting in trouble for something perked Sybil right up.

Darius offered his best confused look in response. "I haven't a clue. I'm sure I'll find out."

In a half sing-song voice, Sybil teased, "You're in trouble!"

Darius gathered his notebook and pen, scowling, and left the smaller office, being sure to close the door behind him. He moved with confident if not slightly hurried steps that began to erode his self-assurance the closer he got to his superior's office. He already felt an odd sort of exposure, one he had to fight for every step between his office and that of Lead Monitor Powell's.

"Monitor Adair," Powell all but shouted before Darius had even reached the man's office door. "Come in and take a seat."

Darius moved quickly across the threshold and lowered himself into one of the two chairs. The Lead Monitor, who had been seated at his desk, rose and moved to close the door with a swift, impatient gesture. As Darius watched, the man traced his fingers over a line of sigils that had been carved into the frame. There was a soft glow, and the air in the office changed. It felt slightly heavier and smelled of lavender and roses. A glamour of some sort.

"Sir?" Darius asked.

Ty Powell turned back to him and smiled, though he looked exhausted. "A simple spell to turn prying eyes and ears away." His smile brightened, making his lean face look boyish. "The floral scent was my idea. I find them calming. Plus, they remind me of my wife, Cady, and that always helps. But we aren't here to talk about me." He strode back to his desk, taking his place behind it and leaning forward. "Your message sounded sensitive, among other things. Are you all right? Are you safe?"

Darius was struck by the man's concern. He hadn't had many opportunities to speak one on one with the Lead Monitor beyond the occasional assignment. Even now, in the office, Darius realized he had never taken the time to really get an impression of him beyond his professional loyalty and work ethic. He had expected brusque professionalism dampened by simple courtesy. What he saw was a man very much invested in Darius's own welfare. Darius just couldn't figure out why.

He cleared his throat. "Yes, sir. I am safe."

Ty raised a hand. "Please, right now, it's just you and me. Call me Ty if you want. We can leave the professional niceties at the door with the glamour. I'm assuming, from your message tone, this is about more than just work."

Darius studied his superior, again thrown by how open the man was. He was about Darius's height, lean, with dirty blonde hair kept in a deliberately unkempt style and blue eyes that professed honesty and sincerity as they met Darius's own gaze. He didn't sense any deception here, despite knowing, or at least thinking he knew, that people weren't this nice. He was surprised at how personable the man was being, but he was even more surprised by how much relief and appreciation he felt for having a safe place to let his guard down. How long had he been keeping those walls up? His entire life? He was equal parts wary of letting anyone see even the smallest flaw in his defenses and just damned tired of holding them up. "Very well. Ty."

"So, what's up?" Ty asked.

Darius pursed his lips, still unsure of how much it was wise to share. He pondered his words carefully before he spoke. "In the hypothetical, what would you do if someone came to you and told you that they had knowledge of..." Darius trailed off. He was hedging. Distrusting. He needed to be able to speak freely, and that meant making the decision to trust.

Ty waited, patient but expectant.

Fuck it.

"The evening before last, I woke in the middle of the night. I sensed there was something unusual happening, and upon utilizing a quiet scan of the mindscape, I discovered a person," Darius began. Out poured most of the story about Morgan, though he kept himself from revealing Emily's role in it. She was easily omitted, and Darius wanted to spare the Slavin family further involvement.

He shared finding Morgan, bringing him home, the claims Morgan had made, and the possible future they could be looking at. Darius made sure to outline the evidence he had mentally cataloged, including the necklace under the man's skin, what Trinity had said about his aura, and Ines's estimation on his health, though he kept their identities vague. His few glances at Ty's face told him that the man was listening to the outlandish tale of the time traveler without judgment. Darius was grateful for that much.

When he finished, Ty sat back, his hands folded against his chin. "And you believe this Morgan?" he asked.

"I do," Darius said without hesitation.

Ty considered this answer. "Why didn't you want your partner to know?" The question was edged, and the Lead Monitor was watching him carefully for an answer.

Darius felt some of the color drain from his face. "Sir?" he asked, slipping back into a more formal address.

"I received your message seconds after your partner, who was uncharacteristically late this morning, stepped off the elevator and an instant *before* she entered your shared office space." Ty grinned, fox-like, at Darius's surprise. "There are reasons I've made it to my position in the Protectorate. I am fairly good at my job."

Darius nodded and shifted, unsure how to address the issue of his partner. He hadn't intended to discuss it.

Ty read his discomfort. "Darius, as long as no one is in imminent danger, nothing leaves this office."

Darius nodded. "Well, Monitor Diluna has a tendency to look for opportunities to further her position where they arise. I was worried that if she learned of Morgan that the news wouldn't be something kept secret for long. That isn't to say I meant to keep it from the Protectorate, but her history with delicate matters isn't a pristine one and—"

"You don't trust her," Ty interrupted flatly.

Darius wanted to argue. He hadn't come into Ty's office with the intent of getting Sybil in any trouble. Nevertheless, he heard the truth in Ty's conclusion and couldn't argue it. He still tried to soften the blow. "In Monitor and Protectorate matters, she is a great resource. In matters that may be closer to home, more personal... No, I do not."

"And this is personal?" Ty said.

Darius could feel his face heat. "To some degree, yes, it is."

Ty considered this for a moment. "You discovering him coincided with the power surges that Cosmology told us about, yes?"

Darius felt his gut churning. "It's possible, but I don't know for sure."

Ty leaned forward again, resting his elbows on the desk as he thought. His eyes were sharp when they cut over to a moderate pile of files on his desk, then back to Darius. "All right." He reached out and took the pile in hand, holding it out to Darius. "This is Indagator Decker's fieldwork. Hasn't been entered into the database because we had to scramble to get coverage for this energy surge event. Take it. Work from home while I consider everything you've said."

"Data entry?" Darius asked, confused by the sudden turn of the conversation.

"As of right now, you're off of the Cosmology incident. I want you to work from home. If you get some of this entered, that's fine, but primarily I want you to keep close to Morgan," Ty explained. Leaning forward, he spoke in hushed tones. "Between you, me, and this glamour, Cosmology found a lot of irregular magical energy all over Chicago. Unless there are many time travelers coming our way, I think there's more to this than your Morgan. He may be completely unrelated, but I'm not going as far as leaving someone who allegedly broke taboo and passed through time without supervision. I think it's important that you keep an eye on him, but he isn't our main theory just yet. There are Protectorate elders also recently in Chicago, and that adds another layer to the entire issue."

Ty shook his head, and for the first time in that meeting, Darius could see how truly tired the man appeared to be. "There's a lot going on, so for the time being, stay vigilant. If I have a monitor already watching one possible avenue, I'd feel much better." He leaned back. "Besides, your work is stellar. There's no reason not to trust you with this."

Darius blinked, accepting the small pile of folders and staring at his superior. He had thought *everyone* in the Protectorate knew of his mentor's betrayal and tryst into taboo magic. He assumed, every day since he had rejoined the Protectorate, that everyone believed he had willingly joined in his mentor's machinations. That he would one day attempt to betray the Protectorate in some twisted form of revenge. He had gotten it firmly put into his head that he was only in his current position by the good graces of the Protectorate and that no one truly trusted him.

Ty waved a dismissive hand at him, and Darius realized he must be wearing more of his surprise on his face than he meant to.

"Yes, I was briefed on what happened. As far as I am concerned, it's been almost seven years, and in that time, you've done nothing but show yourself to be a solid monitor, a hard worker, and perhaps too tolerant of your partner's idiosyncrasies. The Protectorate believes you free of your past, and so do I." Ty shrugged. "Keep me informed if there are any developments with this person of interest, and if you need any help, don't hesitate to call. Here," he instructed. He took a business card out of his pocket and jotted a quick note on the back. "That's my personal cell. Call if you need to, any time."

Darius nodded, too surprised to vocalize anything close to a reasonable response. He stood, taking the card and the file folders with him as he turned and opened the door. There was a subtle change in the air pressure, and the floral smell vanished as Darius stepped back out into the collective office space. Darius hadn't realized that the glamour had also muted much of the noise from the office beyond Ty's. The sounds of typing, the copier being used, and hushed murmurs of office workers were all surprisingly loud. Darius hurried back to his office.

"So, what was that all about?" Sybil asked. She hadn't turned to look at him when he entered. Whatever she was typing, it took up all of her attention.

"Lead Monitor Powell gave me some files he wants me to enter into the database. With everything going on, they need a Monitor to keep up on Indagator Decker's fieldwork. Apparently, it needs to be caught up."

"Sounds dull," Sybil said. "So, you're not in trouble."

"No."

"And no interesting story? Just extra work?"

"Pretty much."

118

"What a waste."

"At least he said I could do it from home," Darius offered.

Sybil turned towards him, her face a mask of thin sympathy over passive-aggressive intent. Darius wondered why she even attempted the façade. He braced, knowing what was coming.

"You know, someday the people in this office will realize you're not that wretched de Winter woman and stop dumping the scut work on you. Not your fault she was trying to resurrect a dead fling."

Darius hadn't known the barbed compliment would strike quite so deep. He gritted his teeth but didn't flinch. He wasn't going to dignify that with a response. Instead, he simply nodded, saying, "I'm going to be working from home over the next few days. Email if anything comes up."

Sybil's expression never changed. "I'll text you to make sure you're not too lonely."

"Uh, thanks," Darius mumbled. He tucked his laptop into his bag, shouldered into his coat, and left before Sybil could say anything else she thought might be encouraging.

CHAPTER EIGHTEEN

Morgan

He must have fallen into a deeper sleep than he had intended. The next thing Morgan knew, he was hearing the sound of a key in the apartment door, the lock sliding, and the door opening.

He blinked from his place in the bed. "Darius?" he asked, his voice a feeble croak.

There was no response. Morgan tried again but was still met with silence. A quiet dread blossomed in Morgan's chest. "Hello?" he asked, voice small, though as soon as the word left his lips, he regretted having spoken. He'd alerted the intruder to his fear. Now it *knew* he was there and afraid.

Morgan heard a footstep, then another. It was a shuffling sort of gait, each footfall accompanied by a heavy, dragging sound.

He wanted to investigate, to see who or what it was. He couldn't move. He tried to tell his arms and legs to act, but they ignored him. He was trapped in the bed. Fear, deep and primal, flowed through him like liquid ice. Something was coming, something was around that corner, and it might be the end of him.

Morgan gasped, eyes snapping open as he was wrenched out of the dream and woke for real this time. The sound of his name had roused him, and he found himself looking up at Darius, who had a concerned expression on his face and a hand on his shoulder. "Sorry for waking you. It looked like you were having a nightmare."

Morgan blinked and nodded. "Yeah, sorry. Must have fallen asleep."

"You don't need to apologize." Darius looked at him for a moment, searching his face. "Your eyes are red. Are you all right? Feeling any better? Worse?"

"Not sure," Morgan replied truthfully. His heart was pounding in his chest, adrenaline only now fading from the dread in the dream. He needed a minute to calm down.

Darius nodded and stepped back, moving around the bookshelf and into the kitchen, out of Morgan's line of sight.

Morgan let his head fall back on the pillow, taking a deep breath. The dream had felt so real, one of those half-waking imaginings that just hit him in precisely the right way to be absolutely terrifying. He didn't like it. He wasn't one that normally had dreams of anything beyond a pretty someone he had seen or some obscure mixture of too much media. Nightmares weren't his thing.

Of course, after scrambling his very being to pass through time, he imagined his 'thing' wasn't what it used to be.

"Glass of water?" came Darius's question from the kitchen.

"Yes, please." His throat felt raw from the dream as if a scream had gotten caught in it. He pushed himself up to sitting and sighed as Darius reappeared, a filled glass in his hand. He offered it to Morgan, and Morgan accepted. Their fingertips brushed in the exchange, and Morgan couldn't help the small jolt of electricity that ran through him from the contact. Glancing up, he found himself looking into Darius's deep, dark eyes, and he looked away, feeling his face flush.

He took a few tentative sips of the drink before his thirst took over, and he downed the contents, using it as something to distract him from Darius's penetrating gaze. "So how were things at work?" he asked, eyeing his empty glass. No more distractions there.

Darius let out a long sigh and, mercifully, looked away. "I don't know," he said, lowering himself to sit on the bed.

Morgan wasn't sure what his tone was. It sounded flat, with maybe a hint of worry. He couldn't see his face to read it, but Morgan thought Darius's training as a monitor would probably mean he'd learned how to control his facial expressions as well as his tone. "There's not much to go on. A lot of magical energy located all over Chicago." Darius glanced back, nodding towards him. "At first, I assumed it was you, but my LM informed me that there were a good number of power surges, and he isn't convinced it was the work of one person."

"LM?"

"Lead Monitor. My superior," Darius explained, looking down at his hands when he spoke. "I told him about everything except for Emily, and I kept Trinity's and Ines's identities as vague as I could."

"Everything?" Morgan repeated, mouth going dry.

"Yes, but don't worry," Darius hurried to explain. "He seemed to take it all in. He's assigned me to keep you safe and work from the apartment for the time being. He trusts me with this, and I…well, I made the decision to trust him."

Morgan could tell that it was difficult for Darius to speak his last few words. He had the look of a man balancing high above the ground and praying the tightrope didn't snap. Morgan wanted to reassure him, but he was worried himself. Now the Protectorate, or at least part of it, knew about him. Morgan had been taught by his mother what little he knew of the Protectorate. She hadn't painted a very positive picture. Neutral at best. They served a needed purpose, to keep the mundane and nonmagical protected from the magical, but their methods often only took into account the greater good, and that was defined by them. He didn't know if there would be punishment for traveling incorrectly on the space-time continuum. Even Morgan knew that was taboo. How would he be penalized?

"Do you remember moving much when you first arrived? The place that the surges were traced to aren't actually where I found you. A few are close, but nothing right where you were. Did you make multiple attempts to break through?"

Morgan shrugged. He didn't want to think about what he had felt when he'd passed through or if there were multiple attempts. He didn't remember much of the actual passage. How does one, when they're only a broken-up mass of molecules connected only by spell working and hope? He remembered the searing, electric pain that had coursed through him as he came back into consciousness. How everything around him shifted in time and space, how *he* had shifted. He gripped the empty glass he'd been holding tightly. Panic was pouring in as time seemed to Slow and stretch, pain pricking at his skin. He was getting lost. He looked around, trying to hold on to something that would keep him safe and grounded. He needed to know he was all right. He was here. Here was real. Here *had to be real.*

He was staring down at his hand, grasping the glass as if the smooth surface would save him. He felt the bed shift, and then a hand came into view. It wasn't his. It was Darius's. Morgan took it, holding onto it tighter than perhaps he needed to, but Darius didn't flinch.

"Breathe," came Darius's soft instruction. "Just breathe. I'm here."

If he's here, and I'm holding onto him, then I'm here. Morgan forced air into his aching lungs. Slow breaths in, slow breaths out. After a few minutes, the panic began to ebb. He could feel himself relaxing. He loosened his grip on Darius's hand but didn't let go. Darius didn't pull away, either.

They stayed like that, holding hands, until Morgan realized what he was doing and felt himself blush. He cleared his throat, searching for something to say. "So, uhm, what does that mean for us?" He wasn't sure if he was talking about the Protectorate or their held hands.

Darius shrugged, and Morgan felt the gesture through their joined hands. "Either the multiple energies were from you, or something else was also happening the same night you arrived. Whichever is the truth, I'm not investigating it as of today."

Morgan wasn't sure what to say. "Oh," he went with, finally.

"We can talk more later." Darius checked the time on his phone. He let out a long, exhausted sigh. "Why don't we postpone our shopping trip. I don't think either of us is up for being out and about just yet."

Morgan nodded. He was disappointed. He *wanted* to be out of the apartment, but at the same time, he had no control over the panic that seemed insistent on rising up against him. The idea of being in public when he began to lose it, or worse, his perception of time began to turn backward was terrifying. He would rather play it safe.

"Are you sure you're all right with me stealing your clothes?" he asked.

Darius grinned. "Well, maybe we can have Trinity or Ines pick you up a few essentials to tide you over until we can do some serious shopping. I don't know how well my clothing fits you."

Morgan returned his grin with a small one of his own. "It's not my fault you're so short."

"Next time, find someone taller to get you out of trouble."

CHAPTER NINETEEN

Darius

It was another week before Morgan was feeling up to the task of leaving the apartment.

Darius was content to work from home, using the pile of paperwork he had been given as busy work to fill the time. When he wasn't inputting the data for the Protectorate, he was engaged in conversation with Morgan or helping to take care of him. The only thing LM Powell—Ty—had asked was that Darius supply him with daily summaries of any behavior of note or aberrations of magic that he deemed important. Most of what Darius sent him was the same: no new information, person of interest was doing fine. In fact, Morgan seemed to be improving.

Darius had to admit to being impressed with Morgan, who was doing better and better with each passing day. His rewinds, what he had started calling those moments when time flowed backward, were getting less and less frequent, and after only a week, they had all but stopped. He was even carefully testing his magic, though not much past small breezes or chilling water in glasses. Any further would have earned him Trinity's ire.

Darius learned that Morgan worked with a good deal of kinetic spellcraft. Wind, fire, water…anything that could be mastered through the manipulation of movement, Morgan could affect. There had also been some gnosis craft in his upbringing, he could read and affect auras and admitted to knowing some soul work that his mother had taught him, but his real talent was in kinesis. They also discovered that while spellcrafting exhausted him, it also helped him feel more grounded in himself, and Darius was relieved that he had another way of supporting him to feel present.

In fact, Darius found it more and more difficult to get work done. As the days passed, his thoughts would turn from the mundane work of having to transcribe another Protectorate agent's notes, distracted by

Morgan's imperative to stop whatever magical event he had come back to stop. Then they would simply turn to Morgan himself. His voice. His smile. His laugh.

His ass.

After being pent up for the week, Morgan and Darius took their first outing from the apartment. Trinity had been able to drop off a few pairs of pants and tee shirts she'd scrounged up, but Morgan still needed his own clothes, and after a week, he was itching to escape the confines of the apartment. Darius couldn't blame him. It was a small apartment for one. Two people made it feel downright claustrophobic.

So, Darius had called a rideshare, and they were off to avail themselves of some of Chicago's finest shopping. Water Tower Place was Darius's initial suggestion, and since Morgan had no real objections—as long as it was beyond the walls of Darius's home—it was their first stop.

After the first few stores, Morgan was in much higher spirits than Darius had seen him since meeting him. Out and about, and in clothing and shoes that fit him correctly, he appeared much healthier and happier.

Darius was surprised to find that he was having fun as well. He had never liked shopping. He would go for a new suit or whatnot whenever he needed them but made quick and uninterested work of it. Now, having someone to shop for made it all the more enjoyable. He was finding an unanticipated amount of pleasure in the act of choosing ensembles for Morgan. A comfortable sweater and jeans. Dress pants and a button-down. Hell, even khaki shorts and a polo shirt. Summer would be here before they knew it, right? Even in January, the department stores were pushing spring and summer attire; who were they not to partake?

Will Morgan be here in the summer? Darius wasn't sure if he was getting ahead of himself, thinking so far into the future, but it felt good in the moment. For once, he let that be enough.

Besides, Morgan looked damn good in the clothes. He looked good in everything.

Darius felt himself blushing hard. He cast a sideways glance at his companion, but the other man was too engrossed in the mall directory in front of them to have noticed anything.

"Are you sure this is all right? I know this probably cost a lot of money," Morgan was saying, indicating to the new, slim-cut jeans and gray striped sweatshirt he was wearing. He lifted the hand that was carrying the two other clothing bags. "The coat alone was—"

Darius held up a hand to stop him. "It's just money. Besides, it's not like I'm spending much on other things." It was true. He spent his life either at work or in a studio apartment that offered only a hair over three hundred and ninety square feet of living space. The only things he ever spent extra money on were coffee and delivery meals. He wasn't rich by any stretch of the imagination, especially with Chicago's cost of living, but he had tucked away a tidy sum into savings. He even started a college fund for little Emily, something he'd had to fight her father about.

Nick Slavin, who didn't really have money but wouldn't let that stop his pride. Darius knew his own pride had been in the mix as well, but he wasn't about to let the kid go without. What was so bad about wanting to help? He had promised Seren he would, and a college fund discharged only a fraction of that vow.

It was a promise he would never break. Not after what she had done for him.

"Where did you go?"

Darius blinked, realizing that Morgan was staring at him, concern on his face. "Sorry, lost in thought."

Morgan studied him a moment longer, then smiled, and Darius couldn't help but do the same. "So," Darius began, shaking himself out of the past, "where do you want to go next?"

"Honestly? I'm starving."

"What do you want to eat?"

Morgan's eyes widened, and his smile did the same. "Can we get a burger? Please?" He spoke with the expression of an excited child getting to pick his favorite meal.

Darius never stood a chance.

He did roll his eyes, but he couldn't hide his own grin. "Yes, we can." Glancing at the mall directory, he saw a burger place on the mezzanine and nodded toward the listing. "That look good?"

"Absolutely!"

Darius was honestly surprised the man didn't run off, he looked so excited. Then again, he hadn't eaten much since his arrival, and most of it had been smaller snacks or takeout, nothing really resembling a traditional meal. Darius wasn't a very good cook. And really, what was more traditional than a burger and fries? Darius had to admit his own tastes tended towards the utilitarian unless it came to coffee or on very rare nights out with coworkers or, even rarer, with friends.

As he hurried to catch up with Morgan, he wondered how much his isolationist mentality had cut him off from some truly enjoyable company and events. He thought about Trinity and Ines and even little Emily. He realized he didn't know how they had been doing. Trinity and Ines had both helped him all those years before, in his time of need, and he had ignored them. Or maybe his time of need hadn't ever ended, and that's why he had kept himself isolated. He thought it was better, being away and alone. Thought he was somehow safer.

But was he? Or was he just afraid of actually working through his emotions? Not an easy question to grapple with, but he was leaning hard toward the latter as an answer.

And all it had taken was a time traveler from the future for him to start taking a hard look at himself.

He almost laughed out loud at the absurdity of that thought.

Still grinning, he hopped onto the escalator after Morgan and tried not to let his enthusiasm run away with him. He couldn't deny that he was growing attached to Morgan, and it filled him with both awe and warmth. Then again, hadn't Seren had the same effect on him all those years ago?

Hadn't what he had thought was love for Vivian de Winter done the same to him before Seren?

Iciness drenched his enthusiasm. His smile immediately faltered, then vanished, not up to the task of holding up against memories quite that terrible. He tried to push them away, to lock them back into whatever room in his mind had inadvertently released them. He was successful, to a degree, but his enthusiasm for being out, despite it being with Morgan, had paled considerably.

When they reached the mezzanine, it was to be greeted by an almost completely empty burger place. Chairs were all neatly arranged next to tables in twos or fours, the tabletops worn away from frequent cleaning. It had been a long while since Darius had been in a mall food court, and he was momentarily surprised at how deserted it was. Then he remembered that it was three-thirty in the afternoon on a Thursday. Most people were in school or at work. Lucky for Morgan and Darius.

"What do you want? Can I order it?" Morgan asked, his words rushing out. Catching himself, he colored and gave a short laugh. "Sorry. For whatever reason, being out and doing this sort of thing is making me feel more connected to everything." He grinned. "Or maybe I just *really* want a burger?" In his enthusiasm, he didn't sense the change in Darius's mood.

"All right, you order, I'll find us a seat. I just want a chicken sandwich. Mayo and lettuce only."

"French fries?"

"Sure," Darius said, handing him thirty dollars. Morgan took the money and hurried up to the person behind the counter.

Darius found them one of the cleaner small tables made for two and put the shopping bags down next to the chair. The mall around them was sparsely populated, and most of the people there were older individuals walking, shoppers dipping into stores to pick up one or two items, and workers who wished to be anywhere but there. Darius couldn't imagine working retail. It seemed thankless and soul-sucking.

Not unlike my own work, he thought and chuckled. Being stuck behind a desk, fact-checking and note-taking, was not the most fulfilling of occupations, even if it was for a greater good.

"Darius Adair, it has been a long time."

Anything remotely resembling a good mood died at the sound of the voice. Darius felt a tightness close around his gut, anxiety squeezing at him, as he turned towards the person who had spoken.

Walking towards him were two men. Darius immediately recognized Nick Slavin, Emily's father. Nick was shorter than Darius, with an open, honest expression that had always struck Darius as boyish and immature. Now, however, he looked drained. There were circles under his eyes and his dark curls, which reached his shoulders, were limp and greasy. He didn't raise his gaze to meet Darius's. He wasn't who had spoken.

The man who had addressed Darius was slightly shorter than Nick, maybe an entire five feet six or seven inches tall. He appeared young, much younger than his actual years. He looked fourteen, but Darius knew his age numbered more than a hundred years. Possibly much more. He had sandy blonde hair and pale eyes that defied accurate description. In some light, they were a fair blue; in others, an amber-rose color. Despite their opalescence, they were always sharp, always taking in the measure of everyone and everything around him. He was a mage, and a powerful one, a well-known elder in the Protectorate and not necessarily well-liked. Energy practically radiated from him. No one knew his true name. He came from the older schools of knowledge that held that a true name gave others power over one, and he guarded his well. He simply went by Kris. He had been Seren's mentor, the man who had taught her the mage craft of the Cycle, of life and healing and growth. Had she lived longer, Kris may have taught her other disciplines as well. Old, revered mages were often able to master many disciplines within the sphere of spellcraft.

When Ty had mentioned that there were elders in Chicago, Darius hadn't dreamed that included Kris.

Kris did not like Darius.

Oh, the youthful-looking man had never said as much to his face, but Darius had caught snippets of hushed conversations, sideways glances, and rumors around the Protectorate. Kris blamed him for Seren's death and did very little to hide that fact. If Darius hadn't needed Seren's help escaping his own mentor, she would still be alive. As her mentor, Kris would have preferred to see Darius die, not Seren.

In his darker moods, Darius agreed, and it made his guilt much worse.

It was Kris who had spoken, the words cold and snappish. Darius couldn't remember if that was how he spoke normally, or simply to those he didn't like.

Nevertheless, Darius extended a hand in respect. "Kris. Good to see you."

Kris stared at him, amber eyes never wavering. He made no move to accept Darius's hand, and after a moment, Darius dropped it along with any attempt to be genuinely cordial with the elder. Cool civility was the best Darius would muster for him.

Darius turned his attention to Nick, who was still looking down and away, hands shoved deep in his pockets. Darius was fully aware that this could be the time when Morgan would meet his father, and Darius wanted to do his best to keep the situation calm. "How is Emily doing?" Darius asked.

Nick looked up then, and Darius could clearly see his face. Days of stubble lined his jaw and chin, and his normally olive-toned, darker complexion looked pallid. His eyes were red and damp, but whether from tears or exhaustion, Darius couldn't tell. The man looked like he hadn't eaten or slept well in days, but the mention of his daughter brightened him up a bit. He offered an awkward smile. "She's good. Uh, thanks for letting her hang out with you for a bit. She can be a handful. She's better off when she's with Trinity than me anyways."

"She is an amazing child," Darius said, the words feeling odd in his mouth. The run-in he'd had with Nick ended in a shouting match, so to see him now, meek and withdrawn, was strange. It brought up memories of Seren but also thoughts of what Seren would think if she saw him.

"Yeah," Nick said, perking up a bit. The smile that lit his lips was small but genuine. "Was actually here picking something up for her." He lifted the bag he was carrying. It was small, probably a small trinket or accessory. "She, uh, she liked earrings."

Darius nodded awkwardly. "That's great. Maybe we could all get together sometime? Maybe dinner with Trinity or something?" It sounded weak even to his own ears, but Nick was trying, and Darius thought he should do the same. Maybe this could be a chance to let the past go.

Darius was surprised by how badly he wanted it to be just that.

"Doesn't that sound delightful," Kris exclaimed, clapping his hands together mockingly. He had a twisted smile on his face, one that held only contempt. "Though it might get awkward. Conversations with old friends tend to dig up the past, don't they?"

The threat, if it was a threat and not just a barb, was not lost on Darius by any stretch. Kris's meaning was clear. *You're the reason her mother was killed. Do you really want something like that to come up?*

Kris took a step closer to Nick and leaned in as if he was going to whisper something to him. When he spoke, though, it was at normal volume. "Besides, the last time Darius was anywhere near you, you lost the woman you loved." Kris looked at Darius and shook his head, making a mocking *tsk tsk* sound. "I wouldn't trust him around her child."

Darius clenched his jaw but refrained from making any comment or defense. He was now focused entirely on Nick, whose expression had darkened with Kris's reminder. Nick turned away, seething. As he did so, something around his neck caught Darius's eye. It glittered in the dim mall lighting, a small flash of red and gold, and then it was gone. "Come on, Kris," Nick said, voice now shaking with anger. Kris's reminder had worked, and any semblance of civility between Nick and Darius evaporated. "Let's get out of here before I do something I'll regret." There was violence in his words.

Darius was unsure if he was disheartened or frightened by how easily the tentative olive branch between them had been dashed away.

"You heard the man," Kris said, shrugging. "Good day, Mr. Adair." He turned with an unnecessary flourish and walked off with Nick.

Darius watched them go. The entire exchange hadn't taken more than a minute or two, but it felt as if it had rent a hole in the carefully constructed order that Darius had managed to put his life into, or at least convinced himself that he had. Just Kris's voice had brought back enough to prove that conviction entirely wrong. His threat settled in Darius's chest, as did Nick's sudden rejection, both throbbing painfully.

You're the reason Emily's mother was killed.

Let's get out of here before I do something I'll regret.

Darius tried to push the thoughts away, to compartmentalize them and return to a more even mood, but they would not be bullied. Not this time. This time they had reinforcements. He could see all the things Emily would never do with her mother. There would be no learning how to ride her bike or how to swim from Seren. There would be no mother-daughter heart-to-heart conversations about Emily's first kiss or first love. No tearful farewells when Emily went off to college.

You're the reason Seren is dead.

You got her killed.

She died because you were weak.

You took that poor child's mother away.

"No," he said, barely audible as he shook his head to try and dislodge the thoughts. They jumped and jumbled together but only crowded in further. "No."

"Darius, are you okay?" Morgan was standing beside him, tugging gently on his coat sleeve. A tray of food was on the nearby table. "What's wrong? You look pale."

"I…" Darius couldn't find the words. "No, I'm not *okay*."

Morgan pursed his lips. "All right. I'm going to get bags for our food. Then we can go."

Chapter Twenty
Morgan

The streetlights strobed through the interior of the car as it moved through the city streets. The rideshare driver said nothing to their passengers as they navigated the steadily darkening city. They made only one stop on the way—to a cell phone store, where Darius stiffly ordered Morgan to stay in the car when he went in, and fifteen minutes later, he returned with a new phone for him. He handed the phone to Morgan, asked the driver to take them to the apartment, and lapsed into silence.

What the hell happened?

Morgan had stepped away from Darius for only a minute or two to order the food, and everything had been fine. When he'd returned, it was to find a shaking, pale, taciturn Darius who hadn't spoken more than a handful of words to him since. Something must have happened, though he wasn't sure what could have gone on in such a short amount of time. The only thing Morgan did know was that Darius had completely shut down. The quiet stretched between them, and with each second, it looked like the weight of it dragged Darius down further.

Morgan did not like this.

He was the one who thanked the driver when they both climbed out of the car at Darius's building. He then quietly followed Darius into the lobby and onto the elevator. It was only a few floors up, but even the elevator ride felt tense. Morgan tried to use the time to figure out how he would ask Darius about what had happened. He was worried about making this worse. Just because he was interested in the man didn't mean he knew Darius well, and he was afraid he might say the wrong thing and set Darius off or drive him further into his retreat.

The soft ding of the elevator reaching their floor and the sound of the metal door sliding open were the only noises that permeated the soft, warm hallway of the apartment building. Both men stepped out and walked down the hall, to the last door at the end. The silence between them was so deep that, amidst the soft white noise of the heating in the apartment hall, Morgan swore he could hear each tumbler shift as Darius inserted his key.

Then they reversed.

Everything was getting sharper and more jumbled, time unraveling itself on Morgan.

No. Now is *not* the time.

Morgan followed Darius into the apartment and let Darius close and lock the door behind them. Morgan placed the bags of food on the table, trying to focus on something to keep himself from feeling disconnected. He couldn't let this happen now. Not when Darius needed him. He fisted his hand tightly, focusing on the sensation of the straining muscle and using it to keep himself grounded. He felt the feeling of separation start to ebb. Not much, but it wasn't growing, and it wasn't maintaining the same level of pressure. That helped.

Darius moved past the table, and the bed, into the darkened living room space. He sat down on the couch, his back to Morgan, and leaned his head on his hand, supporting it with an elbow on the arm of the couch. He was silent.

Morgan took another minute to collect himself. When he thought he was solid, or at least good enough to help someone else, he moved to the couch and sat beside Darius. He was sure not to get too close, but despite the respectful distance, he saw Darius twitch, almost jump a bit when he did so.

"What's going on?" Morgan asked, keeping his voice soft. "Where are you?"

Darius looked like he struggled to speak. "I...I..."

Morgan noticed that the hand he was using to rest his head on, the same one that covered his eyes, was shaking. Without thinking, Morgan reached out for Darius's free hand and took it in both of his own. He could feel the tremor there. "It's all right. You don't have to speak right now. What can I do to help you?" he asked, trying to keep his voice quiet and calm.

"I don't know," Darius said between breaths, licking his lips. "Just feel panicky."

"Well, why don't we try using the focus trick? Five things you can see?"

In the shadows, Darius shifted, lifting his hand from over his eyes to look around him. "The window. The couch. The coffee table," he began, listing them off mechanically. Then his dark eyes moved to Morgan, and in the shadows of the apartment, Morgan could still see that they were damp. "You. I see you."

"And a fifth thing?" Morgan asked, swallowing under Darius's gaze. He couldn't discern his expression in the half-light, but he felt himself blush nevertheless. He hoped Darius couldn't see.

"I don't know if I need a fifth thing right now."

"Oh."

Darius wet his lips, and Morgan tracked the movement, having trouble remembering what it was he had been saying only seconds before.

"Can I kiss you?" Darius asked.

Morgan's eyes widened a bit, and his mind reeled. Only a second ago, Darius had been having a panic attack. Or was he still?

"Are you sure you aren't looking for a distraction?" Morgan blurted out, voice a bit louder than he'd meant it to be.

Darius let out a soft sigh but didn't look away. "Yes. Maybe. I just know that that's the one thing I'm concentrating on now. It's the only thought that doesn't hurt right now."

Morgan felt his face grow warm. He *wanted* to kiss Darius, or rather be kissed by Darius. Both? Both. He wanted a whole list of things, but he was worried about where Darius was mentally. Still, it was an offer he couldn't refuse. At least not unconditionally. "Only if we talk or at least try to talk afterward. Deal?"

Darius nodded.

Morgan took a deep breath, but it was interrupted halfway through by the kiss, which he hadn't been expecting so quickly. Darius's lips were on his, kissing him. At first, Darius was tentative, and Morgan had the distinct impression that he was testing to see if Morgan was real. Or maybe that was how Morgan felt, his own struggles with reality seeping into the kiss. He wanted to know, down to the core, that Darius was real and that they were there with one another.

That thought spurred Morgan on, and he lifted his right hand to slip it up to Darius's face, then the side of his neck to cup the back of his head, fingers sliding through the man's dark hair. He shifted forward, deepening the kiss, wanting to explore further. He swore there was a moan from Darius, a small, breathy sound that sent fire and excitement to all the right places.

Or all the wrong places if he didn't want to go too far.

And he didn't, right?

Right?

He let the kiss turn gentle again, then broke it. He placed a small kiss on Darius's forehead before pulling back completely. "That was really, *really* nice, but I think we have a few things to talk about before anything else happens, yeah?" he said.

Darius nodded, but there was no missing the disappointment in his expression.

"Besides," Morgan said, laughing, "I'm starving, and no, that is not some sort of innuendo."

Darius smiled, though it looked like he was doing so grudgingly. "My appetite isn't that great right now. Well, not that appetite, anyway," he explained, nodding towards the food at the table. "Which I'm not used to, I have to admit." He sounded embarrassed, though it was hard to say with the shadows covering his face. "You eat. I'll—"

"Talk?"

The heavy sigh that escaped him said that it hadn't been his first choice. Finally, and with resignation in his voice, he said, "Yes, I'll talk."

Morgan hopped up from the couch and moved to the kitchen counter, where he'd left the food. Digging into the bag, he withdrew two burgers and a French fry container. He was too hungry to look for actual plates and instead used the wrapper the burger had been packed in as his plate. He sat himself at the stool and looked back towards Darius. "Well?"

"I didn't think you would be ready so quickly," Darius chuckled.

"I *said* I was hungry!" Morgan's smile slipped a bit, and he sobered. "Unless you need me there?" He pointed to the empty space on the couch beside Darius.

"No, I'll come to you," Darius said. He stood and made his way quietly to the other stool at the counter. The kitchen light illuminated his features, and he still looked pale as he ran a hand through his hair, dark eyes moving over the apartment. He was searching for what to say, how to start. "Do you know who Seren Morgan was?"

"Aside from my namesake?" Morgan asked. "All I knew was that she was Dad's wife, Emily's Mom, my mom's best friend, and that she died. The details were never really discussed, and after Dad... After he died from suicide, we didn't really talk about the past much. It was too much for Mom and sometimes even Emily." Talking about the past choked him up, and his own appetite was beginning to fade. It also brought his anxiety and disassociation closer than he liked. He pushed the thoughts away and stood, retrieving a glass of water before resuming his seat. "That's it."

"Well, they weren't married," Darius said, finding his way to the conversation's start. He wrung his hands and studied them as he did so. His anxiety was still present, still obvious, but he continued. "My mentor's name was Vivian de Winter. She was an elder in the Protectorate. One of its founding members. Hundreds of years old. She was considered one of the wisest individuals that had ever graced its halls. So, when I was chosen as her charge, it was a great honor." His voice took on a sardonic tone, bitter. "I was nine. I was living with foster parents in New York. State, not city," he clarified quickly. "There's more to the state than just Manhattan."

Morgan blinked, confused at the turn the conversation had taken.

138

"Sorry, force of habit," Darius continued, looking a bit sheepish despite his stress. "Anyway, I thought being chosen by Viviane de Winter as a protégé was my chance to do something great, to *be* something great."

Morgan took a bite of his burger, absorbing what Darius was saying. It didn't take much to imagine that this de Winter person was not a good individual, especially given Darius's current condition. Morgan took another bite and waited for the other man to continue.

"She *groomed* me to be the sort of mage she thought I should be," he said, fairly spitting the word 'groomed' as he spoke it. "By the time I was eighteen, I was more talented and powerful than most mages become in their lifetimes. I was also conceited, vain, and obsessed with pleasing de Winter. Everything I wanted was done for her. For her approval. For her...*pleasure*." Darius's voice shook with revulsion. He was wringing his hands so hard that the knuckles were white, and the skin on his fingers was becoming more and more red. His eyes were shining with tears, but they were bitter and angry. He took a deep breath, looking away from Morgan and trying to regain his composure.

Morgan finished his burger but left the other one. He took another drink of the water and stood. "Want to go back to the couch?"

Darius didn't look up but shook his head. "I was twenty-six when I met Seren," he said, his voice quieter but a little stronger. "She was...Jesus, I don't know what she was. Fiery? A pain in the ass? Caring, whether you wanted her to be or not? She came into my life like a fucking bulldozer and tore everything down."

"That doesn't sound *good.*"

Darius chuckled. "But she was also kind to a fault, in her way. She would give everything just to make sure you were all right."

Morgan nodded.

"Just before we met, there was a substantial uptick in magical activity in the city. Strange events. People getting pregnant who didn't or shouldn't have had the ability to do so. Blood rituals. Demonic activity. Basically, it all pointed towards someone trying to draw an enormous amount of power from what exists outside this sphere and not caring who it hurt. Pulling from worlds beyond can lead to energies warping our reality.

"Seren and her friends, who sort of stumbled onto it, thought it was de Winter. Seren reached out to me. Hell, she hunted me down. Told me my mentor was a garbage human being and that she wanted to help me."

Morgan wasn't sure how to react to that. "And, uh, how did you respond?"

"At first? I'm not even sure what my reaction was. I thought her accusations weren't grounded in reality. How could Viviane de Winter, respected member of the founding order of the Protectorate, be doing something so dangerous? I thought Seren was trying to cast aspersions. Her mentor was another elder in the Protectorate, and I thought she was trying to drag de Winter and myself down in some half-baked idea of making herself and Kris look good." He shook his head. "I was so full of myself that I didn't see what was right in front of me the entire time. But she kept at me. She would not go away. She cared with a tenacity that was intimidating, and eventually, I did, too. I fucking cared."

"You loved her?"

Darius nodded. He was still angled away from Morgan, and he wiped at his eyes before taking a steadying breath. "I loved her. And she died for me."

Morgan let the silence fall after that statement. He wasn't sure if he should push it. The story was taking a toll on Darius.

"Vivian de Winter was trying to bring her dead lover back from the beyond," Darius said into the silence between them.

"Necromancy?" asked Morgan. He might not be as knowledgeable as some, but Morgan was still a mage and understood much of the history and Protectorate law that Darius also knew. "But doesn't that take Protectorate approval? Were there even necromancers available?"

Darius chuckled derisively. "No. She wouldn't have gotten approval. Her lover had died rotting in prison. He'd been part of that cult group and had been arrested for the deaths of at least a dozen nonmagical individuals for a ritual he had devised."

There was only one group of mages that were that uncaring for the lives of nonmagical humans. "The Ascendant?"

Darius nodded. "Yes. As a result, when he died, his body was burned, and the ashes were warded and destroyed to completely cut them off from the soul. There would have been nothing for any true necromancer to work with."

"Then how?"

"Who needs the old body when there's a new one to be had?" Darius's voice was hollow, and it echoed in the small apartment. He sounded ragged and wrung out as if there was nothing left. "She had groomed me to be the vessel into which she would force his soul. Cut my hair like him, dressed me like him..." He trailed off and shuddered. "Touched me like him. For *years*." He nearly choked on the words, voice breaking. "All of that, and she only meant to tear my spirit from my body and offer her lost love a new host to walk the world in. I was nothing but a container to her."

Morgan was speechless. He couldn't fathom what finding out something like that would do to him. The mentor he had grown up with, been abused by, been manipulated into completely depending on, had done all of it just to mold him into an object to be used. He moved around the counter to stand in front of Darius. He wanted to reach out, to touch him, but he waited. He didn't know how Darius would react to it, and he wanted to give him a chance to finish. He just wanted to be closer to him.

"I finally went to de Winter's home, to our home, myself. I confronted her. Maybe I thought she would deny it, or I could *prove* she wasn't doing this." His breath shuddered when he exhaled. "I don't remember much. I became a prisoner in my own body. Viviane de Winter, master of mind spellcraft, turned me into a puppet. She wanted to do the ritual right then and there. Started to..." Darius trailed off, putting his face in his hands and breathing for a few seconds. "Seren interrupted the ritual, but the power de Winter had summoned was too much. It dispersed so violently. There was an explosion and...and..."

"I'm so sorry," Morgan murmured.

"So am I," he whispered, tears spilling down his cheeks.

Darius finally looked up, and the expression of grief and frailty on his face made Morgan's heart squeeze in his chest.

Unable to stop himself, Morgan reached out and pulled him into a hug, holding him as tightly as he could. For a split second, Darius hesitated, and Morgan was about to release him and apologize, but then Darius hugged back with equal strength, burying his face in Morgan's shoulder while silent sobs shuddered through him. Morgan kept him close, quietly intent on making sure Darius knew he was not alone. He would hold on as long as Darius needed him to.

CHAPTER TWENTY-ONE
Darius

"How are you feeling?" Morgan asked, voice gentle.

Darius's head hurt, a constant, throbbing pain pulsing behind both eyes. His sinuses were so clogged he couldn't breathe, and he was in a state of utter disbelief as to how he had just broken down. He hadn't experienced such emotional upheaval in years. Had it slowly been building all of this time? Had he isolated himself all these years, thinking that he could staunch the flow? He wondered if he would ever be free of the clawing emotions that his past brought up. He didn't have the answer to any of that, let alone to Morgan's question. He was exhausted and wrung out. He knew he never wanted to forget the love and connection he had felt with Seren, but would it always come with the trauma that his former mentor visited on him?

"Not great," he finally admitted, his voice weaker than he would have liked. "Not as pent up, though."

They were both seated on the couch, the dinner they had brought home long since packed away in the refrigerator for safekeeping. Morgan had turned on one of the bedside lamps, and the space was awash in warm, soft light. Darius was thankful that there was no harsh illumination in his apartment. He didn't think his aching head could handle them.

"I'm sorry about all that," Darius sighed. He felt foolish. A child bawling to an adult over feelings too big to handle. "I don't normally... Well, to be honest, I don't think I've ever said so much to someone that wasn't a therapist or taking my statement." He shook his head. "Definitely not in that way as well."

Morgan waved the apology away dismissively. "With how many times I've been falling to pieces over the past week and how much you've helped me, I think you earned some time to fall to pieces too." He looked thoughtful for a second, then, "Can I ask what it was that brought this all up?" He quickly followed the question up. "You don't have to tell me if you're not comfortable."

Darius scrubbed his hands over his face and let out a small groan. "To be honest, it was someone that I saw when we were out shopping. Remember how I said that Seren had a mentor that was also an elder in the Protectorate? He was there. His name is Kris. Strangely enough, he was with Nick."

"Nick, as in my dad Nick?" Morgan sat up straighter on the couch, leaning forward.

Darius nodded, kicking himself mentally. Of course, Morgan would want to know if he had seen his father. "Yes. I'm sorry, I should have said sooner."

"Why didn't you say—No, no," Morgan said, interrupting himself. "This is about you. We can talk about me later." He sat back. "Any ideas why Kris would be hanging out with my dad—I mean Nick?"

"No." It was a very valid question. Darius knew more of Kris from rumor and second-hand accounts than anything else. He had only met the man once, and it was only in a passing introduction when Seren had been with him. She had been his prized student, and from the way she had spoken about him, she thought he was a great mentor. Enigmatic, yes, but still an excellent teacher. To Darius's knowledge, Nick and Kris had not had the best chemistry. In fact, Kris disliked *anyone* getting close to his pupil. He had felt anyone with Seren was little more than a worthless distraction from her spellcraft, or so she had said. Then again, perhaps Nick and Kris had bonded in their grief when Seren passed away? Darius had difficulty imagining someone like Kris feeling anything akin to grief. He had lived so long, survived so much. He had always appeared to be too powerful to be susceptible to the emotions that the rest of them possessed.

Darius realized he was basing much of this supposition on his experience with Vivian de Winter. He knew that wasn't fair. Plenty of creatures—mages and otherwise—lived long lives and maintained their capacity for love.

After all, the stories of vampire love were endless.

While he was lost in his own thoughts, Morgan had decided to speak his aloud. "I only ever heard Kris mentioned once or twice. Mom brought him up but said she didn't like him, especially as Seren's mentor. She thought he was too high and mighty and wanted to drag Seren along the path he chose for her—by the neck if he had to."

Darius blinked, and a realization struck him like lightning from a clear sky. "What did you just say?"

"That Trinity didn't like Kris?"

"No, not that part," Darius said, his mind trying to grasp onto what Morgan's words triggered.

"That he would drag Seren along by the neck?"

The neck.

Darius leapt up, suddenly energized by a flash of a memory. He moved to his dresser, to the small wooden box he kept on top of it for the few little trinkets that he picked up over the years. Opening it, it revealed very little. A small smooth stone he had had since he could remember, a pin that indicated his rank in the Protectorate, and the gold necklace that Ines had extracted from around Morgan's collar bone. It had been cleaned, dried, put into the box for safekeeping, and promptly forgotten about. Moving over to the bedside lamp, he studied it in the light before turning to Morgan and saying, "Nick had this necklace around his neck when I saw him earlier today."

Morgan stood up, walking over and taking it in his hand, turning the glittering piece of jewelry over in the light. As he studied it, Darius saw his eyes turn sad, and Darius lost a bit of his enthusiasm.

"This was Emily's. My Emily's," he said quietly as if recalling a distant memory. "She gave it to me when she was dying." He scoffed, his free hand moving unconsciously to the spot where the piece of jewelry had been embedded around his collarbone. "She pushed it into me. It was supposed to be the anchor back to a specific time. She said it would call to itself, back to when it was made, because it had been made from an imbued stone."

"Imbued with what?" Darius asked, treating the topic with a bit more reverence than previously. Amid all the chaos, he hadn't thought to examine the necklace for magic. He silently berated himself for not doing so earlier. He should have treated it as a piece of evidence, but instead, he had been too preoccupied with his connection with Morgan.

Morgan shrugged. "I don't know." He blinked, and his eyes flashed as he studied it through his spellcraft. His voice took on a dreamier tone when he spoke again. "A soul, maybe, or part of one? It feels incomplete." The light vanished from his gaze, and he clenched his eyes shut, wavering on his feet. Without thought, Darius reached out a hand to steady him, and Morgan clung to it, taking deep breaths. "Sorry," he said, opening his eyes. "Got a bit dizzy there."

"It's fine."

"Not really," Morgan grumbled. "Am I ever going to be able to access my magic without feeling like I'm going to vomit and pass out? Am I ever going to feel reconnected to reality? Fuck, at this rate, I'd settle for existing without panicking constantly."

Darius thought for a moment, taking the necklace from Morgan's hand. He put it on the bedside table. It could wait. Not for long, but for a bit. "I don't know," he replied simply. "There may be improvements, but the mind comes up with strange and not always great coping mechanisms." He saw Morgan's face fall further and hurried to find some sort of hopeful response that wouldn't be sugarcoating but also wouldn't be quite so bleak. "However, you have been feeling better. You've been up and around more today than any other day, and your appetite has improved. Progress like that, in a week, is definitely encouraging."

"Thanks." Morgan's tone was dismissive. "Nice of you to say."

Darius stepped closer to him. "I'm not *just* saying it, Morgan," he said, locking eyes with him. "I am telling you that it will get better."

Darius never thought he would hear himself say those words to anyone. Why was it so difficult for him to believe them for himself?

Morgan's eyes went wide, and his smile softened a bit. "Thank you."

Darius now realized how close to Morgan he was standing. He could feel the warmth coming off the other man and feel the brush of his breath against his cheek. The heat he had felt earlier, when he had kissed Morgan, returned and he blinked, looking from Morgan's eyes to his mouth, then back. He could tell Morgan could feel it too. "May I—"

"I wish you would," Morgan breathed, barely audible.

He didn't need to be told twice.

Their lips met in a kiss that had none of the previous timidity. Darius felt freer from his despair and loneliness. It left room for want to fill the void. He slid his arms around Morgan's lower back, holding him close without, he hoped, being too forward.

Those worries were quickly laid to rest when Morgan's hand slid up behind his head to cup the back of his neck, and his other snaked around his shoulders. Darius relished the feeling of being held as he was pulled against Morgan, and the kiss grew deeper, needier. It was hot and glorious.

Darius was surprised at how quickly his body reacted. He was flushed and wanting, feeling simultaneously connected to Morgan and desperate to be more completely and utterly linked. As their hips ground together, Darius could tell that he wasn't the only one affected. Feeling Morgan's hardness against his own through their clothes, knowing that his need was as strong as Darius's, was as exhilarating as it was arousing.

Just then, Morgan broke the kiss and pulled back a bit, breathless and grinning. "Are you sure you're okay?"

"I think I'm better than okay," Darius said, pressing his hips against Morgan's to bring them both more delicious friction.

Morgan tilted his head back at the sensation, exhaling shakily. "I mean with everything, Darius. With this. With us. This is all... happening quickly... and you said you were..."

"Demi?" It was then that Darius really caught Morgan's gaze. Beneath the haze of lust was concern, and he was searching Darius's face for signs of hesitance. Darius knew he wouldn't find any. There was none to discover. "I am, but I also feel so damned connected to you. I just...I want this, Morgan," he whispered. "I want you." He lowered himself to the bed and lay back, pulling Morgan with him and settling with his weight on him. He liked the feeling. For once, it felt like he wasn't alone.

Morgan leaned down, moving against him as his lips found the sensitive skin on the side of his throat, sending sparks of sensation through Darius. He shivered and sighed against the feeling, relishing it. His arms went up and around Morgan's shoulders, pulling him closer, trying to find that amazing friction between them that had been so arousing only moments before. He arched up against Morgan's hips, and the half-moan, half-growl that elicited from Morgan felt like it set him aflame.

"We are both wearing entirely too much clothing," Morgan said on a breathy laugh.

Darius agreed wholeheartedly. He lifted his head to find Morgan's lips while he helped the younger man slip out of his jacket. Once that was discarded wherever it fell, it was the tee shirt. All the while, Morgan fumbled with the buttons on Darius's dark shirt, and they both attempted to do all of this without breaking the kiss.

It was less than graceful, but neither were looking for grace.

In an attempt to shrug off his shirt, Darius got tangled, the buttons around the wrists of the shirt sleeves catching. Reluctantly, Darius broke the kiss, trying to sit up to extricate himself from the knot of cotton and buttons. Morgan put a hand on his shoulder and leaned in, close enough for Darius to feel his breath hot on his ear. "What if you kept them there?"

Darius stopped, unsure of what he meant.

As an explanation, Morgan tugged at the shirt, pulling Darius's arms back down to the bed and pinning them, tied. "If you're okay with that?"

Darius couldn't deny the thrill that shot through him at the idea of being, to some extent, bound, but he wasn't sure if he could do it. Not yet. He didn't want to disappoint Morgan. It *could* be there, given time. The idea sent blood pulsing to his already hard arousal, but that didn't mean he was ready. "I don't think—"

Morgan heard the hesitation in his voice and held a hand up to stop him, smiling. "All right, we don't do it, then." Without another word, he shifted back and moved to help disentangle Darius from the shirt. Once his hands had been successfully freed, Darius was quick to make use of them, roving over the deep bronze skin of Morgan's chest and shoulders. Morgan did the same in return, tracing the dozens of scars and healed wounds that littered Darius's skin with deft hands before he returned to teasing Darius's neck with his lips.

"Do you have anything, like protection or lube?" Morgan breathed.

Darius froze, then gave a long, exasperated groan. In the past few years, he hadn't had more than a handful of interactions with men or women that could be considered sexual, and even less where protection was really needed. In those few instances, his partners had had what was needed. Darius, who had a moderate to mild libido, was demisexual and mostly avoided dating in favor of work and being alone, had *nothing* prepared should the need actually arise. "No," he said, halfway between a whine and a laugh. "Should I run out to the store?"

Morgan chuckled. "Do you think you could walk with this in the way?" he asked, his hand rubbing Darius's cock through his pants.

Darius gasped, arching against Morgan's touch. "N-No," he breathed. "Probably not."

Morgan grinned impishly. "We'll just have to figure something out, then, won't we?" he asked. With one hand, he unbuttoned the top of Darius's pants and slowly unzipped the fly, sliding down Darius's body and skimming kisses along his chest and belly as he did so. All the while, he would glance back up to Darius, eyes bright, smile beaming with the promise of more to come.

CHAPTER TWENTY-TWO
Morgan

When morning came, Morgan couldn't move.

He was on his side, only able to see as far as his stationary position would allow. He couldn't turn his head, couldn't roll over. Nothing. Dull light filtered through the windows, but he couldn't see past them. There was only a grayish nothing beyond. Fear seeped quickly into the edges of his mind.

What was happening?

Why couldn't he move?

"Who are you?" The voice sounded distant, a rough, full-throated alto that echoed and warbled strangely.

Morgan blinked. It took him a minute to realize that he hadn't actually *heard* the voice with his ears but rather understood it *in his mind,* which was why it sounded so alien to him. Telepathy. Someone or something was speaking to him mentally, feeling around, trying to glean information. The invasion was more frightening than not being able to move, and he steeled himself against it, picturing physically forcing the voice out, keeping it from his thoughts by locking them up deep within.

"You can't hide—" the voice began but was suddenly silenced.

A small chuckle, lyrical and higher pitched, broke through the silence of the apartment. This time he could hear, or thought he could hear, the voice externally. "Good job, Morgan." The person speaking had a clear, calm, almost cheerful tone. "I don't know how, but someone found you and was poking around in your mind." There was a pause and a near sigh. "I chased them away for now but talk to Darius about this. He can help."

A woman stepped into his field of vision. Dressed in tight, high-waisted jeans and a low-cut shirt. She was lightly tanned and had short, blonde hair cut around her head in a halo of a pixie style. Her eyes were large and sparkled the same blue as Emily's. She crouched down in front of him. "Put on the necklace. Call Trinity. She'll know what to do." She moved to stand, to walk out of his vision, but then thought better of it, crouching back down. "Also, tell that asshat that it isn't his fault when you wake up."

"Wake up?" Morgan asked.

He blinked.

Then he woke up.

Gray light rimmed the closed curtains, trying to seep into the apartment despite being blocked. The apartment itself was still in deep shadow, the sliver of light around the curtain edges doing little to chase away the darkness.

"Fuck," he murmured, running a hand over his curls. The dream had felt so real.

Rolling over, and relieved that he could move, Morgan came within inches of Darius, who was still asleep. Morgan bit down a gasp and mentally kicked himself. Of *course,* Darius was in his own bed, in his own apartment, in his own time. Where else would he be?

Letting the surprise pass, Morgan studied the sleeping man. He looked different when he slept. Well, not exactly different. The sharp lines of his face were still there, handsome and dramatic. He was pale, with closed eyelids that hid dark irises. Morgan felt a temporary pang of anger that anyone could look at this man and think to harm him. He had his walls up, walls that had been created from years of manipulation and abuse. Morgan had to thank his namesake for putting a small chink in that armor. After all, would Darius have escaped his fate with de Winter if Seren hadn't intervened? Would the person that Morgan knew as Darius even exist? Or would he have become some strange, magic-twisted creation of a distorted soul in a foreign body? Even worse, what might happen if the two souls were forced to merge? Was that even possible?

Morgan chuckled softly. It was amusing that the mage who had managed to travel through time was questioning what might be possible. If anyone should know that anything was possible, it was him.

"What's so funny?" asked Darius, eyes still closed.

"I'm sorry. Did I wake you?"

"Not sure. Maybe? I've been dozing in and out. Is everything all right?"

Morgan wanted to lie. He wanted to just stay in this quiet moment, with Darius dozing and him thinking about Darius, where there could be no stress. He knew he couldn't; he knew it wouldn't be fair. "I had a dream."

It was then that Darius opened his eyes, focusing them squarely on Morgan. "And?"

"And we need to call Trinity." He went silent, unsure of how to continue.

Darius studied him for a moment longer. "*And?*"

"There was…" Morgan trailed off with a long sigh. Only last night, Darius had been raw and emotional, and Morgan wasn't sure if he was in a place to hear what he had to say. They might not have the time for Morgan to hesitate, either. "In my dream, someone was trying to scrape my mind, learn things."

Darius sat up, his gaze never moving from Morgan's face. "Someone was using mind spellcraft? Are you all right? Did anything—"

Morgan hurried to interrupt him. "Yes, I'm fine. In my dream, there was a woman who stopped it. She, uhm, chased them away."

"Who?"

"Whoever was trying to read my mind."

Darius sighed, his expression flat. "I mean, who stopped it?"

Morgan braced himself. "It was Seren."

"Seren?" The name was dull and lifeless as it fell from Darius's mouth.

"Your Seren. Seren Morgan. She told me to tell you about it, that you could help. She also said we needed to call Trinity and that the necklace is important." Morgan bit his lower lip before continuing. If Darius wasn't upset now, he soon would be. "And she said for me to tell you that it wasn't your fault."

Darius jerked back as if Morgan had hit him, his dark eyes taking on a defensive edge. "What the hell?"

Morgan wanted to reach out, to touch him, to take his hand and tell him that it was all right, but he wasn't entirely sure physical contact was what Darius needed in that moment. "I don't know," he admitted, deciding honesty was the best course of action here. "She just asked me to relay the message."

Darius didn't respond but threw back the covers and climbed out from beneath them. He was only in a pair of pajama pants and nothing else, and he looked damn good with tousled hair and no shirt. Morgan had to slam the breaks on that thought. Darius was obviously upset, and now was *not* appropriate sexy time.

Before Morgan could say or do anything, though, Darius stalked to the bathroom and slammed the door, the sound echoing off the walls of the apartment and no doubt disturbing one of the various apartments that shared walls, ceilings, or floors. Morgan flinched at it and let out a long sigh. Seren's words, or maybe her appearance, had rattled Darius, and he was more than likely still raw from the cathartic venting he had done the night before. His reaction was understandable. Trauma didn't heal itself overnight.

"Still," murmured Morgan, to the empty quiet of the apartment, "He didn't have to storm off."

Sighing, he slipped out of bed himself, shivering as his bare feet made contact with the uncarpeted flooring. He moved over to the bags of new clothing he'd been given, digging through for jeans, a tee shirt, and a sweatshirt. He'd showered the night before, after they had enjoyed each other, and grabbed a shirt and shorts to sleep in. Now he stripped quickly, stepping into boxer briefs before doing the same to the pants. His bladder was making a pressing case for using the bathroom facilities, but it wasn't such an emergency that he would interrupt Darius's shower. Heaven only knew if it was an angry or sad shower, and Morgan thought some space was in order.

Once fully dressed, Morgan pushed the curtains open, letting in the dull gray light of the Chicago morning. The clock read seven-thirty, and the streetlights were only just now flickering off. Still, it was bright enough to illuminate the apartment to some degree, and that was all Morgan needed.

The necklace, the one he assumed the woman from his dream had been talking about, still lay on the nightstand where Darius had left it. In the dull light, the red stone looked like blood, and as Morgan took the jewelry in his hand, he could swear it felt warm despite the coolness of the apartment around him. That wasn't overly surprising, though. He should have known better than to think his Emily had given him a trinket as an anchor. Why hadn't he thought of it sooner? Why had he just assumed that the necklace was just that?

He took a deep breath, almost afraid to unclasp the gold chain and fasten it around his neck. He was no dream reader, he couldn't see the meaning in them, but he didn't think he had to be to know that it hadn't simply been a figment of his imagination. He knew the face of the person who had spoken to him, and it belonged to a dead woman.

It certainly wasn't unheard of for the dead to visit mages. Even the nonmagical had their dead loved ones visit them from time to time. Hell, his mother often worked with a myriad of spirits that had passed on long ago, but he had never heard so much as a bump in the night. When he was younger, he'd wished deceased loved ones had come to him, in dreams or in the wakeful hours. Those wishes had gone ungranted.

Now, Seren Morgan had appeared to him in a dream, and he would be dipped in shit if he didn't follow her instructions to the letter. With only slightly shaking hands, he managed to undo the clasp, slip the warm chain around his neck, and fasten it quickly, bracing himself for what was to come.

For a moment, nothing did.

Then he felt a warmth spread over him from the red stone. It was subtle but comforting. The sort of glow one might get from a weighted blanket or a hot bath. Soothing, calming.

And that was it. Morgan blinked, unsure if he was supposed to do something or if he had missed a step. He thought back to the dream, thought back to Seren's words. Talk to Darius. Put on the necklace and call Trinity.

As if cued by his thoughts, a low buzzing sound suddenly filled the apartment. Darius's phone, which lay on his nightstand, was lit up and vibrated noisily on the little stand. Morgan was in the middle of a debate on whether or not to answer it when the door to the bathroom opened abruptly. Darius, wrapped in a towel and still damp from a shower, strode out and moved to the bed, snatching the phone up without sparing Morgan a glance. "Yes?"

While Morgan waited, he tried to look elsewhere. Seeing Darius half-naked and still glistening with water from his shower was giving Morgan thoughts that would be absolutely useless in the current situation.

There was a pause, then Darius replied, "All right. See you in an hour."

Morgan didn't move. He didn't say a word. He was anxious to see what Darius would say, though the warm feeling of comfort still enveloped him, and he knew whatever it was, he could handle it.

Darius finally turned to him. His features looked sharp, angry. Then it faltered and melted. Darius let out a long sigh and sat down on the bed, holding the towel so that it didn't slip. His back was to Morgan when he spoke. "Sorry about before. I just… What you said surprised me."

"I could tell."

"I'm not *great* at surprises."

Morgan fought his smile. "That is another thing I could tell."

Darius's shoulders sank a little.

"This is about Seren, isn't it?"

"It's always about Seren," Darius said, sounding exhausted. He ran a hand over his face and through his damp hair.

"Are you still in love with her?"

Darius considered the question, then shook his head. "No. It isn't that." He grew silent, and for a few moments, Morgan wasn't sure he would speak again. "I just can't wrap my head around someone willing to do that for me."

"What, die for you?"

"*Yes.*"

The answer was so soft, Morgan almost didn't hear it.

"Not only that," Darius continued, whisper quiet, "I had to... She had... There was too much magic. She was overwhelmed, twisted, turned into a husk of herself, filled with magic and violence."

Morgan knew all too well what Darius might be talking about. He had seen it in his own time. Mundane humans turned to walking scarecrows, bleeding magic and destroying everything they touched. Morgan couldn't fathom seeing a loved one like that. He was by Darius's side in a minute, sitting down on the bed and taking the man's free hand. He squeezed it before resting his head on Darius's shoulder, ignoring the stray droplets of water.

"We're all worth it to someone, you know? I'm sure you can think of a few people you'd be willing to get into harm's way for."

Darius hesitated before replying. "A few, yes." His voice shook.

They sat like that for a bit in the quiet, dimly lit apartment. Finally, Darius let out another long sigh, shaky but not broken. "All right, I should probably get dressed."

Morgan smirked, thoughts from earlier returning as he ran a hand up Darius's towel-covered thigh. "I mean, you don't *have* to."

Darius raised an eyebrow and tried not to smile. "With Trinity coming over, we don't have time for me not to."

Morgan stilled. The idea of being caught by Trinity, even though she wasn't his mother *yet*, had the same effect on his thoughts. "Good point," he agreed, pouting.

"Besides, I'd like to order something for breakfast. We don't have much here to eat."

That perked Morgan up. Good food was always welcome. "Well, when you put it that way, then yes."

156

"Easily persuaded, hm?"

"Where food is involved? Pretty much always."

CHAPTER TWENTY-THREE
Darius

Darius was nervous. He *hated* being nervous.

It was an incessant, tingling itch that pushed him closer and closer to the panic he knew could bring his world to a crashing halt. The night before had been a frightening reminder that it was still there, waiting. It had been a long while since he'd had a panic attack, and he feared that, if he let it, it would consume him. He quietly reminded himself that he had some medication left for those acute moments, should he have need.

Having Morgan with him, however, was proving to be calming enough.

Absently, he rubbed his palms together and checked his watch again. The food delivery had arrived before Trinity, but his stomach absolutely rioted at the idea of putting anything on it, even his beloved coffee. The want of caffeine and the comforting taste and warmth of the hot beverage didn't help his nerves. He sat on the couch, leg bouncing quietly as he attempted to contain his agitated energy.

He tried going over the events of the morning, solidifying them in his mind. When Morgan had told Darius about the dream, Darius's reaction had been instantaneous and reflexive. He closed up. Bring up the walls, don't let anything in or out. The distant, more logical part of his mind had tried to stop him. He could even hear echoes of his therapist's soothing voice trying to guide him out of the overly defensive response, but he'd needed to escape, and he had.

The hot shower had helped soothe the tension in his body, and he'd been able to think more clearly. Somehow, someway, Seren was still connected to all of this. Maybe through the necklace? It was important enough that she had seen fit to reach out to Morgan. He had a soft chuckle at that thought. Even dead, the woman couldn't leave well enough alone. She just had to drag her best friend's future kid into the mix. The amusement didn't last long, though. The words Morgan had spoken to Darius, which had apparently come from Seren, did.

"It's not my fault," Darius had quietly said into the hiss of the water showering down on him. The sound fell flat against the tile wall. He didn't believe it. After all, *he* had been the one in de Winter's thrall. *He* had been the one that hadn't seen through her façade. He had been the one Seren had stuck her neck out to save and paid for it with her life. "It's not my fault," he'd said again, a bit louder.

He'd thought his voice sounded weak and petulant, and he growled to himself as he washed and shaved in the steaming water, trying not to dwell too heavily on his emotional turmoil. He needed to get back into control. He had to focus. He needed to concentrate on something, anything, besides the remembrance of Seren.

Warm memories of their night came back to him for the first time that morning. Considering the rude awakening earlier, these were a welcome change. The feel of Morgan's skin, the sounds he made when they kissed, when he had taken Darius into his mouth and—

Darius tilted his head back, enjoying the rush of arousal at the memory. He knew he couldn't afford the luxury for long and briefly considered taking care of his body's reaction, but there really wasn't enough time. Frustrated, he turned the water colder and started thinking about the dullest piece of office paperwork he knew of in the hopes of calming down. Once he had, he turned off the water and stepped out of the shower.

He had snatched a towel from the rack and began drying off. In the other room, he heard the deep buzzing sound of his cell phone.

Emerging from the bathroom and ignoring Morgan's worried expression for just a moment, he answered his buzzing phone.

The terseness in Trinity's voice had been palpable. She didn't wait for him to respond or give him time to get a word in edgewise. She didn't seem to need it. "We have to talk. Had a dream last night, and I have a feeling that my kiddo from another timeline did, too. I'll be over as soon as I drop Emily off at her father's and pick up a few things. Think in an hour."

He'd had little choice of anything but to agree. He had questions as well. If they were to figure out what this event that Morgan needed to stop was, then they had to explore every avenue.

Blundering through his apology to Morgan, because the whole damn thing felt like a blunder, hadn't been as painful as he'd thought it would be. He still felt raw and unshielded against what was being thrown against him, but there was no reason to take that out on Morgan, and he needed to make sure that Morgan knew that none of this was his fault.

Darius needed him to know that.

Afterward, Darius just tried to busy himself, to find some distraction from his quickly spiraling thoughts. Ordering food was the first order of business. Coffee, maybe some bagels or donuts. Then he had to get dressed. Black jeans, a tee shirt. Part of him hated doing it. The clothes felt restrictive, and he was already having issues with the unsettling sensation that the world was closing in on him. *Thanks, anxiety.* He ignored it. Moved on. Socks, shoes.

Morgan watched it all quietly. He didn't try to stop him. Darius was relieved. He wasn't sure how he would react if he did. To some degree, Darius needed these little routines to make himself feel better, more in control, of a situation that was swiftly careening away from that control.

Still, as he worked, he couldn't stop the thoughts from crowding in. From thinking about what was to come.

Trinity's studies, her spellcraft, meant she worked with dreams and souls. Morgan had dreamt of a particular soul, which could only mean that what Seren wanted them all to do was try to contact her in one way or another.

The thought terrified him.

The sound of the apartment buzzer made him jump, and he pushed himself to his feet to try and cover the reaction. Walking towards the door, he found himself shuffling, almost dragging his feet. Even his physical form seemed hesitant to allow the inevitable through his door. Still, he took hold of the doorknob, icy cold against the palm of his hand, and turned.

"Hey, Darius," were the first words Trinity spoke, but the warmth and worry in them washed over him before he really registered what she was saying. "How are you doing?"

"I'm fine," he said, his voice thicker than he'd expected.

Trinity raised an eyebrow at him and let out a long sigh. "Really?"

Darius shrugged.

"Don't lie," came another voice, this one from behind Trinity. Ines stood, plastic shopping bag in hand and a smile on her full lips. "We're all friends here." At Darius's confused look, she explained. "Trinity called and gave me the highlights. I'm here to help where I can."

Darius felt his chest constrict, dark coils of anxiety and panic winding tighter behind his ribcage. He hadn't known she would be there. He didn't particularly want her to be, but he also didn't want to ask her to leave. He was torn, unable to speak or convey what he was thinking. He knew he had to reach out, to ask for more help, but he was having difficulty doing it. Christ, it seemed like the hardest thing he'd ever done.

"Do you need me to leave?" she asked, all trace of joking gone from her voice.

He tried to speak but couldn't. Finally, he shook his head. No, she could stay.

He stepped aside to let both women in, taking an unsteady breath as he did so. He was still holding the doorknob, clutching at it with a white-knuckle grip that he had difficulty releasing once he had closed the door behind Ines and Trinity. Finally prying his hand back, he rubbed his palms together and took a deep breath. "So, what does this all entail?"

Ines shrugged, and Trinity looked as if she were about to answer when she caught sight of Morgan. She let out a gasp and moved towards him, her hand moving to the necklace he wore around his neck. "This was it? This was what you pulled out of him?"

"Yeah. I didn't know what it was," said Ines, shooting Darius a shrug. "I mean, I knew that it was a necklace, but I didn't know what significance it had."

Morgan looked suddenly nervous. "Emily—I mean future Emily—told me it was an anchor. It would get me back to where I needed to be."

"It's Seren's engagement ring," Trinity explained as she examined the piece of jewelry. "I had it melted down and reformed into a necklace for Nick. Saved the garnet and everything." Trinity took a deep breath, shoulders slumping ever so slightly. "It was just finished a couple of weeks ago. Gave it to Nick myself."

"Morgan's Emily gave it to him. She knew it would call to itself because it was created somewhere around the same time as whatever event started and everything unraveling happened." Darius had meant it to sound like more of a question but heard himself stating it with certainty. He met Morgan's gaze, and Morgan nodded, though there was sadness in the man's eyes. Then it was gone, and he broke the gaze.

"Future Emily is a sharp one," Ines said, pulling two pints of ice cream out of the bags she'd brought and tucking them into the freezer. Darius didn't see what flavors she'd gotten.

"Ice cream?" he asked.

"Listen, these things are unpredictable. It's always good to have comfort foods available." As she spoke, she also pulled two bottles of wine out of the bag, one red, one white. When she saw his continued study, she held them both up. "I wasn't sure which one you went for, and I get the feeling we're all going to need them in a bit."

Darius nodded. Even the little bit of small talk was beginning to help him feel better, and he was now glad that he hadn't asked Ines to leave.

"Ines, it's ten in the morning," Trinity admonished.

"And?" Ines asked.

Trinity cleared her throat, looking around the small apartment. "Can we grab those couple of throw pillows and put them on the floor by the coffee table? This way, we can all sit around it." Trinity nodded. "We don't need much room for a séance, but the closer we can be, the better results we'll have. Everyone all right with casting?"

162

Ines nodded. Morgan was doing the same, but Darius shook his head. "We can. Morgan can't. When he taps too deeply into his magic, it sets him back, and I don't know how much we will need for this."

"Let me try," Morgan said plaintively. "If I start to feel sick or shaky, I'll stop."

Darius didn't like the idea, but he also knew that it wouldn't be fair to exclude the man. Especially if every mage's power could help this work. Darius didn't want to have to try this twice.

"It shouldn't take that much spellcraft," Trinity explained, but she was still concerned. She looked between the two men, but her gaze landed on Morgan. He nodded, trying to convince both her and Darius that he was fit for it. Darius finally relented, adding his own nod, and as a result, Trinity gave in. "All right. Don't push it," Trinity warned.

They all sat around the table. Trinity reached into the messenger bag she'd brought and pulled out a chalice. It was ceramic, obviously handmade, most likely by her. It had been done in dark browns and greens that swirled around each other, mimicking the colors of the deep forest. The glaze was thick and shining and caught the light as she placed it in the center of the coffee table. The cup part of the chalice was shallow and wide, and it reminded Darius more of a miniature bird bath than an actual chalice.

"So, what do we have to do?" he asked, nerves forcing him to speak. He had never been part of a séance. Generally speaking, those who studied what were considered the loftier spellcraft disciplines, those of mind, thought, and reason, among others, found the airier spirit workers to be a bit too close to nonmagical hippies. "Incense or candles or whatnot?"

Trinity's side-eye game was strong, and when she landed it on Darius, he shrank away.

Ines rolled her eyes. "Don't take offense. I'm sure he's been trained to look down on anyone not cooped up in a Protectorate office." She offered a quick wink to Darius, the joke diffusing the annoyance on Trinity's part.

Darius didn't say anything but nodded his gratitude.

All four of them sat around the coffee table. Morgan and Ines sat on the couch; Trinity and Darius occupied the overstuffed throw cushions opposite them. Trinity's deep gaze darted upwards to Morgan, and her tone was measured when she spoke. "Put the necklace into the chalice," she instructed, nodding as Morgan hurried to comply. The gold piece of jewelry made a soft *clink* as it hit the shining clay, and it glittered in the overhead light.

"Now, everyone join hands, and if I get any more remarks, I swear you will catch a beating."

Darius winced, knowing that comment was just for him. He also knew that while he wouldn't be physically accosted, he would have to deal with her wrath. He did as he was told, reaching across to take Morgan's hands and reaching to his right to take Trinity's. He took a deep breath, trying to relax the tightness in his chest. It didn't help.

Trinity rolled her shoulders and cracked her neck, squeezing Darius's hand just slightly before she spoke again. "All right, I'm going to need magical energy, so whatever you can spare me, any little bit helps. It's been a while since Seren passed, and crossing that divide is going to take a lot. The necklace helps, but only so much."

The three of them nodded and went to work.

Darius always felt that reality was a funny thing. It was made up of innumerable threads, each woven with exquisite complexity but ultimately—and sometimes infinitely—malleable. This was why it was so important for mages to be educated and for more powerful, younger spellcrafters to be mentored by their more learned peers. They needed to train, to understand that every action within the weave of reality affected many others. Pulling or tearing at the wrong threads haphazardly could be the difference between life and death, order and chaos. That was what mages did—they walked that line and expertly drew power from the reality around them.

Darius watched the mages around him. Ines's eyes lit with her power, the normal brown glowing the color of sunlight on rich earth in the summertime. Trinity kept her eyes shut, no doubt concentrating on the task at hand. When Darius looked over to Morgan, he felt his breath catch in his throat.

Morgan's usually light brown eyes glowed with a warm amber light, flecks of tawny brown illuminated until they resembled the color of autumn leaves. This was the first time Darius had had the opportunity to really study his companion while working magic. He'd found Morgan attractive before, but with the light of his magic illuminating his eyes, he was breathtaking.

Darius's attention was quickly drawn away from his admiration. A fine, red mist began to rise from the necklace. It was a strange mix of smoke and fog, and it began to coalesce just above the chalice, forming the vague simulacrum of a face. It was imprecisely shaped, incomplete. It almost seemed to try and form a face but couldn't quite obtain the shape. Trinity opened her eyes and took in the sight, then let out an exasperated side. "Damn it," She snapped, her eyes glowing a deep reddish brown.

"Is this as good as it's going to get?" asked a voice from the small, red mist cloud. Seren's voice.

"Looks like," was Trinity's annoyed response.

The voice from the mist took on a note of resignation. "Nothing's perfect."

"Holy shit," breathed Darius, unable to keep himself from speaking. Emotions flooded through him at the sound of Seren's voice. Guilt, happiness, grief, they all coalesced in a nauseating torrent of force. He didn't think he could do this. How could he have ever thought he could do this?

"Take a deep breath, Adair," the Seren-mist said.

Christ, the voice sounded so much like Seren. The tone of it made his throat tighten almost painfully. He couldn't speak; hell, he had trouble breathing. He tried to take the voice's—Seren's—advice.

"Seren," Trinity murmured, eyes still glowing, brow furrowed in concentration. "We need to talk about—"

"I'm not the Seren that you knew, or know, or—fucking time travel," interrupted the mist, annoyed.

A.E. Bross

The words cut through Darius's panic haze. He glanced at Ines, then Trinity. All he saw was confusion. He turned his attention back to the small, glowing orb of smoke. "What do you mean?"

"I'm not actually sure how to explain it," came Seren's reply. "I am the part of Seren's soul that saw time pass." There was anguish in the voice. It shook. "I saw my child grow. I saw my fiancé die. I saw my child die. I saw the world becoming undone."

Darius saw Morgan blinking rapidly, tears welling in his eyes.

"I came back with Morgan. Emily sent me back. Under his skin. This is only a piece. A piece of a whole I was torn from. That I'll rejoin soon."

Darius didn't understand what was being said, and from the expressions on his fellow mages' faces, they didn't either.

"I'm sorry. I hate this cryptic shit as much as you do," Seren snapped. "I just... don't know... how else to put it into words."

"Tell us what you do know," Trinity suggested.

"Nick's despair is eating him alive," came the quiet reply. "His despair creates me. No. He does something, and part of me is snatched into the stone. Gods, it's all so distant and difficult to recall." The small sphere of red smoke pulsed. "He isn't alone. What he's doing isn't allowed. Taboo." A soft chuckle comes from the orb, "Like Morgan moving through time, but worse. Much worse. I don't know, though. The magic is profane, wrong, too much. He isn't alone. He isn't alone. He needs to be with people, but not the ones he is with."

"Darius saw him with Kris last night," Morgan blurted out.

All of them, except for the swirling orb of smoke that was Seren, turned to look at him.

Darius felt the color drain from his face. He now had the distinct impression that he should have said something or done something to Nick, try to pull him away from Kris. He should have put more effort into inviting him away from the danger. But how could he have known? Had he failed another person? Had he cost Emily her other parent, too?

"He isn't alone. He needs to be with people, but not the ones he is w—" Seren's words were suddenly cut off as a heavy cracking sound shattered the relative quiet of the apartment. Involuntarily, Darius

166

snatched his hands up to cover his ears, watching the others do the same. The small sphere of smoke vanished, but before he could say anything to Trinity, the air pressure in the apartment suddenly increased exponentially. It was difficult to breathe, and the air around them grew thick, trying to suffocate them.

Ines shrieked, her fingers digging into her scalp as if she was in pain. Trinity did as well, and Morgan doubled over, clutching his head. At first, Darius thought it was from the sound or maybe the pressure, but then he felt an itch, a light burn, on the back of his head. On the ward tattoo he'd had inked to help keep mages with mental magic out of his mind.

Darius studied the sensation, and from it, he parsed the threads of magic being used to craft it. He could follow them. Moving his gaze around the room, he saw the small tendrils of magic slipping around and into his friends' minds. He isolated them, readied, and snatched at them with his magic, the equivalent of attempting to tear the reins from a horse rider.

For a moment, he thought he had failed. There was no change. Then, as suddenly as it had started, the sensation stopped, and the sound ended. With a sudden jerking sensation, the magic ceased. Ines, Morgan, and Trinity all fell back, collective relief in their various sighs and groans.

Ines was the first to recover enough to speak. "What the fuck was that?"

As if in answer to her question, Trinity's cell phone rang.

CHAPTER TWENTY-FOUR
Morgan

His head was pounding, his ears ringing, and his vision refused to stabilize long enough for his nausea to dissipate. Morgan sat on the couch, though it was more like half-lay, his posture slouched and unmoving. He refused to open his eyes, lest the spinning get worse, but he listened and absorbed what was going on in the room around him.

They had just been attacked. The loud snap, the horrible pain in his head, it had all been blatant spellcraft. It was meant to disrupt and harm.

Someone was actively trying to stop them. It had snapped the connection between them and the part of Seren that they were communicating with. Had Darius not been resistant to the assault, they might have all been in far worse condition than just woozy and disoriented. Morgan shuddered to think what could have happened.

In the aftermath, Ines, Trinity, and Darius had all moved instantly to action. Trinity had called out orders, taking charge before anyone else could think to. "Darius, we need to get through to Nick."

"He isn't going to pick up for me. You're going to have to call."

"Fine," Trinity said through her teeth. Morgan could practically hear her seething as she slipped her phone out of her pocket and dialed. While she waited for him to answer, she instructed, "Ines, make sure Morgan is all right. He doesn't look so good."

Morgan didn't feel so good, either. Using his magic wore on him while they had been talking with Seren, but then the loud sound had felt like a knife to his eardrums. He'd dropped his concentration, covered his ears, then been struck by the most intense, all-consuming pain that he had momentarily thought he'd died. Agony had exploded behind his eyes, and he'd collapsed forward, unaware of anything or anyone beyond the torment in his head. After it subsided, it was all he could do to pull himself haphazardly back up onto the couch, eyes still closed, and try not to vomit.

He felt a cool hand take his arm, two fingers pressing against the hollow of his wrist, feeling for a pulse. "How're you doing?" she asked, her voice more shaken than he'd heard it previously. She also looked pale, the blood drained from her already fair face, her auburn hair a sharp contrast. Still, she was putting on a serious air. She looked as if she needed it.

"I'm all right," he said, though his head was still spinning, albeit much more manageably now. The dizziness was starting to subside, but it hadn't entirely, not yet.

"Pulse is good, but you're diaphoretic. Not surprising, though—"

"What?" asked Morgan, distracted by what she said. "I'm what? Is that bad?"

Ines grinned. "Sweaty. Sorry. Medical speak. You sure you're feeling all right and not just toughing it out?"

"A little dizzy, that's it."

Ines nodded. "No worse than the rest of us, then."

"No answer on his phone." Trinity's voice cut through the din. "Either he's not picking up, or his phone is on mute."

Darius explained, "I'm calling Ty."

"Who?" asked Trinity and Ines in unison.

"His boss at the Protectorate."

Trinity's expression darkened, and Ines furrowed her brow when she spoke. "Are we there already? We aren't even sure what's going on yet. Only that we need to find Nick and keep him away from Kris."

"She has a point," Trinity added. She put a hand over her mouth, considering the options before them. "Why do we need to bring the Protectorate into this at all?"

"Because they might be able to do something about Kris. At least keep him busy long enough for us to figure this whole thing out?" Darius suggested. His voice sounded desperate, like he was grasping at straws.

A tense moment of quiet passed between the four of them. It was clear that Ines, Trinity, and Darius were all wracking their brains for something resembling a plan, and Ines and Trinity were less than enthusiastic about the idea of the Protectorate. Morgan felt useless and wasn't sure what he could do or say to help. He had no real connection to this time outside of the friendships he had been cultivating with Ines, Trinity, and even young Emily. There was also what he and Darius shared, but he wasn't even sure what to call that. More than friendship, that was for sure, but beyond that?

None of those relationships afforded him any suggestions of who to call or what to do in the current situation.

"What about your partner?" Ines suggested.

The expression on her face betrayed that she didn't *like* the idea, and Morgan wondered why. Darius hadn't said much about his partner outside of her name. Morgan didn't know her from his time, either. Judging from the look of disgust on Trinity's face, one that matched Darius, she didn't like the partner much either. It explained why Morgan didn't know her. No one had ever come into his mother's home without her absolute trust, and if her younger self didn't trust this partner, then neither did Morgan.

"No, we can't depend on her for this," Darius replied.

"She can't be trusted with anything," came Trinity's sharp reply. "Bitch is always trying to undermine others to make herself look good."

Trinity probably would have kept going if Darius didn't raise a hand in a quiet request for her to stop. "Telling my boss is the better option here. He trusted me to keep an eye on Morgan without reporting it to his superiors. I believe confiding this development to him is our best option. He might have an idea of what we can do."

There was a long, tense minute before Trinity finally nodded.

"Don't mention Nick," Trinity said hurriedly. "Just say...just say that we need to find Kris. To talk to him. Something about past run-ins, maybe?" She was struggling to come up with plausible reasons that Darius could safely tell his superior.

Darius stared at her, incredulity evident on his face. "How the hell am I supposed to not mention Nick at this point?"

"Distract with something else."

170

Darius looked exasperated. "I don't want to *distract* him. The whole point is to get his help, or at least input."

"What about pointing him towards Kris?" asked Trinity.

Ines jumped on that train of thought immediately. "With a big, important mage like Kris running around, I can't imagine Nick being too obvious on the radar, right?" she offered, shifting her weight from one foot to the other.

"Maybe you could mention something about the power surges that happened the night I, er, arrived?" Morgan suggested, grasping for something, anything, that might be useful. "Didn't you say your office was investigating multiple energy eruptions or appearances or whatever? Maybe make it seem like we think Kris could be the cause?"

"I'm not going to lie—" Darius began, but Trinity interrupted him.

"What if it isn't a lie?" she asked.

"What?"

"What if Kris's appearance in Chicago isn't a lie. Don't you all think the timing is just a bit too convenient?"

Everyone in the room quieted suddenly. A look of dawning realization passed onto Darius's face.

"As far as I know, he made his appearance at the same time, possibly even the same night as the energy reports," Darius said, slowly connecting his thoughts aloud.

Morgan watched, wondering if this was the point in the mystery where the good guys finally put it all together. He liked watching Darius's face as he thought through everything. He could see the man thriving on it.

It did feel like a puzzle piece had fallen into place but was it for the same puzzle Morgan was trying to solve? He had spoken in haste, but could the event he came back to stop have something to do with Kris? The multiple power surges and the appearance of Kris didn't feel like a coincidence. If they hadn't been caused by a temporal rift depositing a traveler from the future, then could an Elder Mage doing something that would be better left undone have caused it? To what end?

A.E. Bross

"It's a bit of a leap to the conclusion that Kris was the cause, especially with zero proof," Trinity said, doubt creeping into her voice.

"Does it have to be completely true?" Ines wondered. "We don't need enough to accuse him, just to gently nudge the Protectorate away."

"I don't like the idea of misleading the Protectorate, but..." Darius trailed off, his voice still heavy with thought. "But it feels too damn well-timed to be coincidental."

Morgan sighed. "Look, it's just a working theory, right?"

"More like a suspicion."

"Couldn't it be an avenue that the Protectorate hasn't thought of?" Morgan pushed. "Aren't the elder members expected to be doing big magic? Don't they get passes or something?"

Darius nodded his agreement. "You're not wrong. It's more complicated than just a 'pass,' but Kris coming to town, then a magic expenditure of that level? He would have to get approval. If he had gone through proper channels, there would be a record of it. Elders might be capable of big magic, but they keep track of it when they do. Only mages who are very old or incredibly talented could do something like that on their own, short of a larger group working magic or someone passing through time." As he spoke, he obviously warmed to the idea. By the end, he shot Morgan an appreciative grin. "That's actually not a bad idea."

"All right, then," Trinity approved, once again taking command of the situation. She checked her watch. "I'm going to swing by Nick's apartment and see if he's there. If nothing else, I was supposed to be there for when the bus drops Emily off after school. Maybe I can get him to come back here with us."

"If nothing else, it might be safer to bring the kiddo around here," Ines suggested.

"So, my apartment is going to be our base for right now?" asked Darius. He didn't sound annoyed. He sounded more matter-of-fact as if he was establishing the safe zone for the next few hours.

"It's pretty much been home base since day one," Ines pointed out. She wasn't wrong.

172

Morgan, still wanting to be helpful, sat up a bit. His lightheadedness had faded, and while he still felt a bit off, he needed to be doing something. He nodded to Trinity. "Let me come. I'll help too."

Trinity nodded. "The more the merrier, I suppose. Besides, if Nick is there, maybe we can talk to him and find out what's going on." She gave Morgan a gentle look. "Maybe you could meet him?"

Morgan swallowed hard. In all the excitement and rush to plan, he hadn't even thought of that. He wondered what it would be like, finally meeting the man he had grown up without. "One thing at a time," he said, finally.

Darius moved to sit next to Morgan, concern in his dark eyes. "Are you sure you'll be all right?"

Morgan smiled. "I think so, yes. Let me help. If nothing else, I can help distract Emily and keep her calm. We can tackle the whole 'you're my future dad' meeting when we come to it."

Darius nodded. "All right. Just be careful?" He leaned forward, tilting Morgan's head down with his free hand so he could gently kiss his forehead. Morgan blinked at him, surprised. He felt a blush heat his cheeks, and he chuckled softly.

"All right!" came Ines's boisterous shout. "You two go. I'll stay here with Darius and make sure things are all right here. Maybe set up some protective wards. Keep in touch and be careful."

Morgan pushed himself off the couch, shouldered into his coat, and forced his feet into his boots. He followed Trinity as she led the way from the apartment.

"Wait!"

Morgan stopped when he heard Darius's voice. Darius came out and pressed a small key ring into his hands. "Here are the keys for the building door and the apartment. Just in case."

"Thanks," Morgan said. He tucked them into his pocket and hurried after Trinity. He offered one last glance over his shoulder and was gratified to see Darius standing at the door, his hand raised in a small wave, the ghost of a smile on his lips.

CHAPTER TWENTY-FIVE

Darius

There were very few people whom Darius thought he'd be able to go to when he needed help or information. While the list had grown over the past week or so, it was still a short list, and Sybil remained absent from it. Despite the confidence he had shown earlier, he wasn't entirely sure Ty was either. What if Darius was wrong? What if this put Morgan in further danger? Still, he had to do something, and if a Protectorate Monitor couldn't depend on their Lead Monitor, then who could they depend on?

He tried not to dwell on the geyser of grief and guilt that had spewed forth when he'd heard Seren's voice. It had been tired, a bit weak, but undeniably her.

Do not think about it. He rifled through his coat pocket and retrieved the card that Ty had given him. He thumbed in Ty's personal number and pressed 'SEND' before he lost his nerve. He was about to bring it to his ear but instead turned on the speaker, motioning for Ines to come and listen. Moving with surprising stealth and quiet, Ines stepped to his side just as Ty picked up on the other end of the call.

"Talk to me, Adair," he said, dispensing with anything remotely resembling a greeting.

"Have there been any more developments in the whole magic surge case?"

There was a deep sigh from the phone. "Not really. A couple more have cropped up over the last few days, but short and difficult to trace. They're not even sure if it's new or echoes of the original phenomena. Cosmology has been working day and night, and a lot of Indagators and Monitors are doing the same."

Darius took this information in. "There haven't been any events here with our person of interest to coincide with that," he explained.

"I figured you would have reported anything if it had. No, the further we get from the event, the more I am thinking that they are unrelated. We may need you to come in, though, once this is resolved. I do have some questions for our time traveler."

"There may be another connection, though," Darius hurried to offer. He didn't want to think about having to go in with Morgan. "Did you know Elder Kris was in Chicago?"

"Well, that's quite a jump in the conversation," Ty observed, though his tone told Darius it wasn't overly surprising. Either he was used to wild discussions, or he knew where Darius might be going with his thoughts. "I did. I'm sorry I didn't warn you. I know there's some history there." A pause, then, "Are you thinking he's somehow involved with the Cosmology matter?"

"The timing does appear to line up."

"You aren't the only one who has suggested that."

Darius blinked. So at least some minds in the Protectorate had contemplated it. "Does the Protectorate view him as a person of interest?"

"Yes." He did not elaborate.

Darius appreciated the honesty. "I don't know to what extent the Protectorate has considered him," he admitted, choosing his next words carefully. He was mentally exhausted, not up for any elaborate deceit, so he decided that the more truth he could tell, the better. "I ran into Elder Kris last night."

"Not an amicable meeting, I take it?" Ty asked, voice mild.

"No. There is some bad blood between myself and the elder." Darius hesitated.

"Because of whom his mentee was, yes?"

Darius took a deep breath, glad he wouldn't have to rehash the whole painful story of Seren and her mentor. "Exactly." He glanced up to Ines, who listened quietly but offered no gesture of expression in reaction to his words.

"Was there an altercation?" Ty pressed.

"No, but…I can't help but worry that he has some ulterior motive or intention and that it isn't a good one. The power surges happened when he arrived in Chicago, as did Morgan's ability to travel to our timeline. Perhaps something that Kris was doing paved the way for Morgan's arrival in our time." The more Darius spoke, the less sure he became. It sounded like a good deal of ifs and maybes, and cases were not built on those. "It's just a possibility. One I don't think we should ignore," he finished.

"And how is the time traveler faring?" asked Ty, changing the subject.

"As well as can be expected." Now it was Darius's turn to keep his replies short and to the point.

There was an awkward silence that followed before Ty broke it by clearing his throat. "All right, I will put some people on the Kris end of this. I'm going to have to assign Monitor Diluna to it, though. We're short-handed as is."

"Understood."

"I'll keep your name out of it," he assured Darius. "If anything happens, update me immediately."

"Yes, sir."

The line went dead.

"That sounded mostly positive, yes?" Ines offered.

Darius nodded. "It did. I don't like having to lie, even small lies of omission. Not in instances like this."

Ines patted him on the back. "Most decent people don't."

"Thankfully."

"What now?"

Darius had been considering the same question. He glanced around the apartment, then out the large windows just beyond the living room. "Scrying?" he suggested. "We might be able to get an idea of where Nick is and if he is all right? Or I can find out who the hell attacked us."

Ines put her hands up. "That would be all you. I fix people, but I'm not much good with following magical energies and trails."

"Well, neither am I," Darius said with a laugh. "It's the mental signature I follow."

"The what?"

"Whoever it was that tried to get into my head, that did get into yours and Morgan's and Trinity's, they leave a mental residue. I can follow that, the thought and pattern that went into the magic." He shrugged. "I also have a pretty good idea of what Nick feels like mentally."

"Incense and questionable life choices?" joked Ines.

"Something like that."

"Ooooh," Ines said, nodding as she drew out the word. She scrunched up her face in disgust. "That makes a creepy sort of sense."

"It's not as strong as actual magical or aura imprints, but it's something."

"All right. I'll man the phones while you're doing whatever you need to do." She held a hand out and took his phone from in front of him, sliding it to her and putting her own phone behind it. She slipped a hand into her pocket and withdrew a set of earbuds, popping them into her ears with a smile before unlocking her phone and commencing silent browsing.

For a moment, Darius didn't move. He was suddenly unsure of himself, unsure of whether or not he *should* try scrying. While the tattoo at the base of his skull had been placed there to make it more difficult for anyone to use magic to affect his mind, it also made using the same magic more difficult. Little things weren't much of a drain, but scrying in any place, let alone a city as populated as Chicago, could prove taxing.

Still, he had to do something until they heard back from Trinity and Morgan.

He snatched a pillow from the couch and moved to the window. He dropped the pillow and lowered himself onto it, staring out the window. He took a few deep breaths, his eyes staring at the gray city street beyond the glass. Then he let his gaze relax, everything in front of him blurring. He blinked, summoning up magic and looking for the threads that he needed to pull to reach out with his mind. Distantly, he felt the tattoo on his skull grow warm, a comfort that told him that he couldn't be watched or detected. Not by any mage that was his equal.

The mindscape had many names, but none of them could truly capture what it was; it wasn't something that could be easily described. It was different for each mage, just as perception of the truth was different for each person. He had been taught to try and see it as his own surroundings. To envision the abstract mindscape like he would the environment he was in. Perceive its form as something familiar and easy to navigate. For Darius, that meant it looked like it bore a resemblance to the cityscape of Chicago itself. He constructed the perception in his head; he formed his impression of each mind within it was a tiny speck of light. Throbbing, noisy light. These lights moved high into the sky in the various skyscrapers and scurried through the street-formed valleys.

He focused on superimposing what he saw onto a mental map of the city, mentally attaching locations to minds, building an easily referenced guide. First, he felt for familiar minds. His own. Ines's. He knew where they were. He kept himself from reaching out for Trinity's or even Morgan's. He perceived them as warmth and familiarity but pulsed away from them. They were moving and would be a distraction. He *knew* specifically touching Morgan's thoughts would break his concentration. Despite that, he could still *feel* Morgan in his mind, an anchor and reassurance.

He sensed further, along streets and through buildings. Countless surface thoughts flew through his mind, and he worked to keep them out, focusing only on the faint memory of what it had felt like when his mind had been attacked.

"DADDY, NO!"

The words, a sharp and visceral shriek in his mind, threw him out of his concentration. He gasped, eyes opening, magic fading along with a single image seen through the eyes of a child.

A closet door closing, the barest glimpse of Nick, exhaustion, sadness, and resignation etched deeply into the expression on his face, trapping his daughter inside while Kris stood behind him and smiled.

CHAPTER TWENTY–SIX

Morgan

Morgan wasn't sure whether to be confident or terrified as Trinity sped through the Chicago city streets. She managed nearly impossible maneuvers, weaving through the midday traffic with frightening closeness. He knew there was no magic involved, either. Trinity's skills, at least his timeline's Trinity, had studied and focused her energy on the spiritual. Nudging a car forward a foot or two, or encouraging a red light to turn green faster, were a bit beyond her abilities. No, this was the practiced expertise of a woman who had spent many a year dodging city traffic.

As nonchalantly as possible, he moved a hand to grip the handle on the door just above the window.

"That's what they're there for," she said, a chuckle in her voice.

"Huh?" asked Morgan, wincing as the car slid between two others in a turn-only lane.

"The oh-shit handles. That's what they're there for."

Morgan glanced up to his hand, then over to Trinity. In his timeline, his mother missed *nothing*, and it seemed this Trinity had the same style. "Sorry."

"Don't be. Just hold on and don't side-seat drive," she murmured, her concentration never leaving the streets ahead of her. She jerked the wheel to the left, making a turn at the last possible moment and barely avoiding a car accident.

Morgan cringed but kept his mouth shut. He knew better than to disobey a direct order from this woman. "So how far is it to pick up Emily?" he asked, trying to keep his voice steady and free of the nerves that tied and untied themselves in his gut.

"Maybe another ten minutes or so? Depends on traffic," she replied, voice mild despite swerving into the tightest of spaces in the flow of the cars.

Morgan nodded and let the conversation lapse into silence for a minute. This was the first time he had been in close, private quarters with Trinity. He cast a sideways glance at her, taking in her profile, studying the younger version of his mother.

"Need something?" she asked as if sensing his eyes on her.

He glanced away and sighed. "I just…" He trailed off, frustrated. "I want to talk, but I don't know what to say." He fidgeted. "I don't want to make you uncomfortable. It can't be easy to find out your future self had a kid that traveled back in time."

"Easy?" Trinity chuckled. "No, it is not."

They lapsed into silence again, but Morgan was still left with the uncomfortable burden of things unsaid. Finally, he blurted out, "You died."

She nodded calmly. "We all do. Doesn't make it easier for those we leave behind." She put a hand out, resting it on his. "After this, we will have time to speak. To bond, one way or another, all right? I just need to focus on one thing at a time."

She didn't look at him, but Morgan felt the full warmth of her focus on him, and he nodded. He didn't speak again. He didn't trust himself not to say something that would distract her from her driving. A buzzing in his pocket soon caught his attention. He dug into the jeans to pull his phone out, immediately seeing Darius's face and name on the screen. He couldn't help the smile that lifted his lips, and he quickly accepted the call, putting it on speakerphone so Trinity could hear. "Hey."

"Are you there yet?" was the terse question that Darius asked, not bothering with pleasantries. Not that Morgan had expected to. Still, the man sounded edgier than when they'd left.

"Still a few blocks away," came Trinity's measured voice.

"Something's wrong," Darius snapped, his voice sharp over the phone's speaker. "I think—I think I saw Emily."

"How did you *see* Emily?" Trinity asked, voice growing louder as she suddenly accelerated.

Morgan's hold tightened on his oh-shit handle, but he said nothing.

"She's all right. She's just, uhm, locked in a closet?"

"In a *closet*?!" Trinity snapped, voice rising even further.

"I'm more worried about Nick. I saw him. I saw Kris in the background. I think they, or at least Nick, was putting her in there to keep her safe."

"Safe from what?" Morgan asked, stomach clenching with anxiety. Was this it? Could this be the event?

"I don't know," admitted Darius, sounding small and unsure through the tinny speaker.

"All right, let's get to Emily first," Morgan suggested, wanting to be proactive and go in with a plan. "After we're sure she's okay then we can plan our next step. Maybe she'll know where they're going or what they are planning."

"And why Nick is with Kris." Trinity said. She said spoke Kris's name through gritted teeth as if it hurt to say, then took another sharp turn. Anger was splashed across her face. Anger and barely contained panic. "They never liked each other. There's no reason for Kris to be slumming anywhere near Seren's ex."

"All right. Do you want me to stay on, or do you want to call when you have more information?" Darius asked.

Morgan wanted to keep him on the phone. Just hearing his voice made him feel closer. Still, he wasn't sure if it would be just one more distraction for Trinity, and he thought it better to err on the side of caution. "We'll call when we know more."

"All right," he replied. There was a hesitation, then he added. "Be careful."

The line went dead.

"We're here," she said, making another quick turn and bringing the car down into a parking garage. She made quick work of pulling into a numbered parking spot, dark eyes roving around. "Shit, I don't see Nick's car."

"Come on." Morgan was already unbuckling his seatbelt and shoving his phone back into his pocket. He climbed out of the car and threw the door closed.

Trinity was out almost as quickly as he was and leading the way to the stairwell door. Morgan kept pace with her long strides and took the stairs two by two to follow her example. She stopped at the fourth floor and flung the door open, vanishing into the hall of the building. Morgan hurried after, almost bumping into her when he realized she had come to a stop only ten feet inside the doorway. Apparently, Nick's apartment wasn't far from the stairs. Morgan had no memories of his father's apartment or if he had even lived there by the time Morgan had come along and was old enough to form memories. Nothing around him was familiar, and it made him feel even more distant from the man who would be his father.

Fumbling with her keys, Trinity cursed, then found the key, jamming it into the lock and twisting with a surprising amount of force. Morgan was surprised the key didn't snap. The door was barely open before Trinity shouted Emily's name.

There was a pause, then the muffled sound of banging from further within the apartment. Trinity vanished through the door, and Morgan plunged in after her, barely aware that he was closing it behind him.

"Emily? Emily!"

Morgan came to the end of the hallway and turned into a small but cheerfully decorated room. The walls were a light blue, and near the top, they were sponge-painted with white to look like clouds. A planetary mobile hung from the light fixture on the ceiling fan, and Morgan could make out the telltale outline of glow-in-the-dark star stickers all across the ceiling's surface. While the wall-to-wall carpeting was the inexpensive industrial type most likely installed by the landlord, a pastel green area rug covered much of it, and was strewn with books, toys, and the odd piece of clothing. A toybox and bed were crammed against one side of the bedroom, across from which was the closet. The closet door was wedged shut with a chair stuck beneath the handle. Trinity was stepping gingerly over toys and clothing on the floor to get to it, and Emily's shouts and banging could be heard coming from behind the door.

"Emily, I'm here. Stop. I'm going to move the chair," Trinity ordered, voice still raised.

Immediately the noise ceased. Trinity snatched the chair away, and after a moment of confusion as to what to do with it, she tossed it onto the bed.

The closet door flew open, and a disheveled Emily threw herself into Trinity's arms. She had been crying, her face flushed and tear-stained, her hair a tangled mass of dark blonde around her young face. She sobbed for a few moments, burying herself in her godmother's shirt. Trinity said nothing, and Morgan knew to let the poor girl get some of her emotion out. He stood against the far wall and, for lack of anything better to do, took the chair off of the bed and moved it out into the hallway.

When he turned back, it was in time to see Emily come to him and throw her arms around him, hugging him close. "Thank you for coming," she said, the words muffled in the material of his shirt.

Morgan felt his heart squeeze in his chest, and he knelt down in front of her, giving her a more level, proper hug. "Are you all right?" he asked, holding her as tightly as he dared. He was enraged that Nick would do that to his own daughter—Morgan's sister, damn it—but it paled in comparison to the relief Morgan felt at finding her unharmed.

She took a deep, shaky breath and pulled away from the embrace, nodding and trying to smooth down her hair. "I think so, but we have to help Daddy."

"What's going on with Daddy, kiddo?" asked Trinity, her voice soft. A single glance up at her told Morgan that she was holding back waves of concern-fueled rage.

Emily turned to look at Trinity, though she kept her hands on Morgan's shoulders. "He's with that other man, Kris. I didn't hear what he was doing, but Kris said they needed to go somewhere that Daddy was connected to Mommy. It wouldn't work otherwise. Then Daddy told me to get in the closet, and I'd be safe." Emily shuddered. "The other man just looked like he didn't care."

In her current state, Emily seemed so young and vulnerable to Morgan. Gone was the precocious young girl that had barged her way into Darius's apartment a few weeks before. Now she was just a small child, confused and afraid. She turned back to Morgan, tears brimming in her eyes. "Why did Daddy trap me in there?"

Morgan gave her another reassuring hug. "I don't know, but don't worry, you can come with us." Without thinking, he lifted the girl into his arms, holding her close and trying to offer her quiet comfort. The embrace reminded him of the countless times that his Emily, from his timeline, had held him when he needed comfort. The way her touch had always been so reassuring. He had always felt that he had the strongest of big sisters, from the time he was old enough to recognize her until the last time he had seen her. He missed her, would always miss her, but right now, this Emily needed him.

Trinity led the way out of Emily's room and down the hall, pulling open the hall closet and withdrawing a child's winter coat from the dark recesses of it. She also grabbed a hat and a scarf, though she couldn't find gloves and quickly dismissed the need for them.

"Where are we going?" Emily asked, voice muffled by the wool of Morgan's coat.

"We're going to go get Daddy," said Trinity as she guided Emily into the coat while Morgan was still holding her.

Emily nodded, somber. Then she looked to Morgan with a shy, questioning expression. "Can I please bring my tablet? For games?" she asked, voice low.

Morgan couldn't help but smile, and Trinity laughed. "You and that tablet," Trinity breathed. "Yes, sweetheart, you can. Go grab it quickly."

Morgan lowered her to the ground, and she ran down the hallway, quickly vanishing into her room.

"Call Darius," Trinity instructed. She kept her volume low, not wanting to alert Emily to any danger. "Tell him to meet us at Promontory Point."

"Are you sure that's where they're going?"

"As sure as I can be. It was where Nick proposed to Seren and where they had planned to have their wedding."

"Why would Kris even want or need something like that?"

Trinity's face worked, and Morgan could see the mixture of anger and worry and grief that passed over it. Finally, she let out a huff. "I don't know if Nick would ever get to this point or if Kris would ever attempt something like this, but what if they were trying to bring her back?"

"I'm sorry, 'back'? You mean necromancy?" Morgan balked at the implication. He recalled what Darius had said about his old mentor and how she had tried to skirt necromancy to bring her old lover back. "Do all elders get to this point?"

Trinity shrugged. "I don't know why else Kris would need a connection like that. He could just petition the Protectorate for permission and assistance. It's a lot of red tape, and there aren't that many necromancers these days, but the man's an elder. He could get his way." She sucked her teeth, obviously trying to puzzle her way through the information.

"But I'm sure the Protectorate would have said something when Darius called them, yes?"

"If it was sanctioned through them, probably. Those are all supposed to be open to all mages. If he didn't get that permission, then what? He's trying to do it himself? Pulling someone back from beyond takes a lot of effort and finesse, and doing anything even slightly incorrect can cause all sorts of issues with the veils between worlds."

"Issues with the veils," Morgan repeated, thoughtfully. A thought occurred to him. "This could be it. This could be the event that starts everything!"

"Just call Darius, have him and Ines meet us at Promontory Point, and pray we get there in time. We have to stop Nick and Kris from doing anything we might all regret."

CHAPTER TWENTY-SEVEN
Darius

"All right, we'll see you there."

As Darius hung up the call, Ines studied him. "What's our next move?" She asked.

"Trinity thinks they're on their way to Promontory Point, so we're going to meet there."

"That's...random," Ines said, but she didn't question it further. "Is the kid all right?"

"As okay as she can be. She was locked in a closet while her father left her alone in the apartment." Darius pursed his lips. He wasn't one for children, never wanted them himself, but even he knew that was neglectful, even abusive. The fact that it was Seren's child made him all the more protective.

"All right," said Ines, "I'll drive. I had to park a block away, so get your coat and let's get going."

"There's more bad news."

Ines was halfway through buttoning her peacoat, and she glanced at him, an eyebrow raised. "More?"

"Trinity seems to believe..." Anxiety twisted his insides painfully. For a moment, he couldn't continue, and to fill the silence, he grabbed for his own coat and scarf. He wet his lips and tried again. "Trinity thinks they might be trying to bring Seren back via necromancy."

Ines stared, every feature of her expression freezing for an instant. Her eyes flashed with disbelief. "Kris wouldn't. He knows the rules, and there's no way Seren would have consented to something like that, living or dead. What is he thinking? He's a Cycle mage, an elder!"

"Trinity feels that it might be a possibility."

As a mage that dealt with healing and life, the very thought of necromancy must have been repugnant to Ines. Much like the idea of mind control was disgusting to those that use magic that affected the thoughts and minds of others. It was a huge breach of any sort of personal right. There was no way for the dead to grant consent to be returned if they hadn't before they died, short of having a Gnosis spell crafter commune with them.

True necromancers had been powerful mages who understood the balance of death and life. Only those most trusted in that understanding were be chosen to learn, and as the years passed, fewer and fewer were entrusted with the secrets. An accomplished necromancer could reconstruct a body from its components and pull the soul back to it. Darius didn't know all the details, it hadn't been his mode of study, but he understood it to require that which makes up the physical form, and the necromancer needed an intimate understanding of the soul it was summoning back. The slightest mistake, and a soul could be imprisoned in a dead body, or worse, the soul could become fragmented, never to be made whole again.

Most necromancy nowadays was calling a soul to a willing host and trading one for the other. It all had to be above board, complete with waivers of consent from all parties. The Protectorate regulated it as heavily as possible. With spellcasting that could force a victim to agree, it could be easily abused.

Darius shivered involuntarily. That was what Vivian de Winter had tried to do to him.

If Kris was hiding this from the Protectorate, it meant he had no intention of using the old, true ways of necromancy. It also meant Nick could be in great danger.

"Come on," she said finally, finishing the fastenings on her jacket. Her voice was icy and hard. "We need to get moving."

They left the apartment quickly, both of them falling into a determined silence. As they made their way down to the lobby and out onto the city streets, Darius focused on what would come next, refusing to allow his thoughts to turn to his own anxieties. First, they had to get to Promontory Point. They would meet up with Morgan and Trinity. Someone would have to stay with Emily when they arrived. Or they would have to figure out some way to keep her safe if things came to violence. Darius hoped they didn't, but he knew that the unexpected and unwanted were often more present than anyone might like to admit.

Ines had her keys out as they rounded the block, and she nodded towards a Honda Civic just as the headlights flashed when she unlocked it. Darius wasn't sure the color on the darkened street, and he didn't pause to discern it before climbing into the passenger seat. Ines barely waited until the engine had started before she threw the car in gear and expertly pulled out of the spot and into traffic, smoothly transitioning from one lane to the other to get them on their way.

Ines guided the car through Chicago traffic like an expert, making it seem more like a dance than a commute. Darius was impressed. He had expected Ines to be much more reckless on the road. Her adept handling of the transit made him consider, and not for the first time, the possibility of getting his own car. These particular situations didn't arise all that often, but he wasn't sure how tenable ride-sharing was when one was dealing with magical issues.

City lights and other cars blended as they traveled, and Darius found himself losing track of where they were. He was instead going into his own mind, trying to prepare himself for whatever they might encounter. He had told his companions all those years ago that he didn't remember anything from the ritual that de Winter had been performing on him.

That had been a lie.

He couldn't forget being trapped in his own body, unable to control his actions as de Winter dictated them. He remembered screaming inwardly, desperate to stop himself even as his body didn't listen and arranged spellcrafting supplies with quiet docility. De Winter had enjoyed all of it, too, the sadistic bitch. She had turned him into an unwilling puppet, pulling on strings and forcing him to go through all the motions of a ritual that would tear his mind and soul from his body. It didn't matter that Seren had helped him stop it; the feeling would be with him forever. In that way, he would always be broken.

"Darius? Darius, are you all right?"

Darius blinked and realized for the first time that the car was no longer moving. "Yes, I'm fine." Then he sighed. "Well, maybe not fine, but for now, I can get through it."

Ines put a hand on his arm. "And after?"

Darius wasn't sure what to say to Ines. He wasn't sure if he would ever be fine again. He wasn't sure he deserved it.

Before he could break the silence, headlights shone in the window and passed by. Darius recognized the dull silver of Trinity's SUV as it passed and pulled in beside Ines's door. He was distantly amazed that she was still driving the same car after all these years. He quickly climbed out of the passenger side and moved around the back of Ines's Civic but was stopped from going any further when Emily ran to him and threw her arms around his waist, hugging him close. "Thank you!" she cried. "Thank you, thank you, thank you!"

Surprised, he put his own hands on her shoulders, unsure of what else to do.

"Thank you for finding me, for seeing me," she continued, holding him tighter.

Darius looked down at Emily, the halo of messy blonde hair reminding him of Seren's short, choppy haircut. He found himself suddenly needing to breathe past a lump in his throat, and he dropped down to one knee to give the child a proper hug. "I told your mother that I'd keep an eye out for you."

"You did?" she asked, voice wet and thick with tears.

"I did, and I will." Darius blinked against the stinging in his eyes.

"Can you keep an eye out for my dad?" she pleaded, not letting him go.

Darius was taken aback by the request and humbled by how young and fragile she now seemed to him. Gone was the precocious girl with quick retorts. In his arms was a scared child, trying to get promises of protection for her father. Darius was only now realizing how difficult all of this must be for her. She depended on the adults around her, and requesting this of him was a serious matter. He nodded. "Of course I will. I promise."

She took a step back and wiped at her eyes before offering Darius a shaky smile. "Look. Trinity and Morgan let me bring my tablet." She held up a smudged iPad, and her grin widened. "It has games."

Darius looked to the two adults she named, who were by now standing just behind her, waiting for her to let Darius go. "That was very nice of them," Darius assured, at a loss for what else to say.

"Hey, Em, want to show me some of the games you have on that? We can sit in the car and wait for Trinity, Darius, and Morgan to go get your dad. I'm sure we can find some music, too." Ines's voice was light and comforting. She pushed herself up and out of the driver's seat and offered Emily her hand.

"As long as it's none of those baby songs," Emily said, a shadow of indignance crossing her face. "I'm not a baby anymore."

"Absolutely no baby songs," she said, nodding. When Emily took her hand, she guided the girl around the car and opened the passenger door for her, closing it once she was safely inside. She crossed back around and moved closer to the waiting trio. "If something comes up, call me. I've got healing hands and I'm not afraid to use them. Besides, a nap would do Emmie some good. She looks exhausted."

"We will," was Trinity's response.

"All right, go. I've got things covered here." Ines nodded and climbed back into the car, closing the door.

"Now what?" Darius asked, looking between Trinity and Morgan.

"Let's start with the Field House." Trinity didn't wait for them to agree; she just set off.

It was a bit of a hike to reach the Field House. Promontory Point didn't offer dedicated parking outside of specially permitted situations when weddings or events took place at the field house, so they would be forced to go from the lot to the west of Lakeshore Drive. They moved quickly, leaving the rush of city traffic behind as they found a park district pathway and took it. It wove through the trees, and the ground beneath them was slick with frost.

"Doing all right?" Darius asked Morgan, being careful to keep up as the three of them gained access to the Lakefront Trail, following it around.

"As good as can be expected," Morgan answered, though Darius could hear the smile in his voice.

"I meant from the magic earlier," Darius clarified.

"So did I."

In the darkness, Darius felt Morgan's hand find his, and they intertwined their fingers. There was no telling what might be waiting for them when they reached the Field House, and the contact was comforting.

The closer they got, the thicker the air became with magic. It was like static electricity, crackling and snapping around them, occasionally with small, sharp sparks that made Darius wince. In the semi-darkness, he could see Morgan and Trinity both reacting similarly. He tightened his grasp on Morgan's hand, trying to offer reassurance.

Ahead of them, they saw the Field House. Even from the distance, it looked nearly deserted. No special events or weddings, but as they grew closer, they could all see the soft, reddish glow through the windows. It flickered and danced but was dim enough that a fire wasn't a worry. More likely candlelight.

"The elders do love their candles," Darius scoffed quietly.

"Hush," Trinity immediately ordered. "And try to stay low."

The three of them continued moving, slower and crouched in hopes of avoiding detection. They crept up the front patio, and Trinity quietly tried one of the great French doors. They were locked. Morgan moved to another set, this one further away, but again there was no luck. Darius moved to the last set that felt far enough away from the flickering candlelight to be safe. As silently as he could, he took hold of the cold metal door handle and turned it slowly. The doors gave a small click and opened.

191

Darius motioned for Morgan and Trinity to follow, and together the three of them crept inside.

The door opened onto a single, large room with dark floors to absorb the light and high, vaulted ceilings. Stone façade covered the walls. There was a small gathering of tables and chairs, obviously stored in haste, and Darius was quick to crouch behind it, hoping to remain hidden. Morgan and Trinity did the same.

The magic in the building was stifling, the air so thick and damp with it that it was difficult to move. It felt as if the gravity around them had increased, making each step and gesture exponentially more difficult to complete. The air was filled with the fading smell of burnt sage mixed with a rich, earthy aroma that reminded Darius of freshly dug earth. Once they were all safe and still, Darius leaned out to see what the situation was.

Nick was prone on the floor, his head moving ever so slightly, mouthing words with no sound. He was dressed only in a tee shirt, jeans, and boots, despite the cold. He looked ill, sweat plastering hair to his flushed face. He groaned, and the sound was pained. The sound tore through Darius, and he remembered the sensation of broken glass reaching into him, pulling viciously at the fabric of what connected his mind–his soul—to his body. That was what it had been all those years before when de Winter tried to evict him from his own physical form. He broke out into a sweat at the recollection.

Kris stood over Nick, his young face contorted with concentration, a hand outstretched high over Nick's body. A glimmering gold necklace hung from his hand, an anchor to the ritual. The glow, which Darius had originally thought was candlelight, was emanating from Kris's hand. They were ribbons of magic thick enough that Darius thought he might see them without his mage sight. Those sinuous strands of writhing magic were buried in Nick's aura, slowly peeling at the layers.

This didn't look like necromancy. Didn't feel like it. It had none of the hallmarks Darius remembered from the rituals de Winter had attempted on him. While no two mages practiced magic exactly the same, there should have still been similarities. Kris wasn't calling to the beyond. His focus was completely on Nick. Whatever magic he was crafting, it was not meant to bring Seren back. Darius didn't know what it was meant for, but if it called for stripping a mage of his aura and energy, it was more than likely taboo. A quick glance behind him told him that Morgan and Ines were just as confused.

Darius took a deep breath and reached out with his own magic, eyes flashing with mage light as he tried to read—without interrupting—the ritual. They needed to know what they were facing; running into danger headlong could get them all killed.

Nick groaned again, writhing to the side as Kris continued his sacrament. Morgan started to move past Darius, but Darius put a hand up without offering him an explanation. He didn't want to interrupt what he was seeing or sensing. Morgan glared at him, but Darius ignored it.

The rite, whatever it was, had no hint of any spellcraft dealing with the mind. It was reaching instead for Nick's soul, slowly decorticating each layer of what made Nick the man he was until it found... something. Darius couldn't tell what.

Another belabored cry came from Nick, but this time the sound held a word. A single syllable. "No." His eyelids fluttered open, and he fought to raise a hand, opening it towards the necklace. "You...promised..."

"Stop fighting," Kris said calmly. "Don't you understand? You're opening the way. Once you're done, then you will see her."

"No!" Nick opened his hand suddenly, and the necklace vanished from above him. Just as abruptly, the strands of magic slowly unspooling Nick's aura vanished. Darius quietly smiled. Nick had worked his own spellcraft and teleported the necklace elsewhere, disrupting the entire spell.

Darius's smile vanished when Nick's hand dropped to the floor, limp. *Oh no.*

Kris's face contorted with rage. "You disgusting waste of flesh and blood. Where did you send it?" He pulled his leg back, aiming a kick at the unconscious Nick. "Where did you fucking send it?"

Before Darius could intervene, he felt a violent surge in the magic around him. Suddenly, Kris was yanked to the side, and through the glass of the French doors he was closest to. The sound of shattering glass splintered across the empty room and out into the cold night beyond. Glancing back, Darius saw Morgan standing in the open, breathing heavily, anger and spellcraft sparking in his light brown eyes.

Darius sprinted forward as the magic dissipated from the room, the ritual now completely ruined. He leapt over the Nick's form and hurried to the doors to check for the elder mage.

He saw Kris clamber to his feet and turn, running into the darkness.

Shit!

Thoughts flew through his mind. If Kris had needed someone closely connected to Seren to complete whatever spellcraft he had been working, did that mean that Emily was now at risk?

"Get Nick," he shouted to Trinity and Morgan as he sprinted to follow Kris, plunging into the darkness beyond.

CHAPTER TWENTY-EIGHT

Morgan

He was breathing heavily, rage and grief and worry coursing through him, mixing with his magic in a nauseating amalgamation that made his world shift. He had seen his father lying prone and defenseless, seen what looked like a teenager standing over that form. The kid, whoever he was, had been using his father, another human being, as a catalyst to rend a hole in reality and pull a soul back to it. What else was Morgan supposed to do? He had reacted without thinking, pulling the magic to him, and releasing it in a gust of air so fierce it sent the young-looking mage flying through the glass of the French doors beside him. The sound was cacophonous and, for Morgan, all-encompassing. Then he saw Darius moving, running. He felt Trinity move as well, going to kneel beside Nick, her fingers at his throat to seek out a pulse.

Before he could think of what to do, Darius was shouting to see to Nick, then dashing off into the shadows. Morgan was momentarily frozen, unsure of what to do. Should he see to the unconscious man or follow the man he was swiftly coming to deeply care for into the dark unknown. No time anomaly he knew of would allow him to do both.

"Morgan!"

He came back to himself at Trinity's sharp address. His mother had always been able to get his attention. He moved, kneeling beside her and helping to assess Nick. His skin was cool and clammy, and he was breathing but with shallow, wheezing gasps.

"We need to get him to Ines," Trinity snapped, her voice shaking.

Had they been too late? Had interrupting the ceremony so violently somehow caused more damage? Morgan's worry blossomed hard and fast as he struggled to control it.

"Morgan, turn around."

He did as he was told, still crouching though barely listening. He wasn't sure he could do this, recover, even if only for a short while. He clenched his jaw, fighting against his panic as Trinity hefted Nick up and onto Morgan's back. The weight helped ground Morgan, and he pulled his future father's arms forward over his shoulders before putting his arms around his back to support Nick in a piggyback carry. Morgan staggered as he tried to straighten up. While Nick was lighter than he'd expected and felt thinner than what was healthy, he was still practically dead weight. "He's going to fall," Morgan worried.

Trinity huffed and grabbed for Morgan's waistband. "Hey, what are you doing!" he squeaked.

"I'm getting your belt. Your pants won't fall, will they?"

"I don't think so."

"Good." She deftly unbuckled the belt and pulled it from around his waist. She did the same with her own, fashioning a longer belt out of the both of them and strapping it around Morgan and Nick. "There, that should help," she said, finishing the buckle around Morgan's chest. "Let's go."

Morgan hesitated, "What about—"

"Darius will be fine," said Trinity, though she didn't sound entirely sure. "As soon as we can get Nick to Ines, we'll come back for him."

Morgan didn't like it. His gut was heavy with anxiety, but he had to trust that Darius would be all right, at least for the time it took them to make sure Nick would be all right. He nodded to Trinity and followed her as she led the way back through the darkness to the parking lot.

By the time they arrived back at the car, Morgan was exhausted. His knees ached and sweat beaded his brow, the January night doing little to cool him off. He moved around to the driver's side of Trinity's car, not wanting to worry Emily with the sight of her unconscious father. Trinity went to Ines, and Morgan could hear them talking softly on the other side of the SUV while Morgan lowered himself and his unconscious patient to the ground and undid the buckle holding them together. He propped Nick up against the car and was surprised to see that his eyes were open and he was studying Morgan.

"Who are you?" he asked, his voice a low rasp.

He hadn't been prepared for his father to be conscious, much less actually speak to him. He wasn't sure what to say. There wasn't enough time to explain things. "Uhm, I'm Morgan. I'm a friend of Trinity's," he blurted out, his brain forcing the first thing that came to mind out of his mouth. Morgan offered an awkward laugh. "Nice to meet you."

Nick's sleepy eyes, the same ones Morgan had inherited, narrowed. He obviously didn't trust what Morgan had said, but he seemed to lack the energy to do anything more than glare at him.

This was not how Morgan envisioned meeting the man who had been his father in his own timeline. He was awash with anxiety and longing to make his identity known to him, but adrenaline and panic still rushed through him, closing his mouth until a better time could present itself.

Still, things could have been worse, he supposed.

He heard footsteps rounding the front of the SUV, and Ines appeared, kneeling down next to the seated Nick. "Damn, Slavin, you really know how to get yourself into trouble, don't you?"

"Ines? What are you doing here? And who is he?" asked Nick, pointing weakly at Morgan and ignoring Ines's barb.

"A friend," she said. Her eyes flared with magic, lightening to a brown-orange that called to mind sunlight filtered through autumn leaves in the midst of a deep forest. Putting her hand on Nick's neck, she looked him over while counting the beats of his heart. Her brow furrowed. "What did he give you, Nick?" she asked, glowing eyes still studying him. "Looks like you've got something in your system."

"What? What is it?" asked Morgan, unable to hide the worry in his voice.

"Not sure," she said. "Not enough to overdose, I hope, but enough to knock him on his ass." She continued to count out his pulse for another few seconds, then let out a sigh. "All right, we need to get you in the car.

You're getting checked out at the hospital, then I think Trinity plans on murdering you for locking your child in a closet and leaving her."

Nick groaned, his eyes sliding shut. He lightly banged his head against the car door behind him but said nothing.

Ines patted Morgan's shoulder to grab his attention. "Help me get him up and into the front seat?"

Morgan nodded, and together they maneuvered the half-conscious mage up from the cold ground and around the SUV, opening the passenger door and somehow managing to get him into it. They reclined the seat for him, and once he was belted and leaning back, somewhat upright in the seat, they closed the door.

Satisfied that her patient was secure, Ines turned back to Morgan. "All right, Trinity is going to take him to the hospital. She's also taking the kiddo someplace safe." She gave Morgan a hard clap on the shoulder. "We're Darius's backup."

As Ines spoke, Trinity carried the slumbering Emily to the SUV, opening the back door and putting her into her seat. None of the jostling seemed to wake the child, and once she was buckled, she moved her head to the side to rest on her booster seat's headrest. Trinity quietly closed the car door and offered Ines and Morgan a worried look. "Are you sure I shouldn't stay here?"

Ines shook her head, "No, go. You have Slavin people to take care of. We'll be fine." She cracked her knuckles as she spoke, her eyes still alight with magic.

"Call," demanded Trinity, climbing into the driver's seat. "As soon as you're all safe, call."

"Yes, Mom," Ines drawled but sobered up when she caught Trinity's withering look. "Go take care of that man and the kid. We'll call—don't worry."

Trinity hesitated a moment longer, then closed the door and started the car. Ines reached over and took Morgan's arm, leading him back towards the path and the fieldhouse beyond.

Ines's eyes glowed unnaturally in the darkness, and she gazed around. "Do you need a flashlight?" asked Morgan, regretting he hadn't thought about it earlier. He fumbled in his pocket for his phone, which would have one.

"Not for me. I can see just fine," she said, voice smug.

Morgan had almost forgotten that Ines crafted in cycle magic, which often included body augmentation for those accustomed to the spellcraft. Adjusting her vision to see better in the low light was no far stretch for her. He chuckled softly and finally retrieved his phone. He activated the built-in flashlight and brandished it as a weapon amid the darkness. Quietly the two continued towards the Field house, but just as they reached the French doors, there was a shout. A raw, strangled sound that came from the shoreline.

Almost immediately, a burning pain ripped through Morgan's head. He groaned and dropped to a knee, the cold stone patio meeting him with uncomfortable hardness. Ines was beside him in an instant, but he couldn't hear what she was saying past the burning pain. Just as suddenly, it was cut off, as was the shout they had both heard.

"Are you all right?" asked Ines, hissing the question.

"Darius. I think that was Darius," he raised a hand, pointing towards the waterline. "We have to get to him. Now!"

CHAPTER TWENTY-NINE
Darius

Darius knew he was making a mistake. More than one. Hurtling into the darkness without light, advantage, or additional support in pursuit of an elder mage who may or may not have been engaging in forbidden spellcraft was beyond foolish; it was deadly.

His second mistake had been assuming that he was in the same condition that he had been when he was in the field as an Indagator seven or so years earlier. He most definitely was not. His lungs burned, and his legs ached as he emerged from the Field House in his pursuit, hoping that he was still on the elder mage's trail. He caught sight of Kris and pushed himself to run harder, the grass beneath his shoes slick with frost. The flashlight on his phone was a poor defense against the darkness of the area around him, and even though the city lights of Chicago reached him, it was only just barely. Darius had to depend more on sound than sight during the chase.

So, he listened. He listened as his suspect fled, the sound of dry branches being knocked aside, and followed without thinking. His quarry had taken off running south from the Field House, through the trees and grass, crossing the pavement, and closer to the shore of Lake Michigan. Darius didn't slow until he reached the great limestone slabs, skidding to a halt to get his bearings. He was forced to move cautiously, the changing terrain beneath him calling for a slower approach.

The night had gone quiet. Aside from the distant din of the city and the gentle lapping of water against the stone, he heard nothing. No hint of retreating footsteps. He strained to detect even the softest sound of flight, but there was nothing. *Did he get away?* Adrenaline and panic combined in Darius's gut, making it twist painfully. Would he go after Nick again? Or worse, Emily?

Wielding his flashlight as a weapon against the semi-darkness, he shone it around him, willing his eyes to adjust and find some sign of his quarry. They didn't obey. Kris was nowhere to be found.

An itch at the back of his head was the only warning he had before searing, stabbing pain ignited violently. The tattoo on his scalp burned white-hot, and he clutched at it, letting out a sharp cry at the sudden agony. Without intending them to, his thoughts went to Morgan, an unconscious plea for help.

The burning vanished as abruptly as it had flared, but Darius had no time for relief. A strong hand wrapped around his throat, squeezing with merciless purpose. He blinked against the pain to see who was on him, who was attacking him, as he was lifted up, high enough so that he couldn't touch the ground, his assailant with a powerful grip around his neck.

Kris. It was Kris. He hadn't gotten away at all. He had just waited.

"Do you have any idea what you just cost me, you little shit?" he asked. His lips were curled back in a vicious snarl, and he squeezed Darius's throat. "Do you have any idea how easily I could kill you, you insignificant piece of absolute garbage?" He suddenly brought Darius down, slamming him hard onto the slick rock beneath them as if he weighed nothing. Stars exploded in Darius's vision as his head connected with the limestone. He went limp for a moment, dazed by the pain and confusion the blow had brought.

Fight, he told himself. *Fight, damn it.*

Kris brought him back up, their faces so close that Darius could feel the heat from the other man's skin. Kris studied him for a moment and smirked.

Darius realized there would be no getting the hand to release physically. Cycle mages could augment their own strength. Instead, he reached out with other means, calling on his magic to attack, but the attempt only renewed the intense pain behind his eyes. The hand on his throat tightened in response, and Kris laughed, shaking him. "You Mindscape mages. It's amazing how easy it is to incapacitate you. You think everyone thinks like you. Mental attacks and all. You never consider how vulnerable you leave yourselves to everything else." His eyes flashed, glowing with light as he began working magic, his lips moving inaudibly.

Agony erupted in Darius's chest, so sharp and overwhelming that he couldn't make a sound. It felt like his ribs were being pried open, pulled up. He let out a short, shocked gasp when he felt a rib crack. It broke away from the sternum, searching for freedom by pushing against his flesh. The pain was so severe Darius couldn't scream.

"Should I do this one rib at a time or all at once?" asked Kris. "Or maybe turn them inward, pop your lungs like a fucking balloon, and leave you to drown in your own blood?"

"Darius!"

Morgan's voice rang through the air. Kris turned towards the noise, his lips stilling and the mage light going out of his eyes.

The pain in Darius's chest lessened, though the broken rib was still aflame with agony. Relief flooded through him even as the edges of his vision began to darken, his breathing still restricted behind Kris's grip.

"Come any closer, and I will kill him," Kris said. His hold on Darius's throat loosened slightly, enough to let more oxygen into Darius's burning lungs. He gasped at the air in a deep coughing breath and writhed against the pain that it caused. He saw Morgan at the top of the embankment, and next to him was Ines, her eyes glowing preternaturally in the half-light.

"Let him go," she growled, sounding more like a wild cat than a person. "Now."

Kris hesitated for a second, then let out a low chuckle that only Darius could hear. That did not bode well for him. "What would I get out of the deal?"

"Your life," Ines spat back.

Darius thought she must be joking. Did she just threaten an elder?

"Protectorate is on their way," Ines continued, somehow appearing haughty in the face of one of the most powerful mages in existence. "They would probably be curious as to why you're beating one of their Monitors into oblivion."

"E-especially after what we witnessed in there!" Morgan added, though his voice was not filled with quite as much solid steel as Ines.

Kris looked decidedly less smug. "I don't have time for this," he said, more to himself than anyone else.

Bringing Darius's face close to him, Kris grinned. "This isn't over. I can't wait until it is. You are going to pay for this."

With what seemed like the flick of his wrist, Kris threw Darius, sending him into the air for ten yards before he crashed down on the steps.

Darius tried to protect his head when he landed but couldn't lift his right arm, the injured rib too painful to allow him the freedom of movement. His skull impacted with the limestone again, sending fresh waves of pain and nausea through him as he tumbled across the stone. His momentum was only checked when he hit the icy water, but the blow to his head had rendered him half senseless. The freezing water flooding his nostrils and ears felt like pinpricks, the algid Lake Michigan coursing down his throat. He wanted to cough, his lungs burning, his ribs throbbing.

Then the cold began to fade, and the pain wasn't as bad as it had been.

Somewhere in a part of his mind still capable of logical thought, he knew he had to get out of the water. This was shock. He had to fight it, had to try and get back to the safety of the concrete and limestone that surrounded Promontory Point, but he found that as the dark waters of the second-largest Great Lake closed over him, he didn't have the strength to do anything but succumb.

CHAPTER THIRTY

Darius

"This was it. This was the moment I fucked up."

Darius was no longer in the icy waters of Lake Michigan. Instead, he found himself in a room he didn't immediately recognize. It was a bedroom. The walls were covered in faded wallpaper, white with small pink flowers that peeled at the edges. He propped himself on his elbows in the bed he was in and realized he was naked beneath a thin sheet that half covered him. He wasn't alone, either. Someone else was in the room, rushing around. She was gathering her clothes, which had been strewn about the room. A bra here, a crumpled pair of jeans there. She was speaking to him, but he couldn't hear what she was saying, her words blending in a soft murmur as she tried to find everything she was looking for. She began to dress, haphazardly hopping on one foot as she pulled jeans up over her naked thighs and ass. She slipped into her bra with all the finesse of a drunk gymnast and offered him a goofy smile once she'd finally managed to right the undergarment.

Seren.

This was her bedroom in the shitty little one-bedroom apartment she'd rented when she had first come to Chicago. The same one she'd shared with her on-again-off-again boyfriend, Nick. The same one that had hers and Nick's sleeping toddler in an alcove that she had made into a nursery. Seren Morgan, in all her morning-after glory. Her heart-shaped face surrounded by the halo of a messy pixie cut with blonde ends and dark roots. Those large blue eyes, wide and awake despite their lovemaking, which had gone well into the night.

"Oh, stop ogling me," came an order from the other side of the bed. Darius startled, turning his head to see another Seren.

This one was fully clothed, leaning against the corner of the bedroom with arms crossed over her chest, watching the other Seren as she struggled to find the rest of the clothes she'd discarded so carelessly the night before. The fully dressed Seren gave Darius a playful grin. "I know I was a looker but have some decency."

"Am I dead?" Darius asked, unsure of what else to say.

Fully clothed Seren came and sat next to him on the bed, offering him a handful of the bedsheet to cover himself more fully before letting out a long sigh. "Don't know. I hope not. It's hard to tell. I do know that I am, though. Thanks for the reminder." She chuckled, but the sound was sad, maybe a little forced. Running a hand through her hair, she looked away. "I remember this, though," she said, nodding toward her other self. "This was the moment that I realized I had successfully fallen for two men. Talk about a fuck up of epic proportions. Me? I could have been quite happy in a polyamorous relationship, but Nick? I don't think so. Well, maybe, but not then. And I still loved the big jerk. You?" She gave him an appraising look. "You strike me as the one-love kind of person. And I loved you." She gave an overexaggerated shrug. "Monogamy sucks. I was stuck. Now I'm dead." She laughed. "Life's a bitch, and then you die."

He sat up further so that he was upright next to her, their shoulders brushing. "I'm sorry, you what?"

"Loved you. Still love you, despite you being a stuck-up prick. You were back then, anyway. Now you're just a big soft teddy bear," she said, looking back. She leaned her head against his shoulder. "And I still love Nick. I want to see both of you happy, so stop being so freaking stubborn about it."

Darius breathed her scent in, a strange blend of jasmine and powder deodorant. Despite having not experienced it in years, he found it calming. "If I'm not dead, then how am I talking to you?" he asked.

"I said I *hoped* you weren't dead, not that I knew one way or the other. You're probably pretty damn close, though," she said simply. "That badass tattoo that you had put on you, which by the way, is the reason we haven't spoken in your dreams or anything before this, thank you very much, was damaged. The ward was broken. It's how we're speaking now."

Memories began to push in at the edges of the space. Darius could remember Promontory Point, the Field House, and giving chase to Kris. "Oh, gods, Morgan and Ines—"

"Are fine," Seren interrupted. "It's you that's injured."

"I have to get back," he said, urgency moving him to look around for his own clothes. Then he stopped, realizing he wasn't actually in this room or this apartment. Whatever this place was, it wasn't a physical location. A mental or spiritual one, sure, but one didn't need clothing for that kind of place. "Wait, how do I get back? Can I even?"

Seren shrugged. "I don't know. Wake up, I guess?"

Darius eyed her. "How does one 'wake up' from something like this?"

"Listen, jackass, I've been dead for the better part of a decade; I don't fucking know how to do living people shit anymore." She laughed when she said it. Pushing up to her feet and moving to the window, she gazed out. Darius couldn't see anything beyond it but light. Seren, silhouetted against it, looked much like he remembered her. A wiry firebrand, ready to force her way into one's life and help, no matter what.

"I'm sorry," he said, spellbound by the visage of her in the light.

"For what?" she asked, not turning.

Grief blossomed in his chest, and he let his head hang, unable to face her as he spoke. He had to say this, though. He had to. "You died because of me. Because I refused to see the truth of your warning. You—" Tears choked his words, and he cleared his throat before continuing. "You became that thing, and I had to... to..." His voice failed him.

He didn't look up as the silence stretched between them. He couldn't bring himself to until he heard her laughing. "Darius, I died because I made a choice that got me there. My choice. You just did what you had to do. What was left after that blast... It wasn't me." She still wasn't facing him, but her voice was free of any blame or judgment. Cheerful and mildly sarcastic, as always. "It isn't all about you, Adair."

Finally, she turned back to him. She was hugging herself and looking decidedly less fiery. She looked vulnerable and alone. "If you want, make

206

it up to me, then. Look after Emily. She has too much of my stubbornness for her own good. And…" She trailed off for a moment, then took a big breath, preparing for what she said next. "I know it's a big ask, but keep an eye on her dad, too? He feels much deeper than he's willing to admit, and I think it's killing him." She wiped at her eyes and forced a smile. "I don't want to be the reason he can't find happiness."

He wanted to argue, but her open honesty dispelled any fight he might have put up against the request. Besides, he owed her, and he would make it up to her. Whether he liked it or not, he was tied to the Slavin family. He wouldn't abandon them. Not again. "You know, you're the second person to ask me to look out for Nick," he said, breathing a laugh. Quietly, he nodded. "All right, I will."

The room around him started to fade, the lines and edges of the furniture and walls growing soft, then white. In the span of a breath, everything had faded to white, and the last thing Darius heard was Seren's soft, smug voice, whispering, "I knew you'd figure it out."

CHAPTER THIRTY-ONE

Morgan

They pulled Darius from the water less than a minute, maybe, after he'd gone in. Morgan thought he'd died. He was pale, lips blue, and blood was gushing from the wounds on his head and chest. Morgan's stomach roiled violently when Ines lifted his shirt to reveal the horrifying sight of a rib protruding from Darius's flesh, the wound bubbling as water, air, and blood mingled in his chest cavity and around the glistening bone.

Ines shoved Morgan away and went to work immediately on Darius. She'd had to use all of her weight to press the broken rib back into place, and her eyes glowed with her spellcraft as she healed it there. She drew the water from his lungs as well, and he'd coughed and vomited.

He was alive, but barely.

Worse, he still wasn't waking up.

"Hospital, now!" Ines snapped, picking Darius up as if he weighed nothing and moving back towards the car.

"But...how?" stammered Morgan.

"Cycle magic, remember?" Ines huffed. She gestured for Morgan to open the front passenger door when they reached the car, and she laid Darius down, reclining the seat as much as possible. Only then did the mage light fade from her eyes.

Morgan couldn't remember the drive to the hospital beyond sitting in the backseat of the car and holding Darius as still as possible as Ines rushed to the nearest emergency room. He let Ines lead the way, saying nothing and only doing what she expressly told him to do. She was in control from the moment they pulled him from the icy lake all the way to the hospital, shouting to the ER staff what had happened and what might be needed. Morgan wouldn't have known she actually worked at a *different* hospital if she hadn't been asked to step back and let their medical staff work.

And so had begun the waiting game.

Neither Ines nor Morgan was particularly adept at waiting patiently. They took seats in the small, sterile-looking waiting room. The walls were white and, besides a generic painting or two, were bare. The chairs were stiff and uncomfortable. Nothing in the room made it a comfortable place to wait for them. Ines sat for twenty seconds, thirty tops, before bounding back to her feet and pacing the small space. Morgan kept his seat, sitting forward to rest his elbows on his knees. He couldn't keep himself from bouncing his leg, and after half an hour of the both of them burning through their anxiety at the wait, Ines cracked first.

"Fuck it, I'm going to find their cafeteria or a vending machine or something. Want anything?" she asked.

Morgan shook his head. "I don't think my stomach could handle anything."

Ines nodded and vanished down the hallway, returning ten minutes later with a chocolate bar and soda for herself. She handed Morgan a bottle of water, shrugging. "It's better than nothing. We might be here a while."

After another hour and a half, a doctor came out to greet them. "You were here with the patient they brought in earlier, a Mr. Adair."

"Yes," Ines said before Morgan could even react. "That's his fiancé." She nodded to Morgan, the lie rolling off of her tongue without hesitation. "I'm their friend. What's happening?"

The doctor, a person who looked to be a bit older than Morgan, offered a winning smile as they tucked a strand of hair behind their ear. "Well, good news. Your friend's fall wasn't as bad as it originally looked. He suffered a few cracked ribs and a nasty hit to the head, but luckily his skull wasn't fractured. We are going to keep him overnight, run some tests, but with any luck, he'll be good to go tomorrow, barring complications. He has a concussion and required quite a few stitches to his scalp and forehead." The doctor pushed their hands into the pockets of their scrubs. "Your fiancé will be fine. They're admitting him now."

"Thank you," Ines said, clapping the doctor on the shoulder. "We appreciate it."

"Anytime," they replied, deftly slipping out of Ines's grasp. "It's late, and visiting hours don't start until tomorrow morning at eleven." They gave Ines and Morgan a sympathetic look. "You may want to go get some rest and come back then."

Ines nodded as the doctor walked away, then turned to Morgan. "We have a long haul until tomorrow morning. Want to come back to my place and get some rest?"

Morgan shook his head. He wanted to stay here, but sleeping beneath the glaring lights of the ER waiting room wasn't ideal—or allowed, he supposed—and he wanted to get some things for Darius. "Could you drop me off at his place? I have the spare keys."

"All right. Let's get going, then."

Morgan didn't think about much on the drive home. Ines was quiet as well. Maybe a half hour later, she pulled into a parking spot not far from Darius's building and turned off the car. "Mind if I crash here?" she asked. "I'm too damned tired to drive home."

Morgan had no issue with it, and within a few more minutes, they were in the apartment.

"I'm calling the couch!" Ines said, then vanished into the bathroom. She was out seconds later, dressed in sweats and a t-shirt she'd apparently brought from her car. "I always keep a bag in the car for an emergency. You never know when the shit is going to hit the fan."

As if in a trance, Morgan made his own way to the bathroom. He stripped out of his clothes, washed his face and hands, brushed his teeth, but he didn't have the energy for an entire shower. Instead, he changed into a pair of pajama pants and a tank top and made his way back out into the apartment.

Snoring immediately alerted him to the fact that Ines was already asleep. He chuckled softly and grabbed a throw blanket, laying it gently over her sleeping form. Moving around the couch, he climbed onto the bed but couldn't bring himself to get under the quilt and sheets. He had only slept in the bed by himself a handful of times when he had first been brought back to the apartment. The last time he'd been in it, it had been *with* Darius. Some superstitious part of him didn't want to get under the covers until Darius was home and with him. So, he laid himself atop the comforter, sighing into the pillow that smelled of the familiar bergamot and sandalwood cologne, and let his eyes fall closed.

~

The next time he opened them, it was to Ines gently shaking him. She looked freshly showered and dressed in hospital scrubs.

"What happened?" he gasped, sitting up in the bed. He was disoriented. Had he fallen asleep? It felt like time hadn't passed. Panic flared up, but he fought through it, remembering Darius and the hospital. "What time is it?"

"Time for me to go to work. Come on, I'll drop you off at Provident on my way into work, so you can see your man."

Morgan nodded, but he was shaky. "I just need a shower." He hurried into the bathroom and blasted the shower, the hot water nearly scalding but a good reminder of where he was and that he and the steaming water were real. Afterward, he was calm enough to shave and dress without panic gripping him. Twenty minutes saw him out, in his coat, and ready to go. Ines gave him a look that told him he wasn't fooling her into thinking he was fine. He didn't have the energy to try harder.

Forty-five minutes later, Morgan was pacing outside of the hospital gift shop, waiting impatiently for them to open. Apparently, they shared their opening time with the beginning of visiting hours. Ines had given Morgan a bit of cash to get something overly cheery and cheesy for Darius. He had his eye on a pink teddy bear with a heart that had bandages around it. However, it was now five after eleven, and still, the doors hadn't opened. Morgan wanted to be with Darius as soon as he could.

"Fuck it," he murmured. Gifts could wait. "I'll come back for it."

Hurrying to the elevators, he bypassed them and took the stairs, two at a time, before he reached the floor he was looking for. He made sure his 'VISITOR' badge was clearly visible when he stopped at the nurse's station. "Hi, I'm looking for Darius Adair?"

"And you are?" asked the nurse. She was tall and broad, a short gray bob framing attractive facial features, one slender eyebrow arched as she waited for his response.

Morgan swallowed, suddenly nervous that Ines's lie from the night before wouldn't hold without her present. "I'm his fiancé."

The nurse checked the computer, then nodded. "Night nurse said you'd be visiting today." She pointed to the closest door. "In there, sir. Looks like his bloodwork and tests came back looking good. The doctor should be in shortly to give him a last evaluation and talk to you both about aftercare, but it's a formality at this point."

Morgan beamed and thanked the nurse before striding to the door and opening it.

The room was darkened, the blinds drawn though light still filtered in around them. Despite the dim light, Morgan was surprised to find that Darius wasn't alone.

A woman that Morgan had never seen was seated in a chair in the corner. She had long, titian hair and pale skin, and she turned to look at Morgan when he entered the room. Her eyes were a steely blue, sharp and icy in a way that immediately put Morgan on edge. "Uhm, hello," he said. "Are you a friend of Darius's?"

The woman let out a long, measured sigh and stood up. Her movements were graceful and controlled when she extended a hand to Morgan. "Sybil Diluna. I'm Darius's partner at the Protectorate. And you are?"

"Morgan," he said simply. He remembered how Darius spoke about her, and despite the disarming smile that slid across her red lips, Morgan thought it better to keep his guard up. "I'm his fiancé." He kept his tone casual, laid back. He thought the lie would sound better that way. He wasn't sure of this woman, of why she was there or how she had known

Darius was there. After the night he'd had, Morgan was suspicious of everything.

"Fiancé?" Those red lips turned down in a frown. "He never tells me anything. Here I thought he had just gotten some action. I come to find out it's all sorts of action. Well, congratulations. Very happy for you two."

Morgan felt his guard slip a bit, even if the joke felt a little crass. Maybe she wasn't as bad as Darius had said. Maybe she was just awkward? After all, she *was* visiting.

How had she known he was there?

She quirked an eyebrow but said nothing for a moment. Then she nodded toward Darius, who was sleeping in the bed. "My superior told me Darius was here, and I wanted to make sure he was all right. Didn't know I would find him sleeping like a baby." She chuckled. "Doctor said he would be discharged later today."

"You spoke to the doctor?" Morgan asked. He thought they wouldn't give that information out to anyone but next of kin.

She gave Morgan another appraising look and smiled again, ignoring his question. "I'll leave him in your capable hands. Tell him not to worry about work; I'll cover for him." She moved to the door and paused just slightly before adding, "Nice to meet you, Morgan."

"Nice to meet you, too."

She was already gone by the time he'd returned the sentiment.

CHAPTER THIRTY-TWO

Darius

The arrival home from the hospital came with an unfamiliar amount of being fussed over, something that Darius was inexperienced with. After getting his discharge papers from the doctors, he'd helped Morgan call a rideshare so they could get back to his apartment. Afterward, he'd been gingerly helped into the apartment, sat down, and given a large glass of water to sip from. All the lights had been dimmed, shades closed, and harsh lights disallowed. No television, no physical exertion, and no deep, difficult thoughts.

Concussion and all that.

Darius thought every restriction was doable, save for the last. That one was laughable.

"How are you feeling?" asked Morgan, sitting down next to him once the apartment had been suitably dimmed.

Darius hurt. That was the truth of it. His head was pounding, the stitches itched, and his ribs ached with every breath he took. He had nothing beyond acetaminophen to take for it lest he risk masking worsening symptoms of the concussion or an intracranial bleed.

But he was safe and with Morgan.

"Tired," he said after a sip of water. He was realizing how long he had actually felt tired and how long he had been ignoring it. "In a bit of pain. Also trying to figure out how to not think about anything too hard or distract myself from doing so without a screen." He chuckled.

"Well, we could talk," Morgan suggested. "I could read something to you, maybe?"

"Actually, that second one sounds nice." He adjusted in his seat, wincing at the pain in his chest. "No offense, but I don't have the wherewithal for actual conversation."

Morgan helped him up and to the bed, where he gently laid down and got under the covers, nestling in. Morgan made sure he was comfortable, then put his water on the nightstand, along with two of the white acetaminophen pills. He circled around the other side of the bed and slipped beneath the blankets as well. Darius tried not to grimace as the bed shifted beneath the weight, and it sent small shocks of pain through his ribs. Morgan noticed, though, and winced through an apology.

"It's all right," Darius replied through clenched teeth. "What are we reading?"

"What do you like?"

Darius thought for a moment, then gently shook his head. He hadn't sat down and really read for pleasure in a very long time. Maybe even since Seren had died. He wondered if part of him had died with her. He wondered if he could get that part back. "You pick one."

"You all right with contemporary romance?"

Darius hadn't expected that genre to come from Morgan. Then again, he wasn't sure why he didn't. He couldn't think of an argument against it, either. "Sure," he said. "Any good ones?"

Morgan was browsing on his phone. "How about a novella about a superhero's ex-boyfriend who is looking to find love?"

Darius pondered for a moment, then shrugged. "Sure, why not? As long as it's low stress."

"Don't worry," Morgan laughed. "I'm pretty sure it will have a happy ending."

They stayed like that, Morgan reading, Darius occasionally breaking in with a comment or request as he went. It was, much to Darius's surprise, a lovely way to spend the afternoon. Being pain-free would have made it better, but in the soft layer of bedding surrounding him, with Morgan's reassuring presence and voice beside him, Darius felt cared for in a way that he hadn't for a very long time. Possibly ever.

~

When Darius awoke the next morning, he could see gray light filtering in around the edges of the closed curtains in his apartment. He was in his apartment. In his bed. He must have drifted off the night before.

He sat up a bit, trying to get his bearings. When he did, his head pounded, and he quickly lay back down. His throat was sore, and his neck aching.

Darius realized he wasn't in the bed alone, either.

Morgan was curled up on the bed beside him. He was on top of the blankets, dressed in a pair of sweatpants and a hoodie, thick socks on his feet. He was fast asleep, the hood hiding most of his hair. Darius smiled. He looked so peaceful, deep in restful sleep. Darius wanted to return to that as well, but his bladder had other ideas, so he slowly slid out of bed and availed himself of the bathroom.

Once he'd finished and was washing his hands, he paused for a moment to look at himself in the mirror. He looked pale, maybe a bit more than usual. Stitches came down from his scalp and over his forehead, all the way to his left eyebrow. He knew he had some on the back of his head, too. The bruising on his neck also stood out to him. It had formed in the vague shape of a handprint, no doubt from the strength that his assailant had had. Unnatural strength. He supposed he shouldn't be surprised at Kris's power. He was, after all, an elder.

He ran a damp finger over the purple and black skin, shaking his head slightly as he did so.

He wondered how close to death he really had been. Close enough to see Seren. He still remembered their meeting. The details of it were foggy and vague, but he knew it had been no dream. The only way he would ever truly see the dead would be to join them. He had almost done just that.

Still love you, despite you being a stuck-up prick. You were back then, anyway. Now you're just a big soft teddy bear.

That's what Seren had said. Darius stared hard at the mirror, studying each line of his face, how his hair fell so haphazardly. He didn't feel different, but Seren Morgan, of all people, had called him a teddy bear. When had he changed so much?

Drying his hands, he emerged from the bathroom to see a bleary-eyed Morgan sitting up in the bed, staring at him. "You're awake. How do you feel?"

"My head is killing me. So are my ribs," Darius said, though he barely recognized his own voice. It was soft and grating, his throat not only sore but dry. "And I could use a drink."

"Here, come back and lay down. I'll get more water." Morgan pulled the covers down while he gave his instructions, then jumped up to go into the kitchen. He smiled as he returned with a glass of water, which he placed on Darius's nightstand. "Remember, you're supposed to be on complete rest. No investigating, no physical exertion. Nothing."

Darius took the glass and brought it to his lips, taking a sip of the cold liquid. It was icy relief to his aching throat, and before he realized it, he had drained the glass. He put it back on the nightstand and laid back down, resting his aching head on the pillow and closing his eyes. "Thank you."

"Welcome." He pulled his phone out of the pocket of his hoodie and tapped out a quick text message before putting it on his own nightstand. "Ines wants me to give her daily updates on your condition."

"My very own personal nurse."

Morgan nodded and settled back into the bed.

"Is Nick all right?"

Morgan shrugged, but he couldn't hide the sadness on his face. "He's alive. Trinity said he had some depressants in his system, but not a lethal amount. He doesn't remember taking it. He doesn't remember much of anything from before Trinity and I lugged him back to the car."

"And does he—"

"Know about me? Yeah." Morgan looked away. "Trinity said he wouldn't shut up until she told him about me."

"And?"

"And nothing. She thinks he needs some time to absorb it all. He has a lot on his plate."

Darius nodded but didn't push for any more from Morgan. He was happy Nick was alive. Much longer, and he might not have been. Darius didn't want to think about what Kris had been about to do to him. It hit too close to home and reminded him far too much of Vivian de Winter. He shuddered, then winced at the pain in his side.

"All right...now how are you *really*?"

Darius couldn't help the small smile that lifted his lips at Morgan's question. How perceptive. "Relieved that we stopped whatever Kris was trying to do." Eyes still closed, he reached out and found Morgan's hand, intertwining their fingers. "Glad you're all right. Intensely happy you and Ines found me when you did."

"You and me both," Morgan said, lifting their joined hands to his lips to place a kiss on Darius's knuckle. "I was a bit scared there."

"And with no windows to toss an assailant through," Darius teased.

"I'm useless in an outdoor setting, apparently." There was a laugh in Morgan's voice.

"So now what?" Darius asked.

"Now, we rest," Morgan announced, finality in his voice. He rolled onto his side, and leaned in, planting a kiss on Darius's cheek. "No strenuous activity, just rest and relaxation."

Darius raised an eyebrow, finally opening his eyes to give his lover a playful gaze. "Nothing *strenuous*?"

Morgan rolled his eyes. "Don't tempt me. The most strenuous activity you're going to be doing for a day or two is cuddling while we read or listen to audiobooks. That's it."

Darius let out a long, resigned sigh. "Well, I guess so."

Morgan shifted closer, moving to rest his head on Darius's chest and gently throw an arm around his midsection. "Hush. You rest some more," he instructed, yawning. "Maybe I'll nap, too."

Darius dozed off with a smile on his face, feeling safe and warm and loved.

CHAPTER THIRTY-THREE
Morgan

He tried not to shift in his seat, not wanting to betray how nervous he was. The clothes he'd put on at the apartment and felt confident in now felt itchy and claustrophobic.

The Protectorate building in Chicago was intimidating. Not as much from the outside, but inside, the floor-to-ceiling windows and matching office walls made Morgan feel exposed from every angle. It was the first thing he noticed when he stepped off the elevator. Disconcerting, to say the least.

It had been a week since the events at the Field House at Promontory Point. Darius was healing, though Morgan was constantly reminding him to rest. Even now that Morgan was out of the apartment, he was worried that Darius was pushing it. Knowing that man, he was more than likely typing up reports or had decided to reorganize his bookshelves. He couldn't just rest. It had taken everything to convince him to stay home. The meeting with Lead Monitor Ty Powell was something Morgan thought he could handle alone.

At least, that's what he had thought when leaving earlier. Now, he wasn't so sure. He stood nervously at the front desk, trying to breathe deeply without looking like he was breathing deeply. The attendant at the desk, who had held up a single finger when Morgan approached to tell him it would be a minute before continuing his phone call, finally ended the call and looked up at Morgan. "Can I help you?"

"Yes, hello," Morgan said, forcing himself to speak. "I'm Morgan Slavin. I was supposed to have a meeting with Lead Monitor Ty Powell at noon?"

The man raised an eyebrow and glanced at his computer, making a few keystrokes before saying in a disinterested voice, "Someone will be out for you in a moment. You can have a seat over there." He nodded towards two chairs against the wall, then went back to pretending that Morgan no longer existed.

"Cool," murmured Morgan, at a loss of what else to say. He sat and waited.

After five minutes of trying not to squirm, he was relieved when a fresh-faced individual strode towards him. Morgan had to admit that he hadn't been expecting pastel-colored hair and facial piercings, but he certainly wasn't going to judge. He extended a hand, relieved to have someone to connect to. "Hi, Mr. Powell?"

The individual broke into a huge smile, their cheeks pinking as they took Morgan's offered hand and shook it firmly. "Oh, oh no, I'm not the lead monitor. I'm Baylee, the LM's administrative assistant. You're Morgan Powell?"

"Ah, sorry about that," Morgan laughed. "Yeah, that's me."

"Don't be. Not a lot of people think I look like management material," Baylee said, chuckling. "I appreciate the vote of confidence. LM Powell was just finishing up a phone call but asked me to greet you and bring you to his office." They moved to turn and motioned to Morgan. "If you'll follow me?"

Morgan did, keeping pace while chatting brightly with Baylee.

"All glass, huh?" asked Morgan, gazing around. He didn't want to seem like he was staring at the office workers, but he wasn't sure where else to look.

"It takes some getting used to," Baylee sighed. "Luckily, LM Powell isn't into micromanaging. He doesn't care if you check your phone or social media as long as your work gets done."

"Sounds like a great boss."

Baylee beamed, the hero worship obvious on their face. "He really is."

Morgan smiled. It felt good to talk with people outside of the small circle of friends he'd made since arriving in Chicago. He treasured them all, especially Darius, but Morgan had always considered himself more of an extrovert, and conversing with others boosted his mood considerably. He found himself looking at the offices around him in a slightly brighter light. It felt more open and freer than he had originally thought.

"Sir, Morgan Slavin is here to see you," Baylee said after knocking on the open-door frame to an office at the end of the walk.

The man behind the desk slid out of his chair, standing straight before buttoning his suit jacket. He was two or three inches shorter than Morgan, with blonde hair in a neat style and sharp eyes that took in every detail. Despite his height, he had an imposing energy about him, and Morgan found himself bracing for what might come next.

Ty Powell strode to the door, ushering Morgan in before closing it behind the both of them. He paused, his right hand tracing runes on the back of the door. They glowed momentarily, then faded, and Morgan thought he could smell flowers.

The LM turned from the door and motioned to a seat. "Please, sit. Try to make yourself comfortable. I have a spellcraft on the door. No one will hear anything we're saying." He shrugged as he retook his chair behind the desk. "I figured that would be better for our meeting."

Morgan nodded along with the explanation, trying to relax as he lowered himself into the chair opposite the imposing desk.

"So, I'm Lead Monitor Ty Powell. I don't know how much Monitor Darius told you, but I'm basically his manager. I'm in charge of the work that gets done here and gets passed on throughout the Protectorate." He held up a hand, sensing Morgan's growing anxiety. "I also use my judgment on what can be handled without involving others and what needs to be escalated."

Morgan's mouth went dry, but he continued listening and nodding along. He tried to remember that Darius trusted this man. He took a deep breath, steadying himself, and once the lead monitor went silent, he began. "A pleasure to meet you, Mr. Powell. I'm Morgan Slavin. I'm not entirely sure what Darius told you about me, so I'm not sure where to begin or what you'd like to know."

"The start is usually a great place to pick up from. Also, you can call me Ty."

"All right, Ty," Morgan replied, trying out the name. "But you would be surprised how difficult it is to find a beginning to all of this."

"Take your time," Ty replied, sitting back. "There's no rush."

Morgan wracked his brain for a place to begin, then finally decided to tell it from his own time. Once he had a starting point, it all spilled out of him. Everything that he witnessed. Magic and spellcraft running wild, the struggles, having to pass back through time in his sister's stead. All of it. He was relieved that speaking on it didn't bring up the immediate panic or nausea that it had in times past, but he could feel his chest tighten as he spoke. He was not beyond his own anxiety, just getting slowly better at dealing with it.

When Morgan's explanation reached the timeline he was currently in, he slowed his pace. He wanted to make sure he got all the facts right. He wasn't sure if Trinity or Ines would be angry with him for disclosing their involvement, but he wasn't going to lie. Not to someone who had been trained by the Protectorate to weed out dishonesty and wrongdoing. Since they were guilty of none of it, Morgan thought it would be safe to share. Besides, Morgan still didn't have a strong enough foothold in his new timeline to think up any lie that would be halfway believable, let alone hold up to scrutiny.

Ty listened with rapt attention, only interrupting here and there to ask a clarifying question. When Morgan finally finished his story, Ty stared at him for a long moment, obviously weighing what he had just heard. Finally, he let out a long sigh, leaning against his desk with a thoughtful expression. "That's quite a story."

"It's true," Morgan insisted.

"I wasn't suggesting that it wasn't," Ty continued, holding a hand up. "I can tell that it's the truth, or at the very least, you believe it's the truth. Unfortunately, I'm not sure there's much we can do to corroborate it." He took a deep breath, absently rubbing his temple as if to soothe himself while he spoke.

Morgan's heart sank, and his gaze went with it, dropping to the floor beneath his feet.

"*But.*"

"But?" asked Morgan, chancing a glance back up to Ty.

"But that might be a good thing. It's clear to me that, regardless of how you came to be here, you're here now. If you did travel from the future, that future no longer exists, and you are here to stay."

The words hit him harder than he'd thought they would. Somewhere, deep down, Morgan had known his journey was a one-way trip. Him coming back and affecting change would either make it so that his original timeline had never existed, or it would close it off in an alternate future, one whose time stream was now completely separate from the one Morgan now existed in. Either way, the timeline he had landed in was now his own, whether he liked it or not.

There was grief in knowing he would never see his own timeline again. He wouldn't see the people he had known. Not as they had been to him. He mourned for that.

Ty was still speaking, and Morgan snapped out of his own reverie, realizing he should be paying better attention. "That being the case, here." While Ty had been talking, he'd opened a drawer in his desk and now dropped a manila envelope that he'd retrieved on the desktop. "Those are for you."

Brow furrowed, Morgan reached forward and pulled the folder to him, undoing the clasp and opening it. "What's all this?" he asked, letting the official-looking papers slide out and onto his lap.

"Birth certificate, social security card, school records, high school diploma—"

Bewildered, Morgan flipped through the papers. "But, how did you know...?"

"Trinity reached out to me. Her and I have had one or two run-ins over the years. Nothing bad, mind you. I think that's why she felt comfortable contacting me." Ty explained. He pointed to the paperwork. "We kept a familial tie between her and yourself, though cousins were the safest option. I know you're a little bit older than your traditional undergrad, but you could enroll in classes if you would like and try to find something to help get you on your feet."

"I thought she hated the Protectorate," Morgan blurted out.

Ty laughed heartily at his confusion. "She does. Well, most of it. She also gave me an earful. Her and I met years back through my wife, and I think Trinity holds me in *mostly* neutral esteem."

"Why do all this for me?" The question was out before Morgan could stop it, but it was an honest one. After all, he had just met Ty. They didn't owe each other anything.

"My wife says I'm too nice," Ty said with a shrug. "The reality is that there's too much difficult shit out there as it is, so if I can help, then I will." He sat back, resting his elbows on the armrests of his chair. "I can't discuss specifics with you of ongoing investigations, but I am making sure that Nicholas Slavin, his daughter, and Trinity all have Indagators posted nearby. I don't think that Elder Mage Kris will attempt anything at this point in time, but it never hurts to be safe."

Morgan's grip on the papers tightened.

"My sources tell me that he is no longer in Chicago, but now that the Protectorate has been alerted to possible illegal spellcraft, an investigation has been opened." Ty nodded. "If I have any further questions for you, would it be all right if I reached out?"

"Of course." Their meeting was coming to an end, and Morgan slid the papers back into the envelope. He had come to the Protectorate feeling anxious, dreading this conversation, but now there was just relief. "Listen, I cannot thank you enough for all of this and for your understanding. I'm honestly just floored by all of this." As he stood up and extended a hand to shake Ty's, he caught a glimmer of something in the man's gaze when it met his. A deep understanding of hardship and a genuine want to help.

They shook hands, and Ty smiled widely. "Anytime. And tell Darius I look forward to seeing him back in the office no sooner than next week. Is that understood?"

"Yes, sir."

"Good, now get out of here and make sure he takes care of himself."

CHAPTER THIRTY-FOUR

Darius

March had come to Chicago with pouring rain and temperatures not quite freezing. While this meant far less snow and subzero temperatures, the change did little to warm anything up. Darius almost preferred the colder weather. At least snow didn't drench one to the bone.

"Hope you have a good night," Baylee offered as Darius strode towards the elevator bank at the Protectorate. "Stay dry."

"I'll try. Have a good night."

Work had become more tolerable over the past couple of months. Sybil had taken a promotion in New York and was quick to pack up and take off. She'd seemed distant when he got back, and Darius could only assume that her having one foot out the door meant she didn't want to socialize with the people she would be leaving behind. There was no party, no sendoff, just a quiet sigh of relief the day after her final day.

Darius paused in the foyer of the Protectorate building to button up his peacoat and prepare his umbrella. Beyond the glass doors, he saw rain pouring down over the brightly lit city streets, and for a moment, he enjoyed the picturesqueness of it. Then he was out into that night, umbrella clutched tightly above him to shelter him from the rain.

He made it as far as the café on his walk before ducking inside for a respite from the cold night. The coffee shop was surprisingly empty, though given the weather, he couldn't blame patrons for wanting to be home sooner rather than later. He left his umbrella by the door and moved to the counter. It was a small shop with precious little seating, and the walls had been done in blackboard paint before being covered with chalk drawings of mugs and coffee beans just above a warm wooden chair rail and wainscotting. A quiet electronic take on ambient jazz settled in the background of the place. It radiated coziness.

"What can I get you?" asked the barista from behind the counter, flashing a smile that was all customer service.

"Can I get a medium decaf café mocha and a hot chocolate?"

"For here or to go?"

Darius looked around. The comfortable, well-lit café was inviting, and he wanted to dry off a bit. "Can I get the mocha for here and the hot chocolate to go?"

The barista didn't bat an eye. "Sure. Total is twelve eighty-two."

Darius swiped his card and took a seat not far from the counter. He didn't want to make the barista travel too far. Unlike the local Starbucks, which Darius didn't mind on occasion, this coffee shop had no issue bringing your order to you when it was reasonable.

Sitting down, he took his phone from his pocket and keyed in the passcode, opening his texts.

DARIUS: Stopped on the way home to warm up.
MORGAN: Aww...
DARIUS: Grabbed you a hot chocolate.
MORGAN: Yay!

Darius chuckled, amused at Morgan's quick turn of mood.

"Here's your order," the barista said, putting a large, foamy mug of coffee in front of him along with a cardboard to-go filled with hot cocoa.

Darius nodded his thanks and was about to go back to his phone when a familiar voice stopped him.

"Is this seat taken?"

Nicholas Slavin stood across the small table, waiting for permission to sit down. He looked drenched, dark curls sticking to his skin. Despite resembling a drowned cat, he looked decidedly healthier than when Darius had last seen him. The bags below his eyes weren't as deeply set, and he was clean-shaven.

"How did you find me here?" Darius blurted, unable to contain his surprise.

Nick offered a weak smile. "I was going to catch you at the Protectorate, but that place makes my palms itch. Happened to see you leave while I was pacing back and forth outside, trying to decide to go in."

"Ah. Well then, by all means," Darius said, pocketing his phone and sitting up a bit straighter in his chair. "Sit."

He did, slouching down in the chair for a moment and glancing around but saying nothing. The awkwardness was palpable. Darius took a long sip of the coffee that had been placed in front of him, unsure of how else to fill the steadily growing silence between them.

"Ah, fuck, I don't even know where to start." Nick fell silent, rubbing the back of his neck and staring down at the table.

Not in his wildest dreams did Darius think he would be confronted with the situation where he would have to initiate a conversation with Nicholas Slavin. He was a strange mixture of open to the idea and defensive. He felt he had to walk on eggshells without wanting to. Despite this, he thought through a few different options, then settled on one. "How is Emily doing?"

Darius had a pretty good idea of how the child was actually doing. Morgan had taken to babysitting her on occasion when Nick and Trinity couldn't. She had even made an appearance or two at Darius's apartment, but he thought this might be a safe topic on which to engage Nick.

He brightened a bit, his back straightening ever so slightly. " She's good. Better than when I..." He trailed off, wiped his mouth, and gave a rueful chuckle. "She's good. Really loves third grade, despite, you know, everything."

So much for that being a safe topic. Darius took another protracted sip from his coffee, using the time to figure out another way of opening communications. At a complete loss as to what might be innocuous enough not to set Nick off, he went with what came to him first. "How are you doing? Recovering?"

There was a pause, a beat, then Nick responded. "I am. Trinity finally got me to see someone. Been talking. Think it'll help." He glanced up through his wet curls, meeting Darius's gaze. He laughed, a sound that wasn't entirely without mirth. "This is fucking weird, isn't it?"

Darius had to agree. "It is a bit."

"And how's that other guy doing? What's his name?"

Darius winced inwardly. "You mean Morgan?" *The guy who knows you as his father.* He bit back the words, though. He understood that in this timeline, Nick didn't owe Morgan anything, but some contact, maybe even friendship, didn't seem overly difficult to Darius.

Nick flinched. "I should have known that. Trinity told me his name."

Darius hummed quietly but didn't say anything else. He was doing his damnedest not to get angry on his significant other's behalf. If fate kept throwing Nicholas Slavin into his path, Darius thought it best to get used to it.

"How is Morgan doing?"

"He's also improving. Seeing a therapist as well."

"Yeah, Trinity told me he had a bit of a hard time when he first came here." Nick ran a hand through his wet hair and let out a frustrated grunt. "Listen, I have no idea how to handle this situation, but I want to. I want to get to know him. I just need to get my head on straight. Need a little bit of time."

"Is that something you want me to tell him?" It was getting harder and harder for Darius not to get angry at the man sitting across from him.

"Yes? No? Dude, I haven't the slightest fucking clue." Nick stood up suddenly, jamming his hands into his jeans pockets. He pulled his right hand out and placed it on the table, leaving a gold chain with a red stone behind when he withdrew it. "Listen, I want you to have this."

It was the gold necklace with the red stone. Identical to the one that Morgan had brought back from the future, only this one belonged to this timeline. Before Darius could refuse, Nick continued.

"It's just a thing, an object, and now it reminds me of what that bastard tried to do. Whatever it was, I'd probably be dead if you, Morgan, and Trin hadn't been there to stop it. So, it's yours. You can do whatever with it." He chuckled again. "In some twisted way, I think Seren would have wanted you to have it."

Despite the attempt at nonchalance, Darius had the distinct impression that this gesture had a lot of meaning behind it. He nodded quietly and reached for the piece of jewelry, gently lifting it from the table and tucking it into the inside pocket of his suit jacket. There was another awkward pause, and Darius felt the need to fill it. "Can I get you something to drink or something?"

"Man, I'm good. I'm just going to go. I'll... Maybe I can just... I'll be in touch." Tripping over his words, Nick quickly made for the door and was out into the rainy night before Darius had the opportunity to object.

~

"I believe I was promised hot chocolate."

Darius smiled as he shrugged his coat off and hung it on the hook near the front door of the apartment. Morgan emerged from the bedroom area of the apartment, a pair of reading glasses perched on the bridge of his nose. He had discovered that staring and screens did little for his eyes, and blue light-blocking reading glasses had been one of his first purchases.

Almost as soon as Darius had his coat and shoes off, Darius swept him up into a hug, planting a kiss on the side of his neck and smiling. "I missed you."

"No work today?"

"Got my shift covered so I could go through more of these college pamphlets. It's a Tuesday anyways. I don't even know why they open for lunch on Tuesdays."

Darius placed the coveted to-go cup of hot cocoa on the kitchen counter and moved to the refrigerator, his mind both on the interaction he'd had on the journey home and the Chinese food leftovers he knew awaited him. "See anything you liked?" he asked, head still in the refrigerator as he reached for the fried rice container.

"University of Illinois Chicago has a bachelor's degree in design studies. I thought that might be cool." He sounded sheepish, and when Darius closed the refrigerator, he could see his partner's cheeks getting red. "I haven't been able to do much art, what with my timeline falling to hell and traveling through time."

"I can see how that might present a problem," Darius agreed, grinning.

"Plus, it's a lot. A lot of information, a lot of classes, a lot of money."

"Well, you can take as much time as you want getting there, if you even want to—"

"Oh, I want to," he said. "I've always wanted to. Just didn't have the opportunity to finish." Morgan took a seat on the stool at the kitchen island and sipped his hot chocolate. "So maybe part-time work, part-time school, part-time mentoring?"

Putting the rice into a bowl, Darius popped it into the microwave and set it to rewarm the food. He turned, leaning against the counter to face Morgan. "It is a lot. Just don't think you have to do it all at once."

Morgan nodded, still enjoying his beverage. When he put it down and stopped to study Darius, his eyes narrowed, and his smile slipped, concern creasing his brow. "What is it? What's wrong? Did something happen?" He was immediately on guard.

"Been working on aura reading?" Darius asked, laughing a bit nervously.

"No, just reading your expression."

Darius reached into his jacket pocket and withdrew the necklace that Nick had given him earlier. He placed it gingerly on the counter, watching Morgan's face as he did so. He saw the confusion pass over it like a cloud, and recognition followed it. His own gold chain was around his neck, the red stone occasionally glinting from it.

"Where did you get it?" he asked, leaning forward to pick it up.

"I ran into Nick on the walk home tonight. He gave it to me."

"Nick?"

Darius nodded.

Studying the necklace in the light, Morgan asked almost absently. "Did he say anything?"

"He said he was trying to get his head on straight. He wants to reach out, just...not yet."

Morgan was quiet for a long while before he let out a quiet sigh. "Can't force it, I guess."

Darius hated the disappointment he saw on Morgan's face. He pushed off of the counter and moved next to him, offering a hug with his arms open. Morgan accepted, and Darius wrapped him in his arms, resting his head against his shoulder. Darius had been more and more open to the idea of physical contact for comfort. Even if it only improved the situation by a fraction, he would take it. "I am sorry. I wish I had better news."

"It's all right." He pulled back a bit and offered a smile, light brown eyes damp with tears. He held up the necklace. "What were you thinking of doing with this?" he asked.

"Honestly, I hadn't thought that far ahead."

Morgan looked from the necklace to Darius, then back to the necklace. "Can I make a suggestion and have you not laugh at how sappy it is?" he asked finally, catching Darius's dark gaze with his own brighter one.

"Morgan, you know me. I never laugh."

The younger man gave a laugh, then took the necklace in both hands and put it around Darius's neck, clasping it and taking a step back to look at his handiwork. "Now you have a bit of Seren, I have a bit of my Emily from my own, and...well..." He trailed off, looking sheepish.

"Well, what?" Darius asked.

"We match."

Darius felt warmth flood through him, the depth of the gesture and the tenderness in Morgan's voice filling him with a sort of contented peace that he hadn't known before. It shook him. He reached out, taking Morgan's hands and holding them tightly. "I like that. A lot." He leaned forward, kissing him soundly. "Now, let me eat something, and then we can figure out what to do with the rest of the night."

Morgan stepped back. "Is it a chill on the couch sort of night or...?" He trailed off and waggled his eyebrows in an exaggerated gesture.

"We'll see, but if you keep doing that, it's going to be an early-to-sleep sort of night."

"Understood!" Morgan said, hands raised in quick and amicable surrender. "Take all the time you need. I'm here for you when you're ready."

ACKNOWLEDGEMENTS

It has been an absolute joy to finally release Darius and Morgan into the world. This novel actually started more than ten years ago, when my brain birthed the idea of a time-traveling mage and how he would interact with the people he met. It went from there, picking up steam, and now, in 2023, you all get to see the results.

And don't worry, Morgan and Darius *will* return.

Thank you so much to Michael, my spouse and critique partner. He is the first person to see my fiction and the one I trust most to be brutally honest (without being a jerk). Also, to my fantastic beta readers: Kara Jorgensen, A.E. Bennett, Cyd Sidney, RJ Sorrento, and Vianna Arenas, most of whom are authors and creatives in their own right. Thank you for taking a look at earlier iterations of my mages and sharing your insight and advice with me. My writing is better because of your input.

ABOUT THE AUTHOR

A.E. Bross is a nonbinary, genderfluid indie author interested in fantasy in all of its forms, as well as romance, science fiction, and horror. When not getting lost in their writing, they are an academic librarian, passionate about open education resources and information literacy. They currently reside in the mountains just beyond the Greater New York area with their family, which includes their spouse, their kiddo, and two kitty grandchildren.

OTHER WORKS BY A.E. BROSS

The Sands of Theia fantasy series
    The Roots that Clutch
    Under Stone and Shadow
    No Light from the Fires

www.ingramcontent.com/pod-product-compliance
Lightning Source LLC
Chambersburg PA
CBHW070744180626
46818CB00007B/2981